To my wife Marion,
my daughter Amelie
and my accomplice Lucy.

BENEDICT BROWN

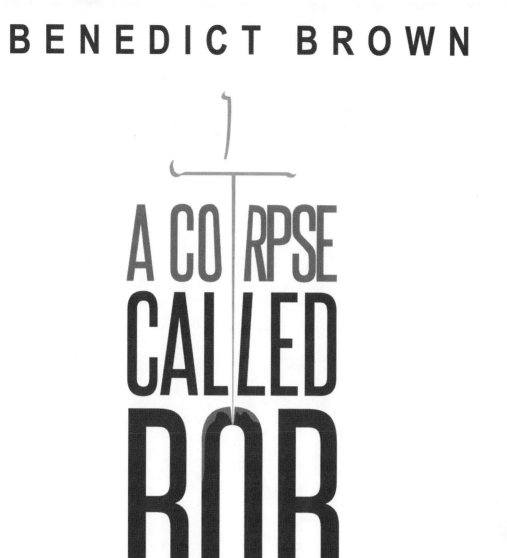

A CORPSE CALLED BOB

IZZY PALMER BOOK ONE

Get **TWO FREE**
Izzy Palmer novellas
with this book.

Copyright

Chapter One

It's amazing that no one had tried to kill my boss before. If anyone was likely to inspire murderous rage, it was Bob.

As I cautiously pushed his door open, I could tell that something was wrong. It wasn't just the stale odour of cigarettes and alcohol that hit me. His blinds were drawn and the lights were still on despite the bright, south-London sunshine streaming into the main office. What really gave the game away though was that my entrance into Bob's sanctuary failed to trigger the slightest grunt of disapproval.

The moment I saw him, I knew that he'd screamed his last insult. His enormous frame was slumped over the desk and his medieval-style letter opener was sticking from his back. He was a giant, struck down by a tiny knight's sword.

There was blood all over his monthly planner and his nameplate looked as if it had been corrected by an overzealous primary school teacher.

R be t H. Th m s was no more.

I stood looking at the body and a strange sensation passed over me. It was like being up somewhere high and feeling the urge to jump. Instead of doing the sensible thing and calling the police, I went in for a closer look.

It's exactly what happens on stupid TV shows. I even heard a little voice in some tucked away corner of my brain screaming, *You moron, what are you doing?* Only, I'd never seen a dead body before and couldn't resist. I sleepwalked over, desperate to understand why someone had gone to the trouble of murdering him with such a small knife.

He'd never been handsome but death hadn't done Bob any favours. His skin was sickly grey and his dark hair looked greasy under the ceiling lights. I was half expecting him to sit up and tell me I was late handing my work in, or make fun of me for falling for his joke. It wasn't going to happen though and, for a moment, I couldn't help feeling sorry for a man I'd previously only had contempt for.

Which was when the urge got too much for me and I jumped from the cliff. I went round the other side of the desk to take in every detail. His head was tilted awkwardly towards me, his gaze intense and focused. I hadn't imagined that his eyes would be open and an unsettling shiver phased through me. It was like he was still checking up on me from the beyond.

Continuing to ignore everything I'd learnt from my life-long obsession with detective fiction, I leaned in close to the body just as Wendy from human resources came in. Wendy, with the coffee-stained teeth and chewed-to-the-quick nails. Wendy, the mini-despot, with her peer review forms and self-evaluation meetings. Wendy, right there, staring at me with a face like a childhood nightmare.

"The Freak's killed Bob!" Clearly much smarter than I was, she immediately ran from the room. "Everyone, Bob's dead and Izzy killed him!"

The news spread across the office in a wave of repeated exclamations. I thought about going out there to clear my name but I couldn't face all those horrified eyes upon me so I pulled my mobile from my pocket and took the obvious next step. Given the circumstances, it was the least I could do.

I could hear Wendy on the office floor, spurring our colleagues on to shock and disgust as an operator answered my call. "Which service do you require?"

I wondered if I should make my voice sound more distressed. I could just imagine the prosecution at my trial playing the tape as evidence of my detachment from the terrible crime. Except, of course, I wasn't the one who'd killed him.

"Police. My boss has been murdered."

In perfect Queen's English, a new voice ran through a series of disappointingly humdrum questions. I figured I at least owed it to my old friend Agatha Christie to take in the facts of the crime scene while I had the chance.

It was incredible just how much blood there was. Bob was surrounded by the stuff and looked like a child who'd got carried away with his finger painting. It clearly wasn't the wound on his back that had killed him. The front of his brown shirt had turned rusty red so someone must have sliced his stomach open. Flashes of violence passed through my mind but I tried not to think about what had happened there hours before.

I wondered for a moment whether whoever had killed him had moved the body, as he was sitting in the wrong place. Deputy director Bob was in front of his desk, not behind it, with shoulders hunched over, like he was in the middle of a drunken nap. His hands were laid flat on the desk, the fingers spread out mid-séance on top of his Porter & Porter headed pad.

He hadn't been a tidy man and there was all the usual debris scattered around him – a bunch of lidless pens, a half-eaten apple, a crumpled second class stamp and some aspirin. There was a wine glass, but no bottle and, sat under his desk, was a fancy box of champagne, no doubt kept there for schmoozing clients.

His computer hummed contentedly, still anticipating its day filled with spreadsheets, inter-office emails and sly searches for *naughty matrons in stockings*. The monitor cast a white glow across the desk but the open search window would go unused. I memorised every last detail and still couldn't shake the feeling that I was missing something important. Where was the vital clue that would reveal Bob's murderer?

I answered the operator's questions and finished the call, but that was the easy part. Next I had to face the whipped-up crowd of my co-workers.

A big group had formed by reception. They stood at a safe distance as I emerged with a hint of red on one cuff somehow. They stared at me like I was the result of some terrible experiment; a dog with a monkey's head.

"You're going to hang for this." Wendy stepped forward to be their spokesperson. "Jack, lock her up."

"Oh, ummmm. I'll have to think about that." Our over-the-hill security guard hadn't left his little cupboard by the entrance.

"I didn't kill him." I held my empty hands out in front of me as if to prove my innocence before noticing more blood and putting them away again. "I only just got here. Half of you saw me arrive."

Ignoring my defence, Wendy paced up and down in front of the crowd like a Nazi general retrained for the modern workplace. "The Freak was standing right over him. I saw it with my own two eyes." To be clear, people normally only call me *Freak* behind my back.

"That's not what happened." The bracelets on my wrist jingled. The reality of the situation had finally got to me and I'd started to shake. "I've called the police, they'll be here soon."

"Oh yeah? The perfect way to hide your guilt." Spittle frothed from Wendy's mouth as her rage peaked. "They'll string you up!" Either she didn't know that the death penalty was banned in Britain or thought my crime so terrible that it would be brought back just for me.

"I arrived five minutes ago. Do you seriously think I could have killed Bob without any of you hearing?" This at least generated a murmur of discussion over the possibility of my innocence.

With his vegetable brush moustache bristling nervously, Jack's eyes flicked between us like he was watching a tennis match. "I think maybe it would be better if we calmed down a tad."

"Don't get taken in by her lies!" Wendy wasn't giving up so easily. In her standard-issue grey twinset, she was enjoying her role as evil-cheerleader and refused to let a little thing like facts spoil her fun. "She probably killed him in the night and came back this morning to cover her tracks."

"What's going on?" Will from consulting had turned up with a couple of his finance bros in tow.

"Urrmmm it looks like Bob might be dead." Jack was terribly polite about the whole thing.

Wendy, not so much. "And The Freak killed him."

Will's face seemed to collapse in on itself. Though he was the kind of guy who spends his free time hunting hamsters and ripping the wings off butterflies, he was also Bob's only close friend in the office. "How could...? What's wrong with you?"

One of the receptionists ignored Porter & Porter's strict anti-smoking policy and lit up a cigarette. Several others copied her, plonking themselves down on top of their desks and loosening top buttons. As if this strange behaviour was a sign of the impending apocalypse, a couple of interns by the entrance started making out.

"I didn't kill him!" I was shouting by now. "And there's nothing wrong with me."

Our deputy director Amara poked her head out of her office to mouth angrily at us. "On the phone! Be quiet!"

Jack the security guard had decided it was time to take action and strode from his cabin. "Perhaps we should put Izzy away somewhere safe. Just until the police get here."

Wendy and Will's faces lit up as they began a creepy pincer movement towards me and I thought about running away.

By 9:05, when our managing director David arrived, I was pinned to the floor under two accountants and the woman who had hired me. From my vantage point beneath Wendy's bottom I could see the smiley-face clock on my desk tick tick ticking away as it smirked at my predicament.

"What's going on?" David yelled as he emerged from the lift. "Why on earth are you smoking?"

With ashtrays having been removed from the office sometime in the 90s, Wendy stubbed out her half-smoked cigarette into a plastic coffee cup.

"*Thank you*. Now will someone please tell me why you're sitting on Izzy?"

It was a bittersweet moment for me. Yes, it stung that my colleagues thought I was a murderer, but it was nice to discover that the head of the company knew my name.

"Bob's dead. The Freak killed him." Wendy's voice faltered a little as she restated her case in front of the boss. "I saw her standing over the body."

David glanced in the direction of Bob's office, but shed no tears. His deceased deputy was not the person to inspire such emotion, even after he'd been hacked up with... with a small letter opener? That didn't seem right but I hadn't spotted any other weapon.

Despite the pressure on my chest making it difficult to breathe, I couldn't help running through the evidence in my head. I knew I hadn't killed Bob (promise!) but somebody had. Given the location of the murder and the fact that most victims know their killers, there was a pretty high chance that it was one of my workmates.

"Do you have any other evidence?" David walked right up to where I was being squashed. "Or any reason to believe Izzy would try to escape?" The crowd had lost its vigilante spirit and his questions were met with silence. "Let her up, please."

I felt a bit of shuffling on top of me as the two accountants got off my back. Wendy was more reluctant but finally teetered up onto her comfy white pumps. David came forward to offer me his hand. Vertical once more, I felt like a battered volunteer in a beginners' self-defence class.

"Did anyone check Bob's pulse?" David's strong, steady voice calmed my firing nerves.

"He's definitely dead." The coagulated sheen to Bob's blood, like leftover jelly after a children's party, told me that he'd been sitting there for a while.

"You made sure of that, you savage."

"Take it easy, please, Wendy." David put his hands out like a referee. "Have the police been informed?"

I perched myself on my friend Ramesh's desk to recover my breath. "Yeah, I called them."

"Okay, good. So can one of you tell me exactly what happened?"

With her henchman accountants standing behind her like trainers at a boxing match, Wendy started her tale. "I went in to see Bob and The Freak was there. She was standing right up next to him and there's blood all over her."

"Thank you, Wendy." David put one hand on her shoulder. "But please don't use such disrespectful language."

As much as I'd grown used to my nickname, which was given to me after a never-ending growth spurt during secondary school, hearing it used so openly could still bring back the electric pang of those early years.

Handsome, approachable David Hughes, with his neat black suit, business-smart haircut and strong Welsh accent, returned to his line of questioning. "Did anyone hear Bob cry out? Is there any other reason to believe that Izzy is to blame for his death?"

Several faces in the pack of rabid finance workers suddenly looked guilty. Some avoided David's gaze while others wore the hangdog frown of punished toddlers.

"I'm not one for puns, but I caught her red handed," Wendy tried one last time as the sound of police cars pulling to a halt in the street below made its way up to us through the cracked-open windows.

Sirens faded to nothing. Doors clicked open then slammed shut. An unnatural stillness gripped the office and it felt for the first time like someone had died.

Right on cue, Bob's secretary burst into tears. "I just can't believe he's gone."

Wendy lit her friend a cigarette to calm him down.

"For goodness sake, Wendy." David really lost his temper this time. "The police are coming."

With the cigarette still glowing in her outstretched hand, Wendy stared back vacantly.

"It's illegal!"

It took another moment for her to cotton on before she crushed the smouldering tube into the carpet with a careless heel. This earned her another bewildered look from our boss just as the lift dinged and the police walked in.

Chapter Two

I can't say I exactly love my job. I've suffered through four years at Porter & Porter and would look for something new if it weren't for my pathological fear of interviews. I've only actually had two in my life but that was plenty to realise that I'm not cut out for them.

During careers week when I was sixteen, our school counsellor asked me to describe myself. I was hoping to come up with something confident like *hardworking and honest with a lot of ambition,* but instead I stood at the front of the class and burst into tears.

As if the stress of the interview wasn't terrifying enough, I'm shockingly bad at self-analysis. Some people are physically incapable of rolling their tongues, I'm physically incapable of knowing anything about myself with any certainty.

When faced with a question like, *What are your strengths and weaknesses?* The only trick I've developed is to take all the things that my biggest admirer – my mother – and greatest detractors – any one of my ex-boyfriends – have ever said about me and try to identify the hard facts.

My mother often tells me that I "have the strength and perseverance to be Secretary-General of the U.N.", whereas my last boyfriend once suggested that I would "make a good test subject for knock-off anaesthetics." Finding the balance between these two perspectives, I can tell you beyond any doubt that I am both somewhat persistent and the kind of person doctors would be happy to include in a medical trial.

I made it through my interview at Porter & Porter because I was the sole applicant for the stellar role of Assistant Data Analyst's Assistant. I got the job despite the fact that, when Wendy asked me whether I was good at problem solving, I reeled off the pin numbers to my bank cards like I was scared she'd mug me.

In terms of physical appearance, Mum claims I have "eyes like a diamond mine". My university boyfriend's parting shot at the end of the relationship was that I had "a face like a plate." Perhaps the one thing they all agree on is that I am tall. "Tall, proud and graceful," Mrs Rosemarie Palmer. Or "like Nelson's column with the body to match," seventeen-year-old Gary Flint, the day after my long-anticipated first kiss. So, I'm tall with eyes and a face. I think that should help you build up some sort of picture of me.

I was definitely taller than the two police officers who took me to the station for questioning on the morning I found Bob's body, a fact they made sure I knew through their upturned glances and the slightly wary way they coerced me downstairs and into their car. *I'm only six foot three*, I wanted to tell them, *not Godzilla.*

Croydon Police station looks like it was made out of Lego by an unimaginative toddler in the 70s. As I was escorted from the car, the thought of what was about to take place filled me with a sense of stomach-aching dread.

I was missing out on the events unfolding back at Porter & Porter but at least I got to sit in an empty room for an hour with nothing to read. The only entertainment was a noticeboard with campaigns *against* shoplifting and *for* community-mindedness. So, with nothing else to do, I tried to picture everything I'd seen in Bob's office.

I'd once read a book called "Twenty Tips to Improve Your Memory" and, if I closed my eyes, I could picture Bob in his ugly brown woollen suit – the only one he ever wore – but with the matching tie missing for once. Bob, with his head resting on the desk, his gaze cast towards the neatly halved apple on an espresso saucer and his mouth hanging slightly open. Bob, with no shoes and only one sock on.

I hadn't thought about it at the time but I could swear that's what I'd seen. One white sports sock on his left foot and his brown slip-ons nowhere in sight.

Like a computer slowly booting up, my brain ran with questions. *Why would he have taken one sock off? Where had his shoes got to? Would such details really help work out who killed him?*

I stopped myself before I could get carried away. My qualifications as a detective extended to one crime fiction module during my English degree and an impressive familiarity with Agatha Christie's body of work. I doubted that it was enough to solve a real-life murder.

Finally, an underling police officer came to collect me and led me through a security door to an unmarked room at the end of a long, featureless hallway. The new space was much less welcoming than the first. Grey plastic chairs, a sturdy rectangular table and blank, white walls without even the colourful lettering of public information posters made me instantly feel like I'd done something wrong.

The next quarter of an hour before anyone came to grill me was tough. Were they leaving me in there to sweat? Perhaps they were observing me on some flickery, black and white monitor, studying the way I sat or the expression on my face, before settling on the perfect moment to make their entrance. It was lucky it only took them fifteen minutes. Any longer and I'd have caved under the pressure and confessed to killing my boss.

"Miss Palmer?" the first detective to enter the room asked. I didn't feel it required a response. "My name is Detective Inspector Victoria Irons and this," she said, with the flair and timing of a stage magician, as her colleague entered the room, "is D.I. John Brabazon."

"It's lovely to meet you," I replied inappropriately.

There was something very Playmobilish about the two of them. She had strangely simple features like they'd been drawn on with a marker and he had no neck. I half expected them to produce a notepad and pen which clicked in to their fingerless hands. They didn't. The woman pulled a remote control from a drawer in the table, clicked it at an invisible recording device and the interview began.

With the formalities out of the way, they sat in silence, sizing me up. I was swimming in a sea of police show clichés, waiting for the good cop, bad cop routine to start.

"What exactly is it that you do in your job, Miss Palmer?" D.I. Irons asked.

"I..." I'd got the first word out. Surely I could cope better than in my previous interviews. I was older now; a proper grown up. "I... I'm... I'm an assistant data analyst's assistant. I studied literature and–"

"How long have you been working there?"

Deep breath. "A little over four years. It was never meant to be permanent but-"

"Why don't you take us through what happened this morning?"

Dear Izzy, my brain said. *No one cares about your dreams of becoming a famous poet. Just answer their questions.*

"I don't know what to tell you." I was beginning to calm down and had perfected the exact right tone to assure them of my innocence. "I got to work at about eight fifty-five, left my bag at my desk, turned my computer on and collected some papers to give to Bob."

"Robert Thomas, the deputy director of Porter & Porter?" Irons checked. Clearly D.I. Brabazon was a silent partner.

"That's right. My colleague Susan Hawkes saw me arrive."

"Very well. Go on." Irons and her partner had matching expressions when they were listening. Brows furrowed, heads tipped forward. They were steely, and hard to read. Skills they'd no doubt honed through years on the job.

"Bob... Mr. Thomas needed me to give him some work first thing. I knocked but there was no answer. The door to his office was ajar and I assumed he hadn't arrived yet, so I went in. I was going to leave the work he wanted on his desk but then I saw him."

I took another deep breath and felt a bit sad again for poor, dead Bob.

"What happened after you went inside?"

"I saw the knife in his back. It wasn't really a knife actually, it was a silver letter opener in the shape of a medieval sword. I remember him boasting about how much he'd paid for it and I thought it was ridiculous that anyone would waste a load of money on a letter opener when our hands come with ten of them built in. I mean, how hard is it to tear an envelope?"

They didn't smile.

"Please continue, Miss Palmer." I felt about six years old every time she spoke.

"I wanted to check if he was dead, so I went closer. When I got to the desk I could see there must have been another wound. There was blood everywhere, it couldn't all have come from the tiny hole in his back." There was a flicker on D.I. Irons' face. It gave me a little buzz and I probably got a bit cocky. "I'm right, aren't I? There was another wound. I knew it!"

"Miss Palmer." She sounded like my GCSE history teacher.

"Sorry, Miss. I mean... Well, I could see that there was no way he'd be getting back up. There was something already very rigid about him like a video set on pause. I leaned over his desk and then I–"

All that confidence drained out of me as I pictured myself right up close to my boss's dead body. I'd been holding it together surprisingly well until now. I mean, it's not every day you implicate yourself in a murder. I hadn't wildly blamed the whole thing on some random colleague. I hadn't even fainted, which, knowing how I get in high-pressure situations, was pretty good going.

"2917!" I blurted and then immediately followed it up with, "Sorry, just ignore that. It's definitely not my pin number."

I felt like a teenager again, trying to get past the bouncers into a nightclub. Even though I'd been a foot taller than most girls my age, I always gave away how young I was through my nervous chattering as I spilled out my life story in the hope of sounding relaxed and natural. Worst of all though was that I hadn't even done anything wrong. I was over eighteen now, with every right to enter a club and I hadn't killed my boss. So why did I feel so jittery?

Mr and Mrs Playmobil were still staring. Still waiting for my explanation.

"I promise I didn't kill him. I had plenty of reasons to and I'm sure that everyone in the office will have told you how much I hated him. Ramesh's probably even mentioned the amazing impersonation I do. But I really didn't kill him. I didn't even help someone else do it, I promise."

Izzy, you're blathering! Stop it this minute.

"I might be an idiot but I'm not a killer. You have to believe me."

My old enemy silence gripped the room. I think that D.I. Victoria Irons might have suppressed a laugh, before finally taking pity on me.

"We do."

I didn't trust her. Perhaps this was the good-cop bit. Perhaps she was singing a lullaby before kicking the baby from the tree.

"You do?"

"Our initial investigation suggests that Mr Thomas was murdered between eight and ten last night. One of your colleagues has informed us that you were in a restaurant up in town."

"I was!"

"Is there someone who can confirm your whereabouts?"

"There is!" I couldn't believe my luck. "I mean, I was hoping I'd never have to speak to him again and it really was the worst date I've ever been on – he took me to Burger Baron and asked me for my blood type – but Dean Shipman from Bromley is possibly my favourite person in the world right now."

"We'll need his contact details." D.I. Brabazon finally spoke up.

"You said that you didn't like Mr. Thomas," his partner helpfully reminded me. "Was this a common feeling in the office?"

"I know you're not supposed to speak ill of the dead but Bob was a total git. He loved making fun of people, nothing we did was ever good enough for him and he made working at Porter & Porter pretty much unbearable. He really had it coming."

D.I. Brabazon frowned and pulled out a completely normal-looking notepad to scribble something down.

"No, I don't mean I wanted him dead. Please cross out whatever you just wrote. I've got a big mouth but I don't even kill spiders. I get Mum to come into my room and take them away."

"You live with your mother?" he asked, which made me feel even more stupid than when I was handing them evidence of my guilt.

"Urrmm, yeah. But it's just temporary, I–"

"Miss Palmer, perhaps we can get back on topic." It was D.I. Irons. She would have made a great headmistress. "You say he was unpopular. Was there anyone that Mr Thomas got on well with?"

I took my time before answering. "He was friends with Will from consulting but I've no idea why. As far as I could tell, Will suffered his insults just as much as anyone."

Irons flicked through some papers on the table in front of her. "William Gibbons?"

"That's right."

"Thank you." She underlined Will's name on what I assumed was a Porter & Porter staff list. "And would you say that Mr Thomas had any enemies?"

I was about to divulge a lengthy list of people who Bob had crossed, when I realised how terrible it would be to incriminate someone for murder because of petty office squabbling.

"Isn't it a bit unfair if I tell you? I mean, he was always screaming at someone. After the last project we worked on, he called me an uppity giraffe and said my mother should have strangled me as a child. No, D.I. Brabazon, don't write that down!"

"Anything you tell us will be used in confidence, Miss Palmer. No one's going to be arrested on the back of office gossip."

I looked at the two of them as they waited for me to spill the news of who hated who and who liked who too much. D.I. Irons had a very trustworthy face. Her partner, on the other hand, scared me. I don't trust quiet people.

"Okay, I'll tell you. But I'm not going to single anyone out. It's all or nothing."

"Tell us what you know, Miss Palmer." Brabazon was beginning to get annoyed.

"All right, I will." I gripped the side of the table and began to deliver a full account of the crimes of Robert H. Thomas. "The fact is that Bob took great pleasure in being nasty. He treated pretty much anyone below him like they were subhuman. He was creepy around female employees, especially the young ones, and if he didn't like someone, he left them in no doubt on the matter.

"After last year's summer social, he uploaded photos to the office WhatsApp of my colleague Suzie kissing Jack the security guard. He couldn't stand either one of them. Oh, and when Amara was promoted to deputy director over him, it kicked off this massive feud. It went on for months until he threatened to sue the company and they ended up sharing the job."

There were so many incidents where Bob had done his utmost to create a perfectly toxic working environment at P&P that it was hard to choose which ones to talk about. "He spent years referring to Ramesh as *the queer one* though Bob knew he wasn't gay. The last time Wendy in H.R. had a new hairstyle he told her it looked like a badger had died on her head and, on at least three occasions, he asked Amara if she was pregnant when she wasn't."

"Is there anything that really stands out in your mind though? Did you personally witness any occasion when his behaviour crossed a line?"

I hesitated then. I didn't want to make anyone's life harder than it already was. "If you're asking me who'd want him dead then I'd have to go with Jack. They had a bit of a brawl at the Christmas party. I don't know the details but they've barely looked at each other since it happened. Or it could be Amara over the promotion. Or Ramesh after the years of bullying. And now that I think about it, Wendy–"

"Thank you, Miss Palmer," D.I. Brabazon said. A slightly conciliatory tone perhaps?

"Wait. There's more. Lots more..."

Chapter Three

Bob wasn't your run-of-the-mill office bully. Behind all his nasty comments, inappropriate behaviour and general thuggishness, he was clever. There was thought behind his actions as he belittled, berated and divided up the office; a coordinated plan known only to him. In my four years at P&P I saw few people stand up to him. Until his final day that is.

I could tell the dynamic detective duo very little about Bob's life outside the office. I'd only met his wife once at a work do. She was sweet and softly spoken, the complete opposite of Bob, who, as soon as he saw us talking, bounded over to make sure the poor woman wasn't saying anything bad about him.

"Selina, do stop boring everybody." Her tyrannical spouse grabbed the half-sipped glass of wine from her hand as he barged between us.

She laughed in reply. It was the sad, defeated reaction of a woman who was ashamed of her husband but didn't want anyone to know it. That was the only time I can think of that I literally wanted to knife Bob. It was lucky for him I'd stuck to finger food.

As I waited outside the police station, I wondered how Selina Thomas had felt when the police brought her the news. Did she break down in the doorway and shed every last tear in her body? Or invite them in for tea, letting out a muffled cheer of joy as the kettle boiled?

On the way to the station, I'd had the full, five-star criminal treatment but, when the police were done with me, I had to make my own way home. I rang Mum and she drove across town to get me.

"This is fantastic, darling!" she said as I got into her tiny yellow Corsa. "I want you to tell me all about it."

She looked as sparklingly pretty as ever. I folded my legs up to fit inside.

"A man is dead, Mother. It's not something to be chirpy about." It was bad enough that I'd gone full Miss Marple. I didn't need her encouraging me.

"Of course, sweetie. You're totally right." She surged away from the curb before having to stop just as quickly at a traffic light. "It's terribly sad but also the tiniest bit thrilling, no?"

I looked at her sternly in the hope it might calm her down.

"My boss was murdered, I found the body. There's not much more to say."

"Oh, come on, darling. I'm dying to know what happened. How was he killed? Who do you think *done it*?"

I do love my mother but sometimes her perky enthusiasm can get a bit much. We zoomed off again and I gripped onto the dashboard, praying we wouldn't crash. It's not that she's a bad driver exactly, she's just not very good when there's someone there to distract her.

"Details, darling! Details!"

"Really, Mother, I could be traumatised for all you know and you're going on like it's my first day at school."

"I've never known you to be traumatised, sweetie. It's not your style. And all I'm saying is that you should feel extremely fortunate. Not everyone is lucky enough to discover a murder."

"I think it's time we put you in a home."

"If it was me, I'd want to uncover exactly what happened." Her car went slingshotting round a roundabout and I banged my head on the side window. "And who's better placed to solve the crime than you, Izzy? You know everything that goes on in that office. I've always said you've got an inquisitive mind. It's about time you put it to use."

If I don't make it as the head of the U.N., Mum has always dreamed of me becoming a private detective. She's never come out with it directly, but she's dropped some pretty big hints over the years. A birthday cake in the shape of a looking glass, a book on improving your memory for Christmas, that quiet word she once had with my high-school careers adviser to steer me in the right direction.

We'd left behind the indelible stamp of over-grown, post-war office buildings and made it to the leafy suburbs beyond the town centre. We lived in West Wickham, a slightly out-of-time commuter town for people who want all the facilities Croydon has to offer whilst still being able to say they live in Kent. Its high street was dotted with cobblers, faded ladies' fashion shops and gentleman's outfitters among the ubiquitous nail parlours and fried chicken takeaways. I never thought I'd still be living there at twenty-nine.

"By the way, Danny's round," my mother announced, once it was clear I wasn't going to cough up any more information on Bob's death.

Danny used to be my neighbour but adopted my family when we were kids and still comes to stay. He's a doctor without borders – though someone really should have set him some. He's far too handsome to look at directly and a terrible flirt. I wouldn't mind so much if we hadn't grown up like brother and sister. It's exhausting; I have no idea whether his flirty comments are childhood banter or a full on invitation for kissy time (sorry, not good at sexy talk).

"Sweetheart?" My mother broke into my thoughts. "I said, Danny's over for a visit."

"Niiiiiiiiiiice," I replied nonchalantly.

Playin' it cool.

We pulled up at the house and mother hooted the horn so that my stepfather Greg glanced out at us through the front room window. A few seconds later, Danny bounded from the house. He was springy and cheerful like a lithe, seductive Saint Bernard.

"You look great, Izzy. Have you been in the sun?" You see what I'm up against?

I looked at the sky and tried to remember the last time I'd seen that big yellow floaty thing. "Must be my naturally swarthy features." I'm about as Latin-looking as mashed potatoes.

He laughed handsomely, then held out his hand to help me from the car. Far too smooth for his own good, you could use Danny as a chamois leather.

"She's been nowhere near the sun. She was locked up in a cell all morning. See if you can get the details from her," Mother called over her shoulder before disappearing into the house.

"Sounds exciting," Danny said, as my eyes lingered a little too long over the deepness of his vee.

Sorry about all this, I really can't help myself. I promise this isn't going to turn into some sordid, steamy affair in which he takes me up to my room to dole out a suitable punishment.

Izzy, snap out of it!

Yes, brain. Sorry, brain. Won't do it again.

"I was nowhere near a cell." I rolled my eyes. "I was merely helping the police with their enquiries."

"Sounds less exciting."

"What about you, Danny? Have you cured any diseases recently? Found a solution to world hunger?"

"No, nothing like that. I've been helping out at a clinic for AIDS sufferers in South Africa. Wait, what did the police want?"

Danny has a lovely smile. If there's one thing in the world I'd like to steal and keep for myself, it's his pretty smile. I'd put it in a box with a padlock on.

I suddenly realised that I'd forgotten to speak. "It was nothing. Just that my boss got killed and I found the body. No big deal."

Which is when he pulled me into his chest and wrapped me up in his big arms. Danny is almost as tall as me and subsequently the only man I'd ever hugged without feeling like King Kong crushing some blonde chick.

"You poor thing. That must have been terrible."

"It was."

His t-shirt was soft against my face and smelt like a bonfire for some reason.

This is the last warning, Izzy. Pull away now or I'll start forgetting happy memories from your childhood.

You wouldn't dare.

I'll do it, you just try me.

Fine, but stop talking to me. You're making us seem like a crazy person.

I pulled away, carefully avoiding the dreaminess of his eyes.

"I'd better get inside. I had an extra-spicy curry pasty for breakfast and I think it's about to have its revenge."

Smooth, very smooth.

I told you to shut up.

"Right," Danny said with an uncomfortable look on his face. "And I should see to lunch."

I made myself scarce, running into the house and up to the bathroom where I sat staring at my phone for five minutes. It was probably the first time in my life I wanted a handsome man to believe I was busy on the toilet. When I'd finished – pretending that is – I went downstairs for lunch.

My stepdad Greg was hard at work laying the table. Greg is Mum's third husband – "One too old, one too young, the third just right," as she likes to explain. They met on an Ashram retreat in Monmouthshire. As well as being a professional painter, he's a trained Yogi, whereas Mum was just there to top up her chakra. They've been married for about five years and I'm sincerely glad they're so happy together, though the fact their bedroom's next to mine also makes me wish they'd never met.

"Have you recovered from your murderous ordeal?" Greg had none of his wife's over the top pep and I liked him all the more for it. He didn't take his eyes off the cutlery he was carefully arranging as I sat down at the table.

"Pretty much."

Greg does everything in his own serious, competent way. He leaves all the interfering to my mother and generally treats me like I have a brain. Though they're about the same age, Greg looks all of his sixty-six years and has the most wonderfully expressive wrinkles across his face and ice-white locks that spring outwards in wiry curls.

"Good." He moved on to the plates and positioned them across the table with all of the care he'd give to one of his watercolours.

Mum came to sit down beside me as our chef appeared from the garden with a small cauldron.

"This is my new discovery. It's called Potjiekos. The only way to cook it is on an open fire. It just doesn't taste the same otherwise." As well as being gorgeous and a saint, Danny is a phenomenally good cook – to round out the package he's no doubt a genius with a feather duster and gives the world's greatest backrubs. Sometimes I'm almost repulsed by his perfectness. Almost.

"Sounds wonderful, Danny." Mum blatantly wishes he was her son.

He set the black pot down on the table and whisked the lid off to reveal a chunky stew which instantly reminded me I hadn't consumed anything since my ill-chosen breakfast. Even Greg let out an *ooh,* as the smell wafted up magically into our nostrils.

"Hello?" a voice called, shortly followed by the sound of the slamming front door. "Hello? Are you there?"

It was my father, who appeared in the dining room, with a bottle of unchilled white wine under one arm. He'd retired several years earlier but still pottered about all day in his oily mechanic's overalls.

"Hello, Ted." Mum was not surprised to see him.

"Dad, why are you here again?"

"Have… Have I done something wrong?" Dad stuttered when he was nervous. "Rosie invited me."

"Do you have your own key?"

"There's nothing strange about it, Izzy." My mother had already grabbed a plate for her ex-ex-husband.

"Yes there is." I tried to sound grumpy but was more or less resigned to his visits. "You broke up twenty years ago. Why can't you be like normal, happily divorced parents and never speak to each other?"

Our chef overruled me. "Don't listen to your daughter, Ted. You're very welcome here."

I was completely outnumbered and Mum hadn't finished. "Izzy, dear, I respect your father as a man and a human being. The fact we're not married shouldn't stop us being friends."

"No, but the fact that you *were* married should."

Back when I wanted more than anything for them to be together, my parents had nothing to do with each other. Since Dad had moved to the neighbourhood a few months before, he'd become a regular caller.

"Ted, our daughter is being terribly mean and won't give us any of the details on her boss's murder."

"Come on, darling." Five years younger than my ever-youthful mother, my father was settling comfortably into old age. The grey eyes that he'd passed down to me crumpled up in a plea that he knew I couldn't resist. "Tell us what you know."

"Oh, all right." I let out a sigh, secretly rather happy to show off in front of Danny. "If it'll shut you all up."

I ran my taped-together family through the gory details, stopping only to field questions from my over-eager parents.

Dad put one finger up like he was about to make a significant point. "Who would have wanted Bob dead?"

"Just about everyone. He was repugnant." I spoke through a mouthful of delicious South African stew. "The question is who went ahead and did it."

"What about clues at the scene?" Greg's interest was piqued.

"I've thought about that. It's hard to know what's relevant though. He wasn't sitting in his own chair, which I thought was a bit odd. He was in front of his desk with his back to the door and his hands were splayed out on top of his notepad."

"Was there a message on the pad?" Mum was a true Christieite at heart. "Were his fingers pointing to anything?"

"Only the name of the company, I don't suppose that could mean much."

"Unless he was pointing to the initials of the killer?"

"His left index finger was over the letter P, so perhaps Pauline from accounts did it, but the right hand was nowhere in particular. To be honest, it seems like something of a challenge to slump in precisely the right direction as you release your final breath."

No one responded. We sat considering the evidence as we slurped Danny's stew.

After lunch I retreated from the world of dead bosses and pointless speculation to my own private refuge. My bedroom hasn't changed much in the last ten years. I'm like the mother of a missing child who refuses to touch the teenage time capsule they've left behind. It would feel wrong to take down the boyband posters and school sports day certificates from my blu-tack-pockmarked walls.

Above my bed is a shelf with forty-one red, leather-bound books on it. Each one has Agatha Christie's scrawling signature in small gold letters on the spine. My mother gave them to me on my eleventh birthday and I'd read every one of them – all sixty-six novels and every short story collection – before my next birthday came around. As a geeky kid, picked on for my glasses, lank hair and the hippyish clothes my mother dressed me in for the annual school disco, they were my portal to another world.

In Christie's books I found all the genteel elegance that my Chinese-burnt, spitball-infested adolescence was lacking – along with scores upon scores of dead bodies. It was hard for me to understand why my mother would encourage me to read such blood-spattered tales which, if it weren't for the presence of well turned-out, elderly gentlemen or nosey old maids surreptitiously investigating the crimes, would most definitely have been considered *not suitable for children*.

From August 2003 to October 2004, I barely slept at night. Mammoth, after-dinner reading sessions stretched into the early hours of the morning, at which point the hunger to know exactly how the showgirl had been done away with or the wealthy widow finished off would overcome my heavy eyelids or submit to a nodding head. Such furious consumption would have carried on much longer if it hadn't been for my ancient former-stepfather (daddy number two) catching me one night, reading under the covers with a torch like a teen boy with a lingerie catalogue. After that, my collection was taken away and I was restricted to one book a week, thereby teaching me the art of moderation.

These days I only allow myself to spend the afternoon with Poirot or take tea with Miss Marple when I really need it. Occasionally, enough time will have passed between readings for me to forget who the killer is and I can luxuriate once more in the thrill of the protagonist's detective work.

Sitting on my bed, I was contemplating pulling down "The Mysterious Affair at Styles", figuring that today of all days I deserved it, when my pocket started to vibrate. I pulled my phone out but didn't recognise the number.

"Hello?"

"Izzy, it's David. How are you doing?"

It took me a moment to work out who David was and why he was calling me.

"Fine thanks, boss." I sounded like some peppy reporter from an old film. I had never spoken to him on the phone before and didn't know what to say. "Just great really."

He sighed down the line. "That's good to hear. I wanted to tell you not to come back in today. The police are busy here and so I've sent everyone home."

"Oh... thanks very much." The thought hadn't entered my mind.

"Did you have any trouble at the station? I hope you could prove you weren't involved?" It was odd the way he phrased it. He spoke about Bob's death like any other office emergency; a broken photocopier or missing courier delivery.

"I was with someone last night when they think Bob was murdered. I should be okay."

"That's a relief." Something in the way he spoke told me that his quiet efficiency was just an act.

"David, are you okay?"

He didn't respond at first. I could hear him breathing but he didn't say anything for a few seconds. "No. I feel guilty actually. I was never that nice to Bob. He wasn't an easy man to get on with, but no one should have to die the way he did."

"Yes, it's a tragedy." Now I was the one who sounded unconvincing.

"He has kids. I know his wife. No matter what I thought of him personally, it's still not fair on them."

"David, I …" I stopped myself from offering advice to the managing director of my company who, until then, had barely said two words to me. "Thank you for looking out for me this morning. It was kind of you."

He cleared his throat and re-engaged his executive persona. "It was purely selfish. I can't have you suing the company for harassment now, can I?"

"It was kind all the same."

The line crackled three times before he spoke. "No problem, Izzy. And thanks for listening."

The phone went dead without either of us saying goodbye, which is weird because I thought that only happened on TV. Our conversation left me with the sense that David's distant tone and distracted demeanour didn't quite add up in the circumstances. He was now firmly placed on my list of potential suspects.

There was a bunch of messages from my best friend Ramesh but I wasn't in the mood to reply. I reached for my book and was just settling in to the warm, familiar tones of Captain Hastings' narration – like slipping on an old cardigan – when the phone rang once more. Again, the number was unrecognised.

"Did you miss me so soon?" I said flirtily and then instantly regretted it. "Oh, I'm sorry, David, that was incredibly unprofessional. I–"

"Izzy?" It was too high and nasal to be my boss's voice.

"Who's that?"

"It's Dean, Dean Shipman from Bromley." He of the Burger Baron date and small talk on my blood type – not to mention a particularly underdeveloped moustache. I wanted to hang up but thought better of it.

"Hi, Dean. How's things?"

"They were fine until the police called to ask where I was last night. I'm a very private person, Izzy. I don't like giving out personal information."

"Sorry about that. I didn't mean to get you involved, but it is rather important you confirm what I told them."

"I already have, for God's sake." Huffing as he spoke, he sounded like a disgruntled gnome.

"Thanks. I really appreciate it."

"Good. So when are we going out again?"

Chapter Four

I've never understood why the men I go out with want to date me. I figure it's more sport than romance. As much for the stories they can tell their friends as a hope for long-term love. Like big game hunting or capturing the great white whale.

I learnt a long time ago that most men don't understand the intricacies of being with someone much taller than them. First kisses are always horrendous so, depending on the height difference, I make a point of only allowing such occurrences when we're both sitting down. This does make it trickier to move the relationship to the next level.

You'd think the solution would be to only date men who are my height, but believe me, I've tried. Either tall men can take their pick and aren't interested, or... well, that's the only reason I've come up with actually.

I started using dating apps about a year ago and, though it helps to stave off the loneliness of staying home every night with my parents, it also increases the likelihood of me being locked up in a stranger's basement. If I was being polite, I'd call the majority of the men I meet a little odd. If I was being honest, I'd call them maladjusted weirdoes with the social skills of a horny polar bear.

There should be some sort of verification system on these apps. It's difficult to sort the online wheat from the digital chaff. Take Dean Shipman from Bromley, for example. His profile had a moody, black and white photo of himself looking like some 50s matinee idol and he listed his hobbies as literature, visual arts and travel. Personally, I don't think that Star Wars comics, erotic robot anime and an annual trip to Bognor Regis fit into the aforementioned categories.

I decided to get my compulsory second date out of the way as soon as possible and arranged to meet Dean that night. I dressed up in my third-best jogging bottoms and sweater combo in the hope he'd get the message that I wasn't interested.

We met at Hayes Station, the closest landmark to my house, chosen to ensure this token rendezvous would take up as little time as possible. He was dressed in a black, military utility jacket with matching cargo trousers. His patchy moustache, baby face and constantly shifting glare made it seem like he'd just come from planning a school shooting.

"You're even taller than I remembered."

"Hello, Dean." I attempted to smile at his silver-tongued opening line.

He nervously moved his weight from foot to foot. "Where are we eating?"

"There's an Indian round the corner."

"Can't." He sounded like a stubborn five-year-old.

"You can't or you don't want to?" It's funny that the one quality I've never considered in a potential partner is their need for mothering.

"Allergic," he replied, with his stupid little unfinished goatee wiggling about.

"How can you be allergic to– Never mind, what about Chinese?"

"Don't like it."

"Okay. What do you like?"

"*I'm not picky*," he said, like I was trying to insult him. "I can do pizza, burgers, kebab or Nandos."

So, after the culinary joys of the night before, we sampled a restaurant I hadn't had the chance to try in a long time. At least this one had cutlery. We went to a Wimpy Burger.

"This is amazing," Dean said as we sat down in their best booth. "I haven't been to one since I was six."

"Shocking."

He wasn't listening. He was carefully studying the menu which a slightly zombified waiter had placed before us. It was three minutes before Dean spoke again, the side orders were a particular source of interest.

"You didn't make much effort tonight. You looked better yesterday."

"That's sweet of you to say." I was trying not to sound sarcastic. It was hard.

"Doesn't matter. I prefer casual girls."

I took a deep breath. "Dean, why are we here?"

"What do you mean?" He finally looked up from his menu.

"In the two hours we spent together last night, there wasn't one thing we agreed on and the evening finished with you telling me I'd have more luck dating if I showed some cleavage. Why did you even want to go out with me again?"

30

"Hang on a sec. Waiter?" He waved the menu about to get the boy's attention. Finally interpreting the signal, the waiter lurched frankensteinishly over to our table.

"Whaaaaaaaat?"

"Double cheeseburger, mozzarella melts, home fries, onion rings, chocolate milkshake and a coke." Dean fired the order off with his eyes closed, like a child memory-whiz on a TV talent show.

Our waiter replied by grunting enquiringly in my direction.

"I'll have the gourmet chicken salad and an orange juice, please."

Having prodded at a tablet to take down our order, the waiter staggered back to his hovel behind the counter.

"This place is just how I remember it." Dean stared around the restaurant, taking in the soft plastic booths and red and white décor. "Wait, what did you ask me?"

"I asked you what we're doing here."

"Oh, yeah..." He let out a long sigh like he was about to reveal some wise and ancient truth. "Izzy, I've been in this game a long time. I've got a profile on four apps and two different websites including a Jewish one that I have no right to be on. I normally meet two to three women a month and in my two years trying, do you know how many second dates I've had?"

I chose not to answer.

"One. Only one."

"Was she deaf?"

"You tell me, Izzy. She's sitting right where you are."

I let out a sigh, as much for his previous dates as for Dean himself. "I'm sorry, but it's hardly surprising. When I asked what you did, you told me I wouldn't understand. Maybe you should change your approach a little?"

The waiter reappeared, made a bear-like moan and put our drinks down in front of us.

Dean picked up his coke and drained it through the straw in one long suck. "I am what I am. My mother says I should always be myself."

"Good advice. And do you still live with her?" I raised both eyebrows accusingly, completely ignoring the fact that people who live in their mothers' glass houses shouldn't throw stones.

"Actually I don't. I have my own apartment. I'm rather good at

31

managing my money, Izzy, which is just one of the things you'll learn about me as we get to know each other."

I might have made an involuntary shudder.

"And what about you?" he asked.

"What about me?"

"I don't see you settling down with your one true love. How many second dates have you had?"

"I've had plenty, thank you. They just weren't to my taste."

"Maybe you should change your approach a little." The nerviness which had characterised him on our previous encounter was gone. The arrogance which replaced it was no more attractive.

"Seriously?" I swirled the unnecessary ice cubes in my orange juice. "You're the one who had to use blackmail to get me here."

"What are you talking about?" His voice spiked higher, like a teenage boy's.

"Oh come off it. You know the only reason I agreed to this evening is because you're my alibi."

His jaw sank, the rest of his face curled up and he stared at me angrily. "You really thought I was going to withdraw my statement if you didn't come?"

"It crossed my mind, yes."

He stood up angrily. "Fine, enjoy your chicken salad – which is a terrible choice by the way – alone!"

He was about to walk off when the zombie-waiter brought two plates filled with breadcrumb-coated goodies. Dean looked back and forth between the food and the door before I finally took pity on him.

"Just sit down, Dean. I'm sorry I thought badly of you."

"You should be." He plucked a bunch of onion rings from the plate and chucked them one by one into his mouth in a simplified game of hoopla. "There's a lot worse out there than me."

"Sadly, you're right."

He gave me another hard stare and returned to his place to consume his deep-fried snacks. When there were only a few malformed cheese melts left, he prepared himself for more conversation.

"So, did you do it?"

"What?"

He took a pallet-cleansing slurp on his newly delivered milkshake.

"Kill your boss?"

"No, of course not."

"I don't care if you did."

"I was with you at the time he was murdered, idiot."

"Doesn't mean you weren't involved. You could've been using me as a cover story whilst your accomplice did away with him."

"I wasn't." The rest of the food arrived and I tucked into my gourmet selection.

"Doesn't matter. It wouldn't have been my worst date."

"Go on then. What was your worst?" My mouth was full so I probably managed a lot less consonants than that.

"A woman once told me there was no way she was going to spend a whole evening having to look at me and that she'd report me to the police for breach of the trade description act."

He'd made me laugh. "Ouch. Still, she had a point. Your profile is a little flattering."

"Thankfully the police didn't think so. They gave her a warning for wasting their time."

I laughed. He was still just as weird as on our last date. He still avoided eye contact as much as possible, like everything he said was a lie, but he could do a much better impression of a human being than I'd imagined.

"Why do we bother trying?" I tossed a carrot baton into my mouth. "This whole thing is such a nightmare."

"Personally, I have a weird fetish for sitting in front of women and talking to them."

"Psycho."

"What about you?" he asked. "What depths have you plumbed?"

I swallowed a chunk of chicken.

"Oh, you know, the usual stuff. It's not often that I make it to a date as so many guys just want to send me naked photos. There is one guy who stands out though. Half way through the meal, he told me that he collected women's wigs and that, if I thought it was strange, we should call it a night."

"Classy. What did you say?"

"In my defence it was a really nice restaurant and I got the impression he was paying."

"You stayed?"

I nodded, smiling at the bad memory that had long since become a funny story.

"And did he pay?"

"Nah, they rarely do."

"So you'd prefer it if we did? I get nervous eating in restaurants with my parents because I'm not sure who should get the bill. With women I'm a mess."

"In an ideal world, I'd have enough money and it wouldn't be an issue. But I'm twenty-nine and still live with my mum because my job pays barely enough to rent a storage container, so I wouldn't say no."

"Izzy Palmer of West Wickham, I'm gonna make your dreams come true tonight. The chicken salad's on me."

"What a gentleman." This conversation had been conducted with ketchup and mayonnaise covered fingers which I now attempted to clean off, almost extracting a serviette from the dispenser with the ball of my hand before giving up and licking my hands clean. "*Now* will you tell me what you do?"

He pushed his glass away and looked around for our waiter. "You wouldn't understand."

"Just when I was beginning to think you were capable of polite conversation."

He didn't smile. "I'm not being arrogant, my job is *very* technical."

"I didn't ask you to teach me how to do it. Just tell me what it is."

"I work with computers at a company that produces surveillance equipment."

"There you go. That wasn't too difficult. Plus telling me you work with computers has the added bonus of me not wanting to ask any more questions. Try that with the next girl you see and you won't have to hope that her boss is murdered to secure a second date."

"And here I am thinking my search for love is over."

After the meal, he paid as promised and we said good night. Despite his psychotic clothes, anti-social personality and general weirdness, it was the best date I'd been on in months.

Chapter Five

Bob's murder was on the local news that night, but the report didn't tell me anything new. There was an appeal for information from the police and shots of our office block. Standing outside the No. 1 Croydon building, a towering, stack of fifty pence pieces where Porter & Porter had its headquarters, the reporter wore a solemn expression on his face as he signed off.

"A real tragedy that no one could have expected in a place like Croydon. This is Haider Jairaj for BBC London."

The next morning, my dear, departed boss made it into the national papers, though only to page nine in the one I looked at. It was a tatty little piece, basically a write up of the TV report with some added interviews with unnamed members of staff who described how popular Bob had been. I can't imagine who they spoke to. Maybe it was the team of Romanian cleaners who come every evening and stand apologetically up against the wall with their buckets and dusters as we march past them on our way home.

I read the paper on the tram into work. It felt strange to be going back. I dreaded seeing my colleagues who had been so quick to believe my guilt and had thrown their insults about to wound me. But having spent the day before feeling like a child bunking off school, staying home was not an option.

I needn't have worried about it. If there's one thing guaranteed to normalise, anesthetise and lobotomise away any drama it's working in finance. I walked up to the office, walked into the office, walked into the lift, walked out of the lift and it was as if nothing had changed.

There was still the constant workplace soundtrack of copiers and telephones, low-level chatter and tapping keys. My workmates buzzed about, few raising their eyes to greet me for another day at the grindstone. Someone dropped their coffee and a short burst of mockery and applause rose up then died away, like the clatter of fallen cymbals. If it weren't for the blue and white X in police tape across Bob's door I might have believed I'd imagined the whole thing. I half expected him to come bursting through it to scream at Ramesh for being too slow and faggy with his work.

I sat down at my S-shaped workstation with my deskmate Suzie on the other side. She made a purring sound to acknowledge my arrival but didn't look up from her screen.

"Morning, Suze," I said, as cheerfully as I could manage.

She chirped in reply, her eyes darting at me for the briefest of seconds as I powered up my computer.

"I need a drink, do you want one?"

She let out a squeak of polite refusal and I headed off to the breakroom. I was immediately seized and escorted over by my excitable best friend.

"Bloody hell, Izzy. Bluh-dee hell!"

Ramesh guided me to a free table and was about to start in on his interrogation when Wendy stormed over. Somewhere between forty and seventy, she had one of those faces that was impossible to make any sense of. Her beige knitwear was twinned with a bright pink skirt with kittens on.

"I've got my eye on you." She looked me up and down, as if searching for proof of my guilt. How could anyone resist her grumpy charm?

"Only one?" I checked.

She poked her glasses back up her nose. "I don't care what anyone else says. I reckon you're just the type to have killed Bob."

"The feeling's mutual, love." Her nemesis Ramesh stepped in to stick up for me.

Offended by the mere sound of his proudly metrosexual voice, Wendy launched herself into one of her trademark rants. "You young people think it's all such a joke, with your polyamorous relationships and your bath salts. I suppose murdering your boss is a bit of a laugh by today's standards but I'm having none of it."

The conversation was already off the rails, so I figured that one stupid question couldn't hurt. "Wendy, could you leave us alone, please? I need to talk to my friend."

"Huh!" She looked at me like I'd suggested she buy me lunch. "I'll leave you alone... when you're locked up where you belong."

She walked back over to her usual group of gossips and stirrers and recounted the whole conversation for their pleasure.

Even this interruption couldn't smother Ramesh's joy and he was soon back on topic. "You do realise this is the most extraordinary thing that has ever happened at Porter & Porter."

"Well I hope it is." I fished in my bag for a coin for the coffee machine.

"Why did it have to be the morning I had a dentist appointment? By the time I got here, Wendy was telling everyone that you were a Stalinist."

"A Stalinist?"

"Yeah." He paused before delivering the punchline. "She thought it meant devil worshiper."

"Close enough."

Ramesh grabbed both my hands in his like we were starting our own prayer circle. "Please tell me you killed Bob!"

My best friend's love of drama clearly outweighed his belief in law and order. The light brown skin around his deep brown eyes was all crinkled up as he awaited my response.

"You're the one who told the police I was on a date when he died. Which is why I'm here today, as free as a sparrow." I went over to the machine to get an extra sweet hot chocolate.

"Oh what a let-down." His voice died away and he peered about at the other tables in the breakroom. "It's so strange to think that the killer could be here with us right now."

I dug my tea stirrer into the little gap between my two front teeth as I took in the faces of our colleagues. "I doubt we were the only people Bob annoyed. We can't be sure the killer even works here."

"Ha, that's where you're wrong." Perking back up again, Ramesh could hardly control his excitement. "I know something you don't."

I gave him a look which said, *go on, get on with it.*

"Okay, but you're going to pee your pants." He allowed a few seconds of silent suspense. "Whoever killed Bob, stole the CCTV footage!"

"And?"

"Oh, come on, Izzy. The hard drives were behind a fingerprint scanning security door. Only five people had access."

A little surge of electricity ran through my brain.

Five suspects, how very Agatha Christie.

"Only Jack in security, members of the board and the head of I.T. could have done it," Ramesh continued but I was already way ahead of him.

"David, Amara, Jack, Wendy and…"

"And me," he said with a grin. He was enjoying this far too much.

I have to admit I was getting pretty excited myself. "That means we've got a twenty per cent chance of identifying the killer right from the start. And there's no way you did it."

"I could have!" He pretended to be offended.

"Not a chance. You're too sweet. You once refused to recycle a magazine with Jennifer Aniston on the cover because you felt sorry for her."

"How dare you, Izzy. I hated Bob as much as anyone. I could absolutely have done him in." He cast his eyes to the floor.

"Fine. Where were you on Wednesday night?"

A smile instantly broke out across his face. "I was at home watching trash on telly."

I let out a tired sigh. "Any witnesses?"

"Well, I skyped my girlfriend for a while but apart from that, only Elton and Kiki can confirm I was at home."

"I'm not sure that the British legal system accepts the testament of cats, but I believe you." I knocked back the dregs of my drink and recycled the cup.

"Great, so what's next?"

It had been fun for a few minutes but he should have known not to indulge my Tommy and Tuppence fantasy. "Ramesh, we're not the police. We can't investigate this."

Accidently tipping his chair over, the drama of his sudden rise to standing was lost. He compensated by angrily waving a rich tea finger at me.

"We're the only ones fit to investigate." At least he was whispering so that Wendy couldn't hear. "We know everything that goes on here."

"Have you been talking to my mother?"

"I'm fabulous and you've read just about every detective novel ever written." He made some good points.

"Yes but this is real life. Whoever killed Bob could come after us."

"Don't you see that this could be our moment? What can you say you've achieved that's more important than walking through that door yesterday?"

I didn't have an answer. His eyes were locked on mine and I

couldn't look away. At some point this had gone from being a joke to something he really cared about.

"I can't do this without you." His expression remained serious.

I resisted for maybe five seconds then picked up my phone and sent him a text. You know, to be subtle.

Fine, we can look into it. But don't let anyone else know.

He was still looking sad when the buzzing came through to his pocket. I was amazed he managed to hide his emotion as he wrote out his reply.

Wooooooooooooooooooooooooooooooo oooooo!

You won't regret it.

I bought a second hot chocolate to take back to my desk and we said our goodbyes.

As the Assistant Data Analyst's Assistant, my job mainly involves proofreading documents or looking over long lists of names for obvious duplicates, spelling mistakes and typos. I am fully aware that there is software out there that could automise most of what I do but luckily Porter & Porter is an old-fashioned company and my best friend is in charge of I.T.

Dan Phillips, the data analyst himself, is some sort of genius and works from home. He communicates with me by single line e-mails that never require a reply. Technically Suzie is his assistant and I'm hers which means I really don't have to know anything whatsoever about algorithms or data mining or any of the other clever things that they do. My work requires about one per cent of my brain function, leaving me plenty of time to daydream.

Jones, Dennis. 55 Cranley Gardens, SW4 5TQ
Jones, Dennis. 32 Blenheim Court, CR0 3RY
Jones, Derek. 6 St. James's Way, SM5 3BW

"Hi, Izzy. How are you doing?" Bob's co-deputy director Amara had popped up beside my desk. I love Amara and, if she turned out to be the one who killed Bob, I'd happily be a character witness at her trial. There's something so inspiring about her. She's not only the first female executive in the history of Porter & Porter, she's a dedicated mother to two phenomenally photogenic children and, from what I hear, a whiz on the tennis court.

I made a sad face because I like it when she's sympathetic. Even though her family are originally from Ghana and she's only about ten years older than me, I sometimes like to imagine that she's my mum.

Weirdo.

I'm not weird. You are!

"How did they treat you at the police station?" Amara was still there and I still hadn't said anything.

"It was fine." I nodded my head and pursed my lips together because I think that's how normal people act.

"Well if there's anything you need, you only have to ask."

"Thanks, Amara. But really, I'm doing all right."

You idiot, you should have pretended that you needed help and maybe we'd have become best friends.

Stop talking to yourself, weirdo.

Amara didn't notice me staring into space again because she'd turned towards Bob's office. "It is unthinkable what happened to him. I know we had our differences, but I wouldn't wish such a terrible death on anyone."

She looked genuinely sad then and shook her head. It was enough to convince me that she'd had nothing to do with the murder and that she should be put forward in the Queen's Honours List as Britain's nicest person.

"I'd better be off. It might sound trite to say it, but life must go on." She squeezed my arm which made me feel all special then walked off to speak to Jack by reception.

You know, we can't just assume that someone is innocent because they've got a friendly manner. First Ramesh, now Amara. There'll be no suspects left before long.

I ignored myself and got back to work.

Jones, Ellen. 15 Thorne Street, SW13 0PT
Jones, Ellen. 62 Bodmin Street, SW18 4PT

As I zoned into my work and out of reality, I wondered who in that office had the guts and savagery to kill Bob. My mind reeled between the five suspects – including Ramesh of course. At home with cats? Even if there was more chance of my mum being the murderer, my brain was right and we couldn't rule him out.

It was just then that the consulting team stalked into the office, twenty minutes late. Ten men aged twenty-eight to thirty-five in over-priced suits and hand-stitched leather brogues all with monosyllabic names like Craig, Dev and Nick. They looked like crack pilots preparing to fly off on some dangerous mission.

At the head of the pack was Will Gibbons. As well as being lead consultant, Will was a misogynistic thug and the man recently voted – by me in my head – as most likely to kick a puppy. He was the only person at work who Bob seemed to get along with and yet I'd seen the two of them screaming their heads off at one another down by East Croydon station just a week before the murder. Okay, Will couldn't have removed the CCTV data so he wasn't the outright killer, but I figured he at least merited a text message to Ramesh.

Are we absolutely certain it wasn't Will? He's just about the worst person I've ever met?

Sitting at his desk in the middle of the office, it took him proximately three seconds to reply.

Good point. Maybe he knows something. We'd better not exclude him entirely.

I could tell he was excited. He finished the message with smiley face, smiley face, kung-fu man, pizza slice.

One of the upsides of Bob being dead was that he was practically the only person who checked whether I was doing any work. I spent the rest of the morning gazing around the office at my colleagues. It was frankly disappointing that I had to rule so many of them out of our enquiries. None of the judgy P.A.s could have done it without an accomplice and while I loved the idea that Suzie, my near-mute deskmate, was the brutal mastermind we were searching for, it sadly wasn't to be.

The whole place was quiet that morning. It felt as if Bob's shouts, grunts and hurled fountain pens had left a hole in the Porter & Porter soundscape. Voices were whispery, like the mumbled condolences of a new boyfriend dragged along to a family funeral. Mobiles buzzed in people's pockets instead of the opening bars to "Eye of The Tiger" screaming across the room. We were in mourning. I doubted it would last long.

"Psssst…" Jack the security guard hissed on the return leg of yet another trip to the bathroom. "What did he look like?"

"Sorry?" I pretended to be hard at work as he arrived at my desk.

"I mean Bob, all cut up. What did he look like?"

In all honesty, despite his pallid skin and the litres of blood splashed about the place, Bob looked more tranquil than I'd ever seen him. I don't think this was the information our moustachioed protector was looking for.

"I couldn't see his face," I lied. "He was hunched over."

"Creepy." Jack shuddered exaggeratedly. On the other side of the desk, Suzie flicked a glance in our direction and let out a similarly terrified chirp.

"Who d'ya reckon done it then?" He scratched one long strawberry-grey sideburn as he spoke.

"It's hard to say. Is it true that someone wiped the video cameras?"

He peered around to check that no one was listening, but then spoke in his usual loud voice. "That's right, the hard drives are gone. Don't know who would've done something like that."

His words died away but he remained there, staring out of the window at Croydon's skyline. After about a minute with no sound except for the scratching of his yellowed nails on his hairy cheeks, he spoke again.

"Was probably kids." He sighed a long, agonised sigh. "It's always bloody kids."

With his investigation concluded, Jack walked back across the office. I was considering whether this slightly doddery relic of an undemanding 1980s employment policy could have brutally slit open my recently departed supervisor when the cartoon hands on my clock told me it was time for lunch.

Chapter Six

As I ate my sun-blushed California salad, I ran through the suspects in my head like a mantra.

David, Amara, Jack, Wendy, Ramesh and maybe Will.

Ignoring for a moment her wonderful temperament and great skin, Amara had plenty to gain from Bob's death but, with two young kids and all the work she had on, it would be difficult to find a moment in her busy schedule to plot a murder.

Ramesh, meanwhile, had been ritually humiliated on a daily basis. Bob had taken a sick pleasure in dishing out cruelty and my bestie was frequently his target. Plenty of people assumed that Ramesh was gay, it wasn't just Bob. They noticed his good fashion sense, love of cheesy pop music and over the top personality and quickly identified his sexuality. The one thing they hadn't factored in was that, for this to be true, he'd have to be attracted to men, a fact that was apparently absent from their criteria.

Bob hadn't started this unhappy phenomenon, but he'd weaponised it. Turning it into a stick to beat my friend with at every possible opportunity. Ramesh told me countless times about the abuse he was put through, perhaps he'd finally done something about it.

Hairy Jack the security guard had hardly been best mates with Bob and their animosity had boiled over into a punch up at the last office Christmas party. The only other way he was remarkable though was in how little he stood to gain from Bob's absence. Of course, according to Christie, a complete lack of motive often provides the most likely suspects so I wouldn't be ruling him out just yet.

Wendy's awful dress sense was almost enough to convince me she could kill a man. And then there was all the fuss she'd made about finding me in Bob's office. It seemed a bit overplayed to me. What better way to hide her guilt than to wait for me to find the body and kick up a stink?

Will from consulting had the temperament, the savage look and the physical strength to slash someone open but it seemed impossible he could have killed Bob on his own as he couldn't get into the server room to delete the CCTV footage. He was still the likely culprit, nonetheless.

And last, but not to be dismissed just because he was the most handsome, what about our managing director? If smooth, capable David was hiding some dark secret beneath his shiny exterior, I guess I'd have to be the one to delve into it.

Six measly suspects; they don't stand a chance.

My spot in the corner of our single floor, open plan office would be a perfect vantage point to spy on our suspects. I was hoping the fact no one knew I was busy sleuthing, (with my over the top sidekick, who would come to all the wrong conclusions and enable me to solve the case) would mean they'd go about their business as normal and reveal all their guilty secrets.

The breakroom got busy at lunch and the rumours and hearsay were soon flying around like bats in a cave. Ramesh turned up and we eavesdropped on several interesting speculations on who the killer might be before getting dragged into one of our own.

"I still say The Freak did it," Will announced as he sat down with a lamb durum from the kebab shop down the road. For once he was not surrounded by his pack of pseudo-yuppies.

"I was in a Burger Baron with about a hundred other people." My panic re-emerged as I was forced to defend myself.

"Classy."

"Says the man stinking up the office with Mediterranean take away."

"Well fine." He licked a spot of yoghurt sauce from his shirt cuff. "You didn't actually kill Bob, but that doesn't mean you weren't involved. Maybe you got your GBFF to do the deed whilst you chomped down on a double cheeseburger."

"Yeah she did!" Wendy screamed across the room. She was huddled together with Pauline from accounts and a couple of others from their gossip gang. "The Freak did it!"

The shining light of the consulting department, Will was most definitely the person I'd get rid of if I was given carte blanche with a letter opener. It wasn't just that he was arrogant, he was his dead boss's protégé – a study in Bob – and everything he said reminded me of his odious mentor.

"And where were you on Wednesday night?" I asked the silver-suited consultant.

"I was with a lucky young lady showing her a good time."

"Does she have a name?"

"Funnily enough I didn't get it. We weren't really there for conversation."

"Who has time?" Ramesh said. "When you're paying by the hour I mean."

"We met in a bar and she wasn't big on talking." Will sounded more insulted by the idea he could have paid for sex than the suggestion he killed Bob.

"How convenient." I stared him down. "So then you don't have an alibi?"

"Not everyone still lives with Mummy and Daddy, Freak. I reckon about half the office would've been at home alone on Wednesday night. That doesn't mean we all killed him. Why would I even want to?" He jutted out his jaw and bared his teeth like an offended Doberman. Despite his swish clothes and slickly styled hair-do, Will couldn't disguise the decidedly canine features of his face.

"Wasn't Bob your boss before he was promoted?" I didn't give him time to answer. "As senior member of the consultancy team, wouldn't that make you the obvious person to replace him?"

Everyone in the breakroom had stopped to listen and the place was now consumed by their anticipation. Suddenly silent, Wendy looked on in wonder, like I'd discovered Will's smoking gun.

"Let's calm down," he said with uncharacteristic restraint. "I'm sorry I said you were the killer and I'm sorry I was rude to Ramesh. I wouldn't kill someone just for a promotion."

"What would you kill them for?"

There was a communal gasp and Will smiled back at me. "Nice try. If you'll excuse me, I have to get back to work."

He picked up his wrap and made his exit to the murmur of suspicious voices. With its ever present assortment of cooing assistants and preening executives, being a Porter & Porter staff member is like working alongside a Greek chorus.

"Pretty damning, don't you think?" Ramesh chimed in.

"No, not really. A less than romantic method for meeting a woman is hardly evidence of a capacity to kill. That and the fact that he couldn't have accessed the CCTV mean we've got no case against him."

"All right, who's next?"

After lunch, the super-boss appeared with the two plainclothes officers who had interviewed me the morning before. David looked exhausted. Whilst I'd been lazing about at my desk all morning – spying, snooping and drinking tureens of hot chocolate – he'd been suffering through a patented Irons and Brabazon grilling.

"If I could have your attention, please." With Amara at his side, he addressed the office. "I haven't had a chance to talk to you all together yet and I'm sorry about that."

David was in his mid-thirties but had always seemed younger. That morning, his face was creased and pale like he'd aged a decade in a day.

"You all know what happened here on Wednesday night. It goes without saying that we are deeply saddened by Bob's death and I'm sure you're eager to get to the bottom of this tragedy."

David stepped back reverentially and Amara assumed control. "The two officers leading the enquiry are here to talk to you today. I'm going to hand you over to Detective Inspectors Irons and Brabazon. We ask that you cooperate in any way you can."

Amara mouthed a few words in the direction of D.I. Irons and she stepped forward to speak.

"I'm just here to reiterate how important it is that you share with us any information which may lead to a better understanding of what happened to Mr. Thomas. We now have a confirmed time of death of nine o'clock on Wednesday night. We haven't had any reports of anyone arriving or leaving at that time but maybe you noticed someone acting strangely, or hanging around the building that day. Perhaps you have info on Mr Thomas that could explain why someone would want to harm him. If anything occurs to you, whatever it might be, please get in touch."

Standing behind the officers, Jack from security was surveying the crowd with his chest puffed out like he thought he was part of the investigation, rather than one of the suspects. When D.I. Irons finished speaking, the room came back to life and my colleagues returned to their desks or opted for post-lunch coffee and more dissection of the facts.

Only one person approached the police. I watched from my desk as Wendy walked over to them, jabbing her finger in my direction, her cardigan shaking with rage. It was ten minutes before D.I. Brabazon came to talk to me. He was surprisingly chatty.

"Don't worry about her. There's always someone who's convinced they know who the killer is." He was looking even more action figure-ish today. His wide, triangular sideburns appeared to have been inked on with a felt-tip.

"Have there been any breakthroughs?" I asked.

"We've plenty of leads to follow." He paused and looked at me as if he'd just noticed I was there. "What about you? Have you thought of anything else that might be useful?"

"The apple."

He looked at me like I was a child. "What apple?"

"The apple on Bob's desk was cut in half. I imagine the autopsy showed he'd eaten half of it and yet there was no knife in his office. Either the murderer washed it and put it back or there'll be a red-handled fruit knife missing. Who knows, there might even be blood traces in the breakroom."

"Hmmm." He clicked on the ballpoint pen in his hand for a moment. "Good point."

"You know, I might be able to help you. If you share what you've already found out, I could keep watch on the suspects here in the office."

"Like an undercover agent, you mean?" He managed a smile for the first time.

"Something like that, yeah."

"Do you have any experience?"

"I, urmmm... I'm a big fan of crime fiction." I might have blushed a little as I told him this.

"Good afternoon, Miss Palmer." He began to walk away.

"I've read every last Agatha Christie," I said a little too insistently, so that everyone in a three-desk radius turned to judge me. "Even the short stories!" It did not make him reconsider.

I watched from my dugout as Irons and Brabazon took over David's office and called people in one by one to talk to them. They were clearly sticking to the theory that one of our five suspects had been involved. David had already been quizzed at the station, which just left Jack, Amara, Wendy and Ramesh to call by the makeshift interrogation room for five minutes each.

I thought that would be the end of it but then a message went out for Will to take his turn. When he emerged a few minutes later, all his macho bravado had deserted him. His face was ashen and he barely raised his eyes as he navigated the maze of desks on the way back to his own. It removed all doubt that we were right to include him on our list of suspects and I wondered what the police had got on him.

The detectives left about an hour later, but not before a team of scene of crime officers had appeared to seal off the breakroom. They removed one red-handled knife in a ziplock bag but there'd been two there last week.

I thought I'd take advantage of the fact that no one cared what I did all day to check out a theory. It made sense that the killer had got rid of the CCTV footage from the office, but they would still have been caught by building security if they'd used the lifts or gone out through the foyer. This surely meant that, as the police were yet to make any arrests, the killer had left through the fire escape.

I traced the path they would have taken to avoid any cameras. Hugging the wall outside the office, I worked my way along the corridor to the emergency exit.

"Got a bit of a bad back," I had to explain when a delivery driver emerged from the lifts and looked at me like I needed a lobotomy.

I wriggled about on the wall like a bear against a tree trunk until he was gone and I could continue on my way. The stairwell down to the rear exit was free of cameras. I walked down all four floors to check and came out at the bottom by the fire doors which were supposed to be alarmed but everyone knew they weren't. Wendy and her mates always went down there to smoke *in peace and quiet.* Just outside, a mound of cigarette butts and heel-stamped drinks cans were piling up on the shabby concrete.

I was about to head back inside when I noticed the remains of a broken bottle among the other detritus. Most of the pieces had been removed, but I could tell it was the narrow-mouthed, wide-based shape common to champagne. Though the main label was missing, the tag around the neck proved that it was the same expensive brand that Bob had in his office. I took a photo on my phone then walked round to the front entrance to go back up in the lift.

On the way, I debated with myself whether it was really my civic duty to let the ungrateful police in on what I'd discovered. Lucky for them, I won the argument.

Chapter Seven

"I could get used to people being knocked off in the office," Ramesh declared after David let us go home again early with the police still busy in the office. "Let's hope it's a serial killer."

I looked at him with my stern, *be-serious-for-once* face as we walked towards the station. "Go easy, Ra. I don't think that a couple of half days are worth more of our co-workers being slaughtered."

His voice got all sombre. "You're right. No one deserves to be hacked up with a fruit knife. Which is why we have to find Bob's killer." Even when he was trying to *be serious for once,* he sounded like he could break out in giggles at any moment.

We walked along quietly and this idea echoed in my mind. It was true. The fact that Bob had treated us like the runts of the office for years, didn't justify his sorry end.

"Come on," I said as we walked past Sainsbury's. "Tell me what the police asked you."

His standard goofy smile was back on his face. "The usual stuff. They wanted to know where I was on Wednesday night and all about my relationship with Bob. They didn't seem too worried that I didn't have an alibi and told me to get in touch if I thought of anything."

"Will was as white as copier paper afterwards. Wish I knew what they'd said to him."

"Totally. He and Bob were always pratting about together and ever since yesterday, he's been acting weird. He's snappy or friendly, easily spooked or all calm. Will knows something, that's for sure, and I don't trust him for a second."

"We're not going to find out what he's up to without a plan," I said as we arrived at our tram stop. "I've been watching the other suspects all day and no one's done the slightest thing of interest. Where's the suspicious skulking? Where's the smoking gun which will lead us to the killer?"

Ramesh let out a miserable sigh. "As far as I can tell there weren't even any footprints around Bob's door. Trust our colleagues to take all the fun out of a murder."

We squeezed in on the bench beside an Adidas-emblazoned woman with a young baby. I looked at the electronic arrivals board which helpfully informed me that my tram to New Addington would be arriving in nine hundred and ninety-nine minutes.

"The police didn't want my help either." I got busy making faces at the baby as we discussed Bob's violent death. "I'm not saying we're experts or anything but you'd think that with all the cuts to public services, they'd appreciate the offer."

"You're right." Ramesh sat up straight and suddenly seemed more decisive than normal. "We need to be more active. We can't just sit around and wait for someone to make a mistake."

"Maybe you can find an excuse to poke around on their computers?"

"It's probably illegal." He looked put out as a tiny Nike-bootied foot kicked his arm. "But I'll give it a go. I should tell you though that, if I'm the killer, I'll plant incriminating evidence to throw you off my trail."

"Thanks for your honesty."

"I mean it. I definitely had the motive. Who else hated Bob more than I did? And my alibi is pathetic. I suppose the police could check CCTV footage in my area to show I went home before the murder but there's nothing to say I didn't jump in a taxi and come back?"

"Good point." The baby was making a cute little gurgling noise which made me want to smush his cheeks. "And I've always thought you had the look of a felon."

Ramesh got all serious for a second. "It's a shame though. Because I know I didn't kill him and I wish I could prove it to make our job easier."

The electronic board suddenly showed *1 minute* and my tram appeared at the end of the street.

"Yeah. Real shame."

"I'll call you tonight," he said over the sound of people bustling forward and the little boy crying.

"I won't answer!" I waved goodbye to the baby and got on board.

It's actually faster for me to go by bus than tram but I love shooting along through stopped traffic and the quiet buzz of the motor as we speed down the tracks. Yeah – no big deal –unlike 95% of other cities in Britain, Cool Croydon has a modern tram system. Take that, *Central London.*

When I got home, Dad's car was outside our house and I could see through the window that he, Mum and Greg were deep in conversation.

"You're being ridiculous, Gregory." My mum's voice reached me before I'd set foot on the drive. "Why would a total stranger walk in off the street and kill a man? We're talking about South London, not the mean streets of Chicago."

I walked along the path and through the door that nobody had bothered to close. *This is South London,* I thought to myself, *not the trusting streets of some small American town.*

"I'm afraid I'm a bit confused by the whole thing," Dad was saying as I went into the lounge to find them looking at three of Greg's easels that had been set up with large flip charts in place of his artworks.

I gave Mum a kiss and plonked myself down on the sofa by Dad. "What's all this then?"

"This is for you." Mum's tone suggested I should be eternally grateful. "There's one for suspects, one for clues and one for hypotheses. We've already got you started."

By *started*, she meant that they'd written up her designated headings in thick black marker on the otherwise blank pages.

"You'll have the case solved in no time." Greg was even more sarcastic than I was.

Never one to sit around for long, Mum jumped up with a marker in both hands. "So, tell us what you learnt today."

I sunk down into the sofa and wished they'd leave me alone to have a nap. In five minutes flat, Mum had extracted the basic information from me and the list of suspects was complete.

"Only six?" Standing in front of the mantelpiece, scribbling away with her markers, she was full of energy. "Six suspects is child's play. You'll have it solved in no time."

"I think that what you need to focus on is the murder scene itself." My Dad had caught up and, in his quiet, hesitant way was almost as animated as Mum. "There's bound to be something there that'll set you on the right path."

I wasn't so confident. "It's not as simple as sitting around and thinking about it."

"The half apple on Bob's desk is interesting," Greg replied as if he hadn't heard me. "It must have been cut in two and yet there's no knife there. Sounds like the missing murder weapon to me."

Yeah, yeah, Greg. I'd worked that out myself, thank you very much. "I mentioned that to the police and they immediately went looking at the knives in the breakroom to check."

Mum wrote, *apple/murder weapon,* up on the clues board. "And what about the absent shoes and the one sock?"

There was a murmur from my two dads.

"You have to ask yourself why he took them off," Daddy number one told us. "Perhaps he'd been having a shower or clipping his toenails."

"All right. That's enough," I interrupted before the others could offer their perspective. "It's like you're doing a jigsaw puzzle for me. You're taking all the fun out of it."

"Really, Izzy. We're only trying to help." Mum showed me her puppy-dog eyes to make me feel guilty. It always worked.

"Fine. I'm sorry. You're wonderful parents and I appreciate everything you do." To counteract the force of her supreme mum-powers, I smiled sweetly.

"Come along, Ted." My stepfather was better at taking a hint than Mum. "How about a cup of tea?"

"Here you go, grumpy." Mum tucked one of the markers into my top jacket pocket. "See what you can figure out without your silly old parents getting in the way."

She began to head out after her– what's the male equivalent of a harem? But I caught her by the hand. "You're not old, Mum."

"Ahh, darling." She smiled at me then in a way that made her pretty face curl up like a fortune telling fish as she squeezed my hand in hers.

"You're silly, but you're not old." Like an emoji at the end of a text message, I stuck my tongue out to make sure she knew I was joking. Her smile held firm and she cantered off towards the garden.

Alone in the lounge, I sat looking at the lists in Mum's neat, ex-teacher's script. I hoped that, if I stared at them long enough, some deep, hidden truth would emerge. The group of suspects was no more than a collection of names, but the clues were different. As I read over each item, I could picture where I'd seen them in Bob's office.

I closed my eyes to beam myself back there. The tiny sword – standing proud from his back like a flagpole on the moon – shone under the fluorescent strip lights. His blood was like a lake in the night

54

time, a black mirror reflecting nothing. But it was the missing items that stood out most. The shoes and sock, his brown woollen tie and the knife for his apple.

The blood covered Bob's desk, but there was no sign of it anywhere else, which means he was killed right where I found him. And yet, there was no sign of a struggle; no smudged bloodstains or toppled picture frames. To me that suggested Bob had been unconscious when the knife went in. So what had knocked him out? Was it the contents of the packet of medicine on his desk? Or had he overdone it with the champagne? Bob was a big bloke and would've needed a good few bottles to get him so drunk he passed out. It seemed unlikely.

I had to wonder again why he'd be sitting in front of his desk instead of behind it. Bob had a huge leather executive chair that would have looked at home in a Bond villain's lair. Whenever I was in there with him, he put on this big show of raising his seat up so that he was much higher than me. He wouldn't have let just anyone sit in it. So who was there? An enemy, a friend or a lover?

My poke around in that neon-lit room in my head was suddenly invaded by foreign objects and inconvenient visitors. There was my father in his dirty overalls telling me he'd looked all over and couldn't find his screwdriver. My teacher from nursery school dropped by too, and for some reason my clothes were covered in milk.

I woke up to find myself laid out on the sofa. The mental sojourn to Bob's office had only been sustainable for so long before I'd nodded off. Though my dream made little sense, I had woken up with one fact finally clear in my head.

I had something to add to the middle flipchart. Underneath the other clues I wrote, *Champagne bottle* and put a star beside all the missing items.

The list of hypotheses was blank but it wouldn't stay that way for long. I held up the marker and started to write.

Whoever killed Bob took away his tie, sock, shoes, the champagne bottle and the knife from his apple to cover their tracks. Is there anything else missing?

I stood back to see how all those disparate threads might come together. It was only the first step but it felt like I was going in the right direction. Suddenly my head was flooded with ideas and I popped the pen lid off once more.

Bob was unconscious when the knife went in. Perhaps someone smacked him with the champagne bottle then finished off the job.

Now all I needed to work out was who he was drinking with?

Chapter Eight

Fridays are my night to binge on bad food and worse cable TV. I try to stick to shows within the range of channels 250-280 which provides me with a healthy selection of food, travel and lifestyle programming. I know I could put on Netflix or iPlayer and watch things I actually want to see, but to be honest that feels too much like homework.

"Come out with me, tonight." Doctor Danny bounded into the back lounge, just as I was settling down to my evening's entertainment.

"No, thanks." I plumped a cushion theatrically. "I just got comfortable."

Danny always threatened to drag me out on the town when he was in the country but I wasn't taking the bait. If he'd galloped into my room, naked from the hair down, and claimed me as his love-woman (sorry, not good at sexy talk) then maybe I'd have gone for it. The thought of spending a whole evening in public with him as I nervously tried to decipher whether his boyish enthusiasm was flirtatious or, of all things, *brotherly,* was not my idea of a good time.

"Go on, Izzy, a load of my college mates will be there. You know Jonesy and Sasha."

Do I?

"And you'd love Lyds and Miguel."

I looked at the muscly arms protruding from his tight, white t-shirt and dismissed the very idea from my mind. "Nope, sorry. Say *hi* to Johnny and Sasha though."

"Oh go on, darling," Mum yelled from upstairs. "Don't be such a stick in the bog."

No matter where my mother was in the house, she somehow knew everything that was going on. I'd long suspected a system of hidden microphones.

She came storming down the stairs to poke her nose in. "You *must* go. Greg and I are off to our therapy retreat." Which I'd already heard far too much about and I'm pretty sure was a nudist convention. "You'll be all alone."

"Exactly."

Danny looked disappointed but Mum wasn't giving up. "Really, Izzy, where's your spirit of adventure? I sometimes wonder whether we brought home the wrong baby and my real daughter is off trekking across a desert somewhere or dancing on a bar."

"Oh, Mother. I'm sorry I never lived up to your expectations. If only I'd known you wanted me to be a globe-trotting stripper."

"Such a sourpuss." Danny had slipped into the voice I can only assume he uses for child patients. "You're missing out, Izzy."

"Come along, Rosemarie." Greg was holding a suitcase and looked tired before the weekend had begun. "We'll miss the special badminton."

Mum ignored her husband in order to make one last plea. "Darling, promise me you won't spend your whole weekend in front of a screen."

"Urrmmm, no." I grinned belligerently at her.

"It's no use, Danny. She's as bull-headed as a farmer."

"That's not a saying and it makes no sense."

"I guess we'll just have to leave old sourpuss to her solitude." Danny made another soppy face and it made me love him both more and less.

"Bye bye, Danny, my angel." Mum moved in for a cuddle. She blatantly loves him more than me.

"You enjoy yourself, Rosie," he replied – that suck-up.

"Oh, I will." With a leer, she sidled out of the room.

"If I can't convince you to come, I'll be off too."

Danny tried one last cutesy look on me and then I was alone at last. I had a jug of pre-mixed mojito at my side, a frozen pizza in the oven and "World's Stupidest Chefs" was just starting on the screen in front of me. I was set for the night.

My phone buzzed. I knew I should have turned it off.

> **Izzy, I've just had a twenty-minute conversation with my cats. Please save me.**

It was my erstwhile sidekick.

> *Sorry, Ramesh. Can't move. The television won't let me.*

58

Please! I'm about to watch the Eurovision Song Contest. Come round and we can pretend we don't enjoy it.

I didn't know it was on this weekend.

It's not.

Sorry. Busy. Send my love to Mr and Mrs Cuddles.

No, Izzy... Nooooooo!

I closed the app and managed to watch five minutes of halfwit cooks dropping things, falling over and messing up recipes before I was interrupted once more by my mobile's angry illumination.

"Hi there," a voice said. I'm not trying to be mysterious, I had no idea who it was.

"Yes?" I replied, equally vaguely.

"Izzy, it's Tarquil."

Ah ha. Tarquil! The only man I've ever started talking to based solely on the ridiculousness of his name.

"Wow. It's great to hear from you."

I'd been chatting with him a month earlier but not heard anything since. It was too good to be true.

"I've been pretty busy with work recently but I'm free tonight if you fancy meeting." His voice was as posh as his name.

"I did have other plans." I looked up to see a chef with his shoelaces tied together.

"Go on, it's my treat. Name the restaurant."

An hour later, I was sitting at a table for two in Croydon's premiere dining venue. Le Sheek is on the top floor of the Porter & Porter building and affords a view across London's most populous borough. I know people give Croydon a hard time for being cultureless, ugly and generally a bit naff but ever since I was a kid I've loved its skyline. Driving into town with my parents I felt like Little Orphan Annie on a night out in Manhattan, with the shabby charm of the long-gone Safari

59

cinema just as glamorous to me as Radio City. Plus Christie's *Death in the Clouds* kicks off at the old Croydon airport and what higher recommendation is there than that?

I was happy to be looking out across the Fairfield Halls and over to the clock tower on Katherine Street, especially as I'd never be able to afford a meal at Le Sheek under normal circumstances. I was almost as cheerful forty minutes later when Tarquil still hadn't shown up. The insistent waiters' glances and suggestions I order something other than a bottle of their third-cheapest wine barely bothered me as I knew that, at any moment, I would meet the polite, handsome man who had invited me.

It was only when I'd been waiting for an hour that I finally accepted he wasn't coming and a tangible channel of anger shot through me. I felt like smashing the restaurant to pieces, tossing glasses of water into the snobby waiters' eyes and blustering out. I wanted to, but I didn't. In fact I sat there for another ten minutes working out the least embarrassing way to escape. I considered faking a phone call and telling the concierge that poor Tarquil had been in an accident but, in the end, I left thirty quid on the table and slunk out when no one was looking.

The lift arrived with a fake retro ding, and I pushed through a pack of eager diners to be alone in the wood-panelled box. I was surprisingly miserable about the whole thing. After all, it wasn't the first time someone had backed out of a date with no word. I could only assume that dear, darling Tarquil had peeked his head into the restaurant and not liked what he saw.

I wouldn't have felt so disappointed if it hadn't been for the time I'd spent imagining the ridiculous names he and I would give our children. And the only reason that I'd allowed Tarquil to fire my imagination like that was because he'd seemed so different from most of the blokes I met online. He actually seemed nice.

With another digital ding the lift stopped at the ground floor and I stumbled out into the street. I would once more board the tram in my completely out of place little blue dress. Rude kids would say rude things and old people would avoid eye contact as I stared out at the blur of streetlamps and kebab shops we were shuttling past. I was actually quite looking forward to the good old cry I'd have when I got home to my cold pizza, but then I noticed someone I knew.

My boss David was walking past the station, thirty metres in front of me. I kept in the shadows in case he turned round – stupid of course as no one could miss a large weirdo in a sparkly mini-dress stalking after them. He continued on down the road before turning into a supermarket. *Trust David to shop at Waitrose.*

I walked slowly past the entrance to make sure he wouldn't be able to see me, before doubling back and going into the shop. It was full of besuited commuters returning late from the office or post-work drinks in the capital. I passed a middle-aged man with an avocado in each hand. His eyes were glazed over and he looked like he'd just finished a stint of audience participation at a Fairfield Halls hypnotist show.

I cut through the cereal aisle, past countless hovering night-ghouls on their last stop before home, before finding David surrounded by glass bottles. He looked as dumbstruck by the selection as anyone else there and, without my strategy to always go for the on-offer £4.99 option with the fanciest label, he was out of his depth. I stopped just in time to avoid walking right into his line of sight and hid at the end of the aisle to watch.

I was tempted to text Ramesh but didn't want to let David out of my sight now that I was on his trail. What I hoped to learn by watching him choose a bottle of wine wasn't clear to me. The fact was though that, as our boss, he'd be the most difficult of our potential murderers to get close to.

He took down a tall, thin bottle from the top shelf – clearly a pricy choice – and weighed it in his hand as if this would reveal its true value. He did the same with another option then attempted to make a selection. I was so caught up studying his intense, serious expression as his eyes flicked between the bottles, that I failed to notice how completely visible my head was.

"Izzy?" he said, catching sight of me peering around from the end of the aisle like a tall woman following her boss around a supermarket.

I pretended to be very interested in the display I was standing next to.

"Izzy?" he said again.

"Oh, David." I looked his way. "I didn't see you."

"What are you doing here?"

"Just picking up a little something." I grabbed a bottle from the shelf before realising it was strawberry flavoured, tongue-tingling lubricant. "Grrrr, always be prepared!" Hoping it would make me seem more normal, I took a pack of condoms too.

"Are you off somewhere nice?" He looked a little worried about me.

"No, no. I was just heading home to bed actually."

"Good idea." His brow knitted closer together.

"Yeah, I should probably be off." I flapped my purchases in the air in front of his face.

"Sure. Have a great weekend."

I walked down to the tills to queue up. Rather annoyingly, David arrived about twenty seconds later with his bottle of wine.

"Is that all?" the old French woman at the till asked me. She had a scowl on her face like she thought I should be stoned to death.

"Yep. No food for me. Just medium-size condoms and Very Berry fizzy lubricant."

"Twelve pounds sixty."

"And this," David said, placing the bottle of wine next to my items.

"Really, David, on your salary you should be able to afford your own booze."

"No, it's my treat." He stuck his credit card into the machine. "I won't let it be said that I never do anything for my employees."

"Ooh, contraceptives and sex aids." My bottle of red at Le Sheek had clearly gone to my head. I was using my completely inappropriate, saucy voice. "You do know how to treat a girl."

He watched me with a look of concern as I failed to open a plastic carrier bag. This drew a scornful glare from the shop assistant. The unnecessary use of the world's resources was clearly a greater sin in her eyes than the fornication she imagined I was about to engage in.

When we got outside, I tried to think of a non-weird way to say goodbye. Nothing came to mind.

"Izzy, will you join me for a drink? There's a pub round the corner where you can actually hear each other talk. It's almost pleasant."

I started laughing and couldn't stop. I didn't think for a second that he was serious until I caught the disappointed look on his face and realised my mistake.

"Is it because I'm your boss? I can always fire you if it makes you more comfortable?" He smiled. I think this was a joke.

Instead of accepting the invitation, I burst into another fit of laughter. I couldn't get a single human word out.

For goodness sake, Izzy. Stop acting like you've been huffing nitrous oxide and say yes!

"Another night maybe?"

Still guffawing like a moron, I almost managed to compose myself. "Yeah, I'd like that."

I was having a seriously difficult time understanding what was going on. Had my inappropriately flirty comments just got me a date?

He was smiling again and so I smiled too and we held each other's gaze. It was insanely romantic and totally unlike the normal end-of-evening interactions I have with men in which they either spear their faces into mine or completely fail to come up with an excuse for why they have to be leaving so quickly.

"I'll call you."

There was a bit more smiling, some backing away without turning, then finally we'd disengaged. He went off on his way home and I walked to the tram stop. So what if there were mouthy teens everywhere and old people who looked like shell-shocked soldiers? There was even a bloke with a beard being sick into a Poundstretcher carrier bag, but none of it bothered me.

Tarquil could push right off. I had the promise of a date with an extremely nice bloke, who already knew how gangly I was. A date with a man who was neither half the size of me, nor – to my knowledge – a collector of ladies' wigs.

At least I think that's what he meant. It had to be, right? Unless I'd got the wrong end of the stick and he was just worried about me as I swanned around Croydon in my ridiculously short dress with my lube and condoms like a woman in a sandwich board, advertising a free sex buffet.

I suddenly didn't feel so confident.

Chapter Nine

Monday morning rushed round once more, complete with insistent alarm clocks and a sleepy-eyed trek to work.

"I can't believe it!" Ramesh was excited. "He totally asked you out, that randy fox. If it was me, I'd have gone with Mr Lover-Lover right then."

"And you wonder why people think you're gay?"

We were sitting in East Croydon station, sipping milky coffees with plenty of caramel, chocolate topping and marshmallows to hide the coffee taste that we weren't ready to handle. The world was thundering past us in a long black raincoat.

"It was a great opportunity. If he'd taken you back to his place, you could have poked through his stuff. Maybe he's left the bloody clothes there or maybe Bob was blackmailing him and you could have found the letters, or... or... no, that's all I've got."

"I'm not going to sleep with every suspect to find out if they're guilty."

"Fine, just the men."

"You know, I'm not entirely sure he *was* asking me out. Maybe he wanted to take me somewhere to get help."

"Or maybe you've finally found a man who's got a thing for really clumsy women."

My coffee finished, I gnawed on the paper cup. "There had to be one out there somewhere. Who knew he was under my nose the whole time? Anyway, what did you do this weekend?"

"Oh, I watched the first three seasons of Poirot and skyped Patricia. I'm not enjoying this long-distance thing." Ramesh's girlfriend is doing a Masters for a year in Edinburgh. "I thought we could cope with it but it's much tougher than I'd expected. I'm lonely and there's no one to stop me eating Pot Noodles all the time."

"Poor baby. But more importantly, did Poirot teach you anything useful?"

"Not really. One episode made me wonder if you'd killed Bob and another made me think I might have done it. For a while I considered growing a moustache too, but by my twentieth hour of watching I was basically losing my mind. It's starting to seem that an intimate knowledge of Agatha Christie plots might not be enough to crack this case wide open."

"You're probably right. Lucky for us I've come up with a plan."

"Oooh, a plan!" He sat up straight and crushed his empty coffee cup in his hand in a surprisingly aggressive fashion. "That sounds much better than waiting for someone to confess."

"Be quiet and listen. There are video camera type things in the office, right?" I didn't wait for his answer, I knew full well he had one after the drama of his am-dram audition tape. "I never understood why Poirot doesn't just tell his suspects one by one that he knows they're guilty and see how they react."

"How d'you mean?"

"At the end of the book the killer always fesses up, so why doesn't he just tell them at the beginning that he thinks they did it to see whether they spill? He wastes so much time investigating. All we have to do is send messages around the office saying we know who killed Bob and maybe we'll get lucky."

"You want to confront the suspects, even David?"

"No, not David, or Amara either. If they found out we were nosing about they would probably fire us."

"Okay, but why do we need a webcam?"

"Don't worry your pretty little head about it. Just set it up tomorrow in the empty office on the seventh floor and do exactly as I instruct."

When we arrived at work, I gave Ramesh his instructions and then got down to the important job of actually doing a bit of my job. I figured I couldn't go much longer without someone noticing how little I was getting done, so I dutifully processed a whole batch of new contacts. It was as mind numbingly interesting as always, but gave me time to think through the various implications and complications of dating my boss.

First, I had to consider the fact that the attentive, rather charming man who was no doubt heels under head besotted with me was also a suspect in the crime I was attempting to investigate. At the same time, I wasn't getting any younger and my mother wasn't complaining about me being single any less, so even the hint of a boyfriend would make my home life a lot easier.

The one thing that worried me was the possibility that he actually was the murderer and was checking that I hadn't discovered his secret. Even then, I couldn't really see a downside to the situation. Either we would go out, fall in love and I'd find fame as an internationally adored poet – a sort of modern-day, Lord Byron – so that we could both leave P&P forever, or I'd find the evidence to prove he was a savage killer and, on the back of that success, launch my own private detective agency. Unless I was overlooking any significant issues it was surely a win-win.

I needed something to keep my mind off David for a while so I went to talk to Jack during the coffee break. He was holed up in his cupboard by the door into the office, watching funny videos on his computer.

"Oi, Izzy. Have you seen this one?" He tilted his screen my way to show me a bunch of baby pandas tumbling over one another.

I admit, we spent the next three minutes laughing our heads off at the funny little animals before I remembered what I'd gone there to talk about.

"So, don't the security doors here keep a record of who came in and when?" I asked. "Couldn't we work out who the murderer was from the time stamps on the doors?"

His face was instantly serious and he peered about to see if anyone was listening. "Your mate Ramesh is more likely to know about that than me, but from what I understand, the system was too old and there was no off-site backup. When the killer took the hard drives, all that data went with him."

Or her, I thought. *It's the twenty-first century, Jack. Women can be killers too.*

"What about the video cameras in the rest of the building? Wouldn't they tell us who was still here when Bob was killed?"

He paused for a moment and looked as if he suddenly didn't trust me. "The police were wondering just the same thing. My mate Len in the basement tells me that they looked through the tapes and everyone but Bob left before nine."

"Wouldn't take much to wedge a door open and get back in through the fire exit though," I said and immediately wished that I hadn't.

Jack was still eyeing me suspiciously. "Reckon you're a bit of a Sherlock Holmes, do ya?"

I prefer Monsieur Poirot actually, I wisely kept to myself.

"I do love me a good mystery." I employed my super ditzy voice. I find it surprisingly effective at making men think I'm not very clever and that they have no need to worry about little old me. Some women use their sexual wiles to get what they want, I pretend to be a moron.

His moustache perked up and he returned to his computer to show me a video of a baby goat going down a slide. I knew I wouldn't be getting anything more out of him so I laughed along and got back to my desk as soon I could.

Between bouts of data analysis – i.e. correcting missing capital letters and the like – I had the chance to stake out David. I didn't gather any incriminating evidence on him, but I did confirm my suspicions that he was tongue-bitingly handsome. David had clean nails, good manners and wore nice clothes. He was pretty much my dream man and it was suddenly shocking to me that I'd never fallen bonkers in love with him until now.

Get it together, Izzy. This man could be a cold-blooded murderer.

Mind your own business, brain.

Just the sight of him put me into a hopeless, dribbly state. Admittedly, when he arrived, he didn't notice me at my desk and when he went to speak to Wendy he was obviously busy but, a bit later on, when he went to get a coffee, he was almost definitely looking in my direction.

"'Oh, hi there,'" I whispered, as I watched him talking to Amara by the photocopier. "'Hi, David. How are you?' 'I'm having trouble concentrating on my work because I can't stop thinking about Izzy.' 'Oh, that's understandable, she's hot stuff.' 'Tell me about it.' 'Oh, yeah. If I was a man, I would be all over that–'"

"What are you doing?"

It was Wendy. She must have snuck up on me to break into my fantasy conversation. It could have been worse. I don't think she'd heard any details.

"My job," I said snootily and pretended to be hard at work.

"You're so weird."

"No, you are."

She'd startled me and I didn't have time to think up a comeback beyond primary school level. Fixing me with her slightly frazzled eyes, she handed me a manila folder.

She was about to walk away but then held herself there, as if she was fighting against a strong wind.

"I'm sorry, all right?" Her words came out as little more than a throaty mumble.

"Pardon?"

"I said, I'm sorry." She coughed rather wetly. "For thinking you'd killed Bob. I'm sorry I told everyone it was you."

"Oh." I wasn't ready for this. "Thanks."

She turned to escape and that day's off-brown cardigan swished round after her, but I wasn't finished.

"Wendy, I don't suppose you could do me a favour?"

"What favour?"

I smiled slyly. "I'll let you know when the time's right."

She looked terrified. "Then, no. If you're going to be weird about it, obviously not."

Inside the paper file she'd delivered was some work for me to be getting on with and a yellow note in David's handwriting saying, "Some work for you to be getting on with." More horrifying than the fact that he hadn't seen fit to include a single X or O, was the dawning realisation that the work was not data to be analysed but data to be entered.

I was furious. Though hardly different in any respect, data entry was way below my job description. I was an established assistant data analyst's assistant with over four years' experience at Porter & Porter, not some unpaid intern to be fobbed off with nothing work. Obviously I didn't really care and was only angry because I couldn't interpret any hidden message of love in David's nine-word note but, for a moment, I strongly considered talking to my union rep about this blatant undervaluing of my talents.

I spent the rest of the day mopily entering the incomprehensible figures. I typed slowly and loudly, like an old person on a free computer training course in a rural library. Whenever David popped out of his office I tried to glare at him, but he barely looked my way. At lunch not even my chicken tikka and mint mayonnaise demi-baguette or Ramesh's new idea for his Downton Abbey erotic fan fiction could cheer me up.

It was odd that, only a few days after Bob's death, talk seemed to have moved on to other things. The chatter in the breakroom was once more centred on sport, last night's TV and Will's latest lucky lady.

That guy was massively overcompensating for something. He sat at his usual table with his band of luxury idiots scoffing down Waitrose sushi like he thought he was king of the world.

"Bla bla bla, girls."

"Bla bla bla, football."

"Blahhhhh, eyebrow sculpting."

This is only a rough approximation of their conversation but I think you get the gist. The whole of the boys club were there, cut off from the rest of us with their jeering and borderline sexist behaviour. Ramesh had persuaded Amara to forgo her usual out-of-office lunch excursion to sit with us and was asking ridiculously leading questions.

"So, Amara, what did you do at the weekend? *Burn any incriminating evidence?*" Maybe he didn't phrase it exactly like that but he might as well have.

If she was hiding something from us, our deputy director certainly wasn't giving anything away. "I didn't do much really. On Friday my husband's friends came over and we spent all night playing role playing games."

"Wow! That sounds fun!" Ramesh replied with more than a hint of sarcasm.

"Yep, and you sound rude." Have I told you how much I love Amara?

I tried to return the conversation to the easy-going feel it had started out with. "How long have you been married?"

"Almost nine years now."

"How'd ya meet?" Ramesh wasn't interested in a casual chat and had already slipped into the New York drawl of a hardboiled private eye.

"We met in an online forum for gamers. It's kind of romantic really. There were people there talking from all over the world and it turned out we only lived two minutes' walk away from each other. My avatar was me dressed as Sophitia from SoulCalibur and Gareth, that's my husband, says he fell in love at first sight."

"That's so sweet." I had no idea what she was talking about but this seemed like a suitable response.

Perhaps I'd have had more luck with men if I'd dressed up as a computer game character. Sadly the only one I knew was Super Mario and I didn't particularly want a boyfriend who found me sexy in a moustache.

"Does your husband hold a grudge against anyone?" Ramesh asked before I could interrupt.

"Did you see Eastenders the other night?"

Thank goodness for TV; the one unifying factor in our divided planet. I reckon that even Israel and Palestine could find common ground if they only spent more time discussing how great Saturday morning cartoons from the 90s were, instead of focussing on the decades of violence, blame and land disputes that have fractured their peoples.

Amara's perplexed look disappeared and she perked right up. Her fringe seemed to smile along with her. "It was so boring. Have you noticed how they have to have a few really dull episodes between anything good happening?"

There was all sorts of information I was hoping to subtly extract from Amara but my idiot friend had wasted the opportunity. I shot Ramesh an angry glare and we joined in a hearty discussion of TV soap trends. It quickly made me forget my troubles until the bell rang for the end of the lunch. No, hang on, I'm not in school anymore. That didn't happen.

Sitting back down at my desk plunged me into a temporary depression. The stack of pages I still had to get through looked just as high as when Wendy had delivered it. I carefully keyed in numbers into the columns in tiny virtual boxes. For all I knew, this was the extension of David's cruel and elaborate joke, which started with asking me out and proceeded to giving me fake work to do. I mean, how could anyone need the information 9982726YL in the column Transaction Data? What did any of it mean?

Eventually I got into the zone and the distractions of the office tuned out. Like a spaceship travelling at warp speed, the world around me blurred and I became incredibly focussed on the task at hand. Time passed by in the most curious of ways; one minute lasted ten before an hour shot by in seconds.

It was almost meditational. My fingers worked away at my computer's keypad like a nest of furious woodpeckers. People called across the office to one another and, at some point, Ramesh came to talk to me, but none of it sank in.

Before I knew it there was only one page remaining and it was past my home time. The smiley clock in front of me said five forty-five and the office was already half empty. Just then, that monster David emerged from his office and looked right at me. A few hours earlier, the smile he sent sailing through the air, across the neat rows of desks and quietly sleeping computers, would have charmed the pants off me. But after the heartless note he'd sent on its smug yellow background, everything about that man had turned to poison. I was now convinced that he was the savage brute who had murdered our beloved Bob.

I pretended I hadn't seen him and busied myself with the last lines of my day's task. It was soon complete and, turning over the final sheet of paper, I came face to face with another yellow note.

***

"You poor thing," an old woman standing next to me on the tram began. "It must be very hard." This was not the first time someone had uttered such a statement to me. "I don't mean no offence like, but... you know..."

She couldn't hurt me. Her words were wind blowing through my pretty hair. Her commiserations were a fine mist of tropical rain on a summer's day. And yes, a woman in her late seventies, wearing a pink knitted bonnet that wouldn't have looked out of place on a Victorian baby, had so much pity for me that she couldn't resist the urge to approach a total stranger to sympathise with my plight, but at least she hadn't been so rude as to specify why.

"I mean, you being so tall and all. I wouldn't wish that on anyone."

People were beginning to stare. A kid in a full Arsenal kit was looking up at me like I was about to eat her. Other passengers were less obvious about it but still allowed their eyes to flick in my direction when they thought I couldn't see.

"Thank you. That's very kind." I hoped this would shut her up.

She made a frowny sort of smile and kept talking. "It's different for men, innit? I mean, with men it's attractive. Sexy, you might say. But for a woman it can't be easy sticking out like that. You're like a Tyrannosaurus Rex in a field of daisies."

And somehow she still didn't get to me. *Giraffe, stick insect, mutated German housewife,* such old chestnuts barely scratched the warm fuzzy glow that surrounded me. Any colour in my cheeks was merely the first flush of new romance. All thoughts of embarrassment were kept distantly at bay.

I was still clutching the yellow square of paper in my hand. "I'll call you tonight," was all it said but it might as well have been a novel-length treatise on my beauty for the joy it brought. My king was restored to his throne.

"It's not that *I* think there's anything wrong with it. But I feel bad for the way people must stare at you in public. Can't be much fun."

I could have broken down in tears or lost my temper. I could have told her that, though I might be tall, at least I wasn't an interfering old hag, clinging on to life by the tips of my yellowed fingernails. Instead, the new inner peace that I had discovered kept me standing there, upright and graceful, bearing her insults like a martyr.

"You know I wouldn't wish that on my worst enemy!"

My stop finally came and I alighted, smiling serenely to my adversary before sticking my finger up at her through the window.

Chapter Ten

I guess David is a believer in the wait-three-whole-days-before-calling approach which in the age of Tinder and WhatsApp is practically old-fashioned. He called me that afternoon when I was a few minutes from home.

"I was going to ask you to dinner at mine but then I thought it might be a bit intense so we can go to a restaurant instead if you prefer."

Ahhhhhhhhhhhhhhhhhhhhhhhhhhhhhhhhhhhhhhhhhhhhhhhhhhhhhh!

Damn, what had he actually said? "Urmmm… The first one?"

"Dinner at mine. Are you sure? I don't want you to be uncomfortable."

Whoops, he might be a murderer. Oh, well. Too late now. "No, honestly that would be lovely."

As I walked along my road, I was finding it very difficult to process what he was saying because I was now about 97%, sure that David Hughes was asking me out.

Ahhhhhhhhhhhhhhhhhhhhhhhhhhhhhhhhhhhhhhhhhhhhhhhhhhhhhh!

"Great. I'll see you tomorrow then." His lovely Welsh accent came on stronger. It made me want to go swimming in his mouth.

I was smiling so much that the muscles in my face were starting to ache. "Perfect. See you then."

Ahhhhhhhhhhhhhhhhhhhhhhhhhhhhhhhhhhhhhhhhhhhhhhhhhhhhhh!

West Wickham suddenly looked bright and filled with promise, like Disneyland Paris on a sunny day. I wanted to sing. I wanted to dance. Sadly I was tone deaf with a propensity for falling over whenever I stepped on a dancefloor. And so, as I skipped along the road, singing the theme tune from Happy Days, I did not impress the group of hipster teenagers who were wandering past on the opposite pavement.

They stopped where they were to laugh at me, but instead of hiding in a bush, or pretending I was coughing as I normally would have, I sang even louder. I leaned into my uncoolness, not caring in the slightest what they thought because I had a date with a truly lovely man who – there was a very good chance – hadn't killed anyone!

I should probably mention at this point that I'm fully aware that finding love is not the only way to achieve fulfilment. I know plenty of women in relationships who are completely miserable. But, still… I got a boyfriend, I got a boyfriend!

Hang on a second. My brain had just about finished yelling for joy. *Is the date tomorrow or another night? When exactly are we meeting him?*

For goodness sake. You're the one who's supposed to keep a track of these things.

Not to worry. He'll remind us at work.

The smell of Danny's cooking led me home and I could see from the garden that my front room was once again occupied by a bunch of howling sexagenarians.

"You're being ridiculous, Gregory."

"Rosie," I heard my stepfather saying as I unlocked the front door. "I'm afraid I have to agree with your first husband. There's no doubt that Wendy was at her stamp collecting meeting on Wednesday night."

"But that's the perfect cover. Why can't anyone see that?" Mum's voice rose indignantly with every sentence.

The Hawes Lane Amateur Detective Society had grown. In addition to my three main parents, Mum's hairdresser and a couple of neighbours were all contemplating the flip charts.

"Ahhh," Dad said upon noticing me. "The woman of the hour."

"Izzy! Don't go on anywhere near your boss." The lady from number 32 seemed very worked up. "He definitely can't be trusted."

From the look of things they'd been busy. The Clues and Hypotheses pages were suddenly covered in neat black lists. Lines ran between different elements and key themes had been circled or underlined in thick felt-tip.

I was feeling a little overwhelmed. "How do you know this stuff?"

"Your friend has been very helpful." Dad gave up his space on the sofa and settled down on the floor.

On cue, Ramesh walked in holding a tray of tea things. I knew I should never have given my mum his number *in case of an emergency.*

"Who wants sugar?" He walked straight past me.

I considered complaining at them for messing about in my life, but I was still on a high so I sat down between the guy from number 27 and the woman from 32 and tried to catch up. "How do you know where Wendy was when Bob died?"

"I went through her computer like you told me." Ramesh didn't look up as he poured out six cups of tea from Greg's giant pot. "There's a photo on Facebook of her at a stamp collector's meeting in North London. It was even shared on the organiser's page so it seems pretty genuine."

"Sounds rather convenient to me." Mum wasn't giving up on her suspicions. "How do we know it's not an old photo which she reposted at that particular time to give her an alibi?"

"Come along, Rosie." At least my Dad was coming out of his shell a bit. "Where's the motive?"

Jumping up from her armchair, Mum began to hold court. "The way I see it, Wendy had more to gain than most. We know she's in debt on her credit cards. Bob owed her a ton of money he wouldn't give back and she's clearly not satisfied with her job anymore. That all adds up to one desperate woman. Whatever was going on between her and Bob, she won't have told the police about it."

"It's not exactly a cast-iron case, is it, darling?" Greg picked up a marker from the coffee table and drew a box around the first suspect on the list. "This is who my money's on. David Hughes is head of the company and well placed to hide his guilt. He's clearly only dating Izzy to find out what she knows."

I couldn't let that pass. "Thanks very much, Stepdaddy dearest!"

"No offence, Izzy, but think about it. Perhaps you saw something in Bob's office that morning and he wants to work out if it meant anything to you." He had a point there. "Perhaps he's got wind of your investigation and he's running scared."

"Haaaaaaaaa!" I failed to hold in an unbelieving stab of laughter but it was quickly drowned out as everyone in the room started putting their ideas forward.

Without any evidence, Mum's hairdresser was convinced that Wendy had done it because she was after Bob's job. Mrs 32 thought that Jack must be the culprit. Mr 27 figured that that we hadn't found a scrap of evidence on Amara because she'd covered her trail so well and the only person who stayed quiet was my beloved best friend, who was handing out fresh, steaming mugs across the room.

"So what do you think, Ramesh?" The fact there was no cuppa for me made me question how great a guy he was after all.

He tried to hold back his goofball grin but it shone through all the same. "Don't ask me. I still think Will's behind it. I found nothing whatsoever on his computer. Nothing on his social media. No communication with Bob of any kind but it still feels like he's hiding something. Anyway, he's younger than the others. Anything incriminating would most likely be on his phone."

Dad wasn't finished with his theories. "One thing we can say for sure is that Ramesh didn't do it."

Daddy number three didn't agree and pointed at Daddy number one with a teaspoon. "That's not a very scientific approach, Ted. Just because he seems like a nice lad, that doesn't preclude him from being a brutal killer."

Dad blew on his tea. "Ramesh wouldn't have brought us information exonerating Wendy if he was the killer."

"Maybe that's what he wanted us to think. There are four other suspects." Greg pointed to the chart once more. "He could eliminate Wendy to put us off the scent."

"Greg's right." From the sound of Ramesh's voice, I could tell he'd burnt his tongue. "You can't rule me out. I've got no alibi for a start."

"I believe you, Ramesh dear." Mum had found another young man to adopt.

I sat for a while longer as the group worked through various theories and even made it to a second page on the hypothesis pad. It felt totally unreal to me. The way they spoke about the people I'd worked with for years turned them into faceless chess pieces.

Once everyone had drunk their tea and shuffled off, it was left to me and Ramesh to clear up.

"I told you this afternoon," he said as he plonked a fistful of teaspoons in the sink. "I sent you everything before I left work. I would've waited for you, but you seemed busy."

"Sorry, I was a bit distracted."

He stopped what he was doing for a second and peered out of the kitchen window at Danny tending to his campfire in the garden. "I wish I could get hold of our suspect's phones. Amara and David have nothing personal on their computers and Will's Facebook is weirdly anonymous. All he posts about is football and beer."

"I'd say that was the breadth of his interests, but even for Will it sounds excessively macho. I keep thinking we can cross him off the list because we've got basically no evidence on him. And it's not as if he gets on well enough with any of the other suspects to be working with one of them. But everything he does is sketchy and I can't shake the feeling that he's involved somehow."

"Absolutely, the guy's dodgy." Ramesh brushed some crumbs into the bin. "The weirdest thing I found today was an e-mail to David from Bob's work account. He wrote it shortly before he was killed but the network was offline that night so it didn't send. All it said was, *It's already done.*"

I put on some rubber gloves and twanged one cuff like a surgeon getting ready to wield the knife. "Not so weird. They could have been talking about anything – a project or some document." The bubbles were getting out of control so I turned the tap off and got to work. "Anything else stand out?"

"You'll see the overdraft reminders from Wendy's bank. God knows what she spends her money on. Her whole life seems to revolve around stamp collecting, which makes her a psycho in my book. The e-mails she sent to Bob are interesting; she was furious with him. Apart from that, Jack spends massive amounts of time watching animal videos online, Amara has the most sparklingly organised e-mail on earth. Oh and David works much too hard."

"Urghh, he sounds awful. I'll probably have to cancel *my date* with him."

"Ahhhhhhhhhhhhhhhhhhhhhhhhhhhhhhhhhhhhhhhhhhhhhhhhhhh!" It was Ramesh this time. He has a worrying amount in common with my internal monologue. "When? Where? Tell me all the details."

"Urrrmmm… I'll have to get back to you on that."

Dinner that night was another exotically named casserole dish and I had to remind myself that I was now practically spoken for and could no longer perv on Danny as he served up the food. It was difficult; his top was so tight that it looked like he'd painted it on.

"You know that I'm heartbroken," he said once we were all sitting down. "Going out with an eligible bloke for once. One day I'll give up on you altogether."

I made a noise like a confused elephant calf and spent the meal once more trying to work out if Danny meant anything he said to me.

I scurried off to my room as soon as dinner was over. Lying in bed beneath my poster of James Blunt, (my celebrity teenage crush, whose accent I still find almost supernaturally sexy) I whiled away the hours looking at the files Ramesh had downloaded from our colleagues' computers. There were screenshots, spreadsheets and whole searchable e-mail logs for all our suspects' work accounts. The email from Bob to David was written an hour before he died but never reached its destination. The subject line read, "The List" but I couldn't find any other reference to it in their earlier correspondence.

I spent about twenty minutes staring at the message in the hope it would reveal something to me.

It's already done.

It didn't give me a lot to go on. All I could think of were innocent, work-related explanations and I realised how hard it was going to be to objectively consider that David could have killed Bob.

The only incriminating evidence I could find on Amara was an e-mail she sent Bob after a meeting they'd both been in.

I swear, if you humiliate me again in front of clients, I'll return the favour and haul you up in front of a tribunal. You might be able to push your underlings around, but don't even think of trying that with me.

It was the last e-mail they exchanged for months before the murder. I could tell how angry she must have been, Bob was supremely good at needling and rankling everyone around him. But Amara's threat was hardly the wild-eyed reaction of a killer; it was the measured and appropriate response of a capable administrator.

I moved on to look through the screenshots of Wendy's Facebook which very much made it look like she'd been at a stamp collecting evening in Finsbury Park on the night of the murder. The event was organised by the London Stamp Fanatics so I set up a fake Facebook account to get in touch with them and find out about the event I was *so sorry to have missed.*

It was true that Wendy was in debt as well. I couldn't log on to her online bank but she had statements e-mailed to her every month and she was in the red by thousands of pounds.

She hadn't sent many personal e-mails to Bob, but the few that Ramesh had copied for me were not friendly.

I'm tired of your excuses. I don't care if your kids get sick, your wife loses her job or your milkman is bankrupt, I just want what you owe me. I've given you enough warnings. Don't make me go to the police.

Wendy always seemed like such a miser that it was impossible to imagine her lending anyone any money. Perhaps they were going into business together or Bob had given her some dodgy financial advice. Why else would he have owed her eight grand?

I looked through everyone's e-mails from the day that Bob died but there wasn't much of interest. The police had his computer so we didn't have access to his personal messages, only whatever was left on the server from his work account. Not being entirely sure what Porter & Porter really did, I wasn't best placed to interpret the businessy stuff that his emails referred to.

One thing that stood out was that Bob had begun to extend his bad manners towards his clients. I ran back through a series of e-mail chains and, around Christmastime, there was a definite shift in the way he worked. From being short but formal in his replies, he suddenly got sloppy – taking weeks to respond to messages, or firing them off in slangy English.

By March, he'd become full-on insulting and if anyone challenged him, Bob would reply in shouty capital letters.

I SEE NO REASON TO RESPOND TO YOUR RIDICULOUS ACCUSATIONS. STOP WASTING MY TIME.

There were companies that we'd been working with for years who got sick of his attitude and took their business elsewhere. His dramatic change in behaviour was best highlighted by an intervention by our company's founder, Mr Aldrich Porter himself – a man who hadn't been seen in the office in the best part of a decade and lived as a practical recluse in his country house near the South Downs. A month before the murder, he sent a personal e-mail, enquiring after Bob's wife and children by name and checking in on the state of the business. If Mr Porter had noticed the problem, things must have been serious, but Bob never even wrote back.

I get annoyed sometimes when people don't respond to my texts, especially when I can see that they've read them. It's hardly a reason to have someone killed though and I didn't feel the need to add Mr Porter to our list of suspects.

It occurred to me that everything I'd been able to get on Bob, the police would've already obtained. What I couldn't be sure of was how thorough they had time to be. Did they really have the resources to plough through the countless e-mails and messages that were sent within the company each year? Still, I couldn't help wishing that I knew what they'd found on Bob's phone and computer that I had no access to.

When my eyes grew tired from staring at my laptop and I couldn't bear to read another boring e-mail about office supplies or leadership training, I shut them tight. I imagined myself back to the afternoon on the day of Bob's death. It wouldn't have stood out from any other day except for the fact it was Amara's 40th birthday and Ramesh had made her a cake. I looked around my colleague's faces as he got busy carving.

"Pink and yellow; subtle colours." Bob's anger-levels rarely dipped below furious and even his sarcasm was undercut with its own brand of simmering rage. "I wouldn't expect any less from Ramesh."

"No cake for you then." My friend's eyes narrowed as he stared down his enemy. "I wouldn't want you to keel over from a massive heart attack."

"Ha, there's about as much chance of me dying from a heart attack as there is of your girlfriend being a girl." The two had never got on but, since January, Bob's would-be homophobic comments and general cruelty had been bumped up a notch.

I watched him cough out a nicotine-coated lung onto his sleeve then continue with his insults.

To paper over the row, Amara was being her usual humble self. "Thanks, Ramesh. You really shouldn't have made a fuss. It looks lovely."

"If everyone could gather round. I'd like to say a few words." Ah, David's the best, isn't he? He's just so authoritative and managerial.

As our super-boss launched into his tribute to the birthday girl, Wendy looked put out that she was still waiting for cake. She paid no attention when Bob flopped down beside her. There was always something very crumpled about him. He sat folded over, his shoulders rounded and his clothes askew. His old, brown suit gave him the look of someone who had given up ever choosing what to wear. It was the uniform of a thoroughly charmless man.

If anyone was acting out of character it was Will. He was standing back from the group, maudlin and quiet as Bob made himself heard over a flutter of applause.

"Ramesh, you're slower than my mother-in-law on a mobility scooter."

Will's eyes darted about the scene. He looked stunned, distant. I'd never understood their friendship; had Bob finally got tired of it and cut his protégé loose? Will had no reliable alibi, maybe he'd found a way to get into the server room after all.

Ever the good host, Ramesh smiled as he handed out slices of cake around the group. Will was comparatively civil as he received his bounty, but when Ramesh reluctantly passed a piece over to Bob, the brown-suited bully had another cough all over the offering and said, "Changed my mind. I don't like girly cakes."

Tossing the plate onto Ramesh's desk, he stomped off towards his office. He still had a little anger left for me though. "Izzy, stop stuffing your face and finish your work by the end of the day, or we'll cut your wages."

Bob had been messaging me the same thing all morning, so I continued to ignore him. I'd worked there long enough not to be scared of his tantrums. Ramesh on the other hand looked like someone had punched one of his cats.

Living through that scene for the second time, it was bizarre that I'd failed to notice how deeply that hateful man got under my friend's skin. It shows what a talented bully Bob truly was. To be able to act the way he did – to harass and demoralise those around him – and not only get away with it but make it seem normal was a kind of mastery. We were trespassers in his realm and, in the kingdom of Bob, even his fellow rulers didn't dare challenge him.

My thoughts were interrupted by Mum and Greg chanting in their bedroom. The time-slip daydream had done the job though and shone a light on something I would've otherwise forgotten.

I opened my laptop to read through the e-mails in Bob's account from the day he died. The morning was full of the usual stuff; newsletters, messages from clients and junk mail was mixed in with shy replies from a few of the underlings who Bob was so fond of screaming at.

It picked up again after lunch but then, from the time they cut the cake until clocking off, there was nothing. Though he received ten or so messages an hour on a normal working day, there was a massive dead spot when not a single message came in. Maybe that wasn't so strange considering the work being done to the server that week. I would have overlooked it myself if I hadn't remembered Bob spending that whole afternoon sending digs my way about being slower than his mother-in-law on a mobility scooter (he was an unashamed repeater of insults.)

I looked in the Recycle Bin but it was empty. The Sent folder was the same. There was no record of Bob writing or receiving any messages for two whole hours, even though he was shut away working in his office that whole time. Whoever had deleted my messages had made sure that no one would stumble across them. And while I wanted to believe I had a secret defender who had tried to hide Bob's clearly dreadful opinion of me from the police, I came to a very different conclusion.

In the aftermath of Bob's murder, Ramesh was the only person with access to the secure server where our emails were stored. It wouldn't have been enough to wipe files locally on Bob's computer, so the obvious explanation was that he'd deleted a batch of messages and mine had gone with them.

If it wasn't my e-mails to Bob, what was he hiding? Besides Ramesh himself, I knew one other person who could help me find out. I'd never imagined having to look up that number again, but I grabbed my phone and dialled.

"Dean Shipman from Bromley speaking. Who's that?"

"It's me, Izzy…" The line remained silent. "Izzy Palmer from West Wickham?"

"Oh, hello, Izzy." His voiced warmed up a fraction but he said nothing more.

"Listen, Dean. I need your help to spy on my best friend."

"Great. What's in it for me?"

Chapter Eleven

I felt pretty stupid that I'd dismissed the possibility of Ramesh being the killer. If there was one thing I'd learnt from murder mysteries, it was always to expect the person you'd never expect. It's practically the golden rule of crime fiction. The guy with the airtight alibi from the beginning? It could very well be him. The old lady who is kind to children and animals? Psychopathic killer! Hospital-stricken invalid in a full plaster cast? Well, that may be genuine, but take nothing for granted.

I was still holding out hope for a simple explanation to why Ramesh was hiding evidence. The only way I could be sure that he was innocent was to investigate him just the same as any other suspect. Of course to do that, I'd need to find a way to get him out of the office for a good long while. Luckily I had the perfect excuse already in place.

The problem with mounting a secret investigation when even your best friend can't know the details is that it's difficult to keep track of all the elements you've put into play. At work on Tuesday morning I had all my ducks in a row and my fingers crossed that nothing would go wrong, which, when you think about it, is a precarious position to be in. Still, after spending far too long not being detectivey enough, the ball had finally started to roll. Okay, that's too many metaphors.

Even if I'd already landed on a prime suspect, there was a bunch of questions that still needed to be answered. In fact I'd made a list of the most important ones.

- **Who killed Bob?**
- **What did Ramesh have to hide? Did he kill Bob?**
- **Why did Bob owe Wendy money and was she really geeking out over stamps on the night he died or did she kill Bob?**
- **Whoever killed him, why did they stick Bob's letter opener in his back if they'd already gutted him with a fruit knife?**
- **When was my date with David supposed to be and how sparkly an outfit should I wear? Oh and did he kill Bob?**

If I couldn't answer at least one of those questions by the end of the day, I decided I would give up and leave it to the professionals.

"I'm looking forward to tonight," David told me as we coincidentally (not a coincidence) rode the lift together up to the fourth floor.

Result! Move over, Miss Marple.

"Yeeeeeah. Can't wait." I said this in far too flirty a voice so then I had to pretend I had a sore throat.

"Is eight o'clock okay?" He looked at me like he already regretted the invitation.

Rather than reply vocally, I faked a really deep, phlegmy cough and gave him a thumbs up.

To answer yet more of my burning questions, I would send Ramesh off on his next techy spying task at ten that morning which was the exact same time that Dean would be coming by the office.

Ramesh had gone to do my bidding in the unrented office on the seventh floor when Dean Shipman walked in to Porter & Porter looking just as pubescent as ever.

"Hello, Izzy. I'm–"

I grabbed him by the entrance to steer him round Jack in his cupboard and beyond the mouthy receptionist who'd been looking at me like I'd eaten her baby ever since Bob died. I certainly didn't trust Bromley's favourite son to bluff his way past them. I could just see him going up to reception and saying, *Hello. I'm Dean Shipman from Bromley. I'm here to help Izzy spy on her friend.* Luckily I managed to smuggle him over to Ramesh's desk without another word.

"Do you know what you're doing?"

"Izzy." He sighed like the weight of the universe was pressing down on his shoulders but he could just about bear it. "Let me do my job."

I watched him pull out a tiny USB drive from one of the infinite pockets on his black workman's jacket and plug it into the back of the computer. Ramesh's assistant Maria paid no attention whatsoever to us and remained hypnotised by her screen, just as I knew she would.

"Okay, all set," Dean said after about three seconds had passed.

"Wow, that was quick." I'd imagined a long, drawn-out process involving wires, cables and perhaps pliers.

"Hey Iz, who's this guy?" Ramesh had already returned. He'd only been gone a minute. I thought computery stuff was complicated!

84

Entirely unsure what to say next, I stared at the two techiest men in my life.

"Hello. I'm Dean Shipman from Bromley. I–"

I interrupted before he could say anything moronic. "Dean here is from Bromley Technology Solutions he's come to look at..." My voice faded away pathetically and I was about to give up and lie down on the floor when my unexpected saviour came to the rescue.

"Cabling." Dean said it very matter-of-factly, like he knew exactly what he was talking about, which, it turned out, he did. "We had a call from one of the bosses to say you were thinking of installing fibre optics across the network. So I thought I'd come to see the head of I.T., which I hear is you, my good sir, to see what sort of spec you're interested in."

My jaw had dropped all the way down to the basement.

Ramesh glanced between us for a second and then let out a cry in the direction of the far corner office. "David, I love you!"

Will poked his head up over his desk divider. "That's a perfectly normal thing to say, everybody." He was back to his usual mini-Bob ways. "Nothing weird about declaring your love to your boss. Everyone get back to work."

Ramesh was so happy that he completely ignored Will's snarky comment. "I've been asking David to upgrade for months. I can't believe this day has finally come."

"Okay." Dean continued with his patter. "So what are we looking at? What kind of speed have you got in mind?"

I left them to talk nonsense to each other and, when my worst ever date had finished lying to my best friend, Dean stopped by my desk on the way out. "That guy is really into cabling."

"That's nothing." I stopped the no doubt essential work I was doing. "You should hear him talk about Shania Twain."

He pulled back his sleeve to reveal the kind of digital watch eleven-year-old boys wear. "Listen, Izzy. This has taken a lot longer than I was expecting."

"You've only been here fifteen minutes."

His face remained serious, his voice flat. "I'm a busy man." He took another USB key out of his pocket and placed it firmly on my desk. "Plug this in. Run the software and you'll be able to view whatever files your friend has on his computer."

"Thanks, Dean. You were really great back there."

"Course I was." He held one nostril closed and blew out of the other into my bin. "Don't forget our deal. You owe me."

He walked out of the office, checking over his shoulder like he thought someone was following him.

One rat trapped, a few more still to bait.

Ramesh, did you get everything set up?

It took him a while to reply. He was probably off doing his job or something.

All done. I gave Jack, Wendy and Will specific times to head up there. We'll go into the server room at lunch to see what happens.

Good work. But play it cool. We don't want to arouse suspicion.

He sent back a detective emoji followed by a little face with a finger to its lips and then a picture of an oven for some reason. Or was it a computer? A VHS cassette maybe?

I'd done about a month's work the day before so I figured I'd earned a morning off. As soon as Ramesh logged onto the network, I ran the software on Dean's memory stick. It instantly gave me access to the files on his work computer. I poked around in his e-mails first in case there was anything there from the day that Bob was killed. His folders that afternoon were just as empty as Bob's were so I moved on.

A year earlier, Ramesh had been phenomenally happy to have created a hole in the Porter & Porter firewall so that he could synchronise everything with his home computer. I'd had no idea what he was talking about of course but the link I discovered on his desktop helped me figure it out.

There before me were all of Ramesh's personal files. There were plenty that I had no interest in even opening (admin stuff for his Cher forum, love letters to his girlfriend Patricia – yuck!) and his fan-fiction novellas would have taken me months to get through. But hidden away at the bottom of a tree of empty folders was one called "Private Hurts."

86

Having spent my adolescence learning to put up with the names and insults that were hurled my way by every bitchy girl and slimy bloke I came across, I'd escaped through escapism. I'd retreated into detective fiction and police procedurals and I didn't let cruel words from cruel people ever get to me.

I'd always assumed that Ramesh was the same, but the haul of evidence I found on his computer said otherwise. There were videos, word documents, audio excerpts and photos documenting the impact of Bob's bullying over the years.

I put my headphones in and clicked on *All Honesty.mkv,* the first video in the list of files. It showed my friend talking into his webcam, his honey brown cheeks running with tears. He'd never spoken about livestreaming his innermost thoughts and it was surprisingly painful to come across a whole part of his life that I knew nothing about.

"I'm here again to talk about workplace bullying." He looked down at his hands like Lady Macbeth searching for blood. "I know in my last video I said that I was going to put an end to what's been happening... Well I was weak."

He was sitting in his bedroom. The decoration behind him was simple, modern, minimal – to contrast with the complicated man, whose long, curly fringe hid his face from the camera. It must have been a live screen capture as hearts and frowny faces occasionally floated up across the footage from the users who were watching.

"I build up all these plans for how to deal with my boss, but when it comes down to it, I always wimp out." Deep breath and then he looked straight into the camera for the first time. "The things he does cut right through me and I end up hating myself for not standing up to him. I've thought about leaving the company but that would mean he'd won. He doesn't even have to say anything to me these days. Just being near him paralyses me."

All of a sudden, Ramesh sat up on his bed. He tipped his shoulders back and looked into the lens with unexpected intensity. "I wish he was dead. And I'm not just saying that. I wish I had the guts to cut his tongue out for all the things he's said to me."

My throat constricted in on itself. My heart was yelling in my ears.

"If I was any kind of man, I'd take a knife and gut him in front of the whole office."

The video was like a signed statement of Ramesh's guilt. Worst of all was that it had only been recorded a few days before Bob's death. What jury wouldn't deem this treasure trove of videos, semi-fictionalised short stories and bad poetry to be evidence of my friend's obsession with the man he'd murdered?

His carbonised stare on the screen in front of me was like a dagger as I ran through the facts in my head.

Ramesh had no alibi. He had a big grudge against Bob and was one of only five people who could have accessed the server room to destroy the CCTV video. The fact that he knew better than anyone else how to remove the security footage was a bit of a smoking gun too. To my knowledge, none of the other suspects had the technological background he had.

"I'm going to do something about the way he treats me once and for all," the pixelated Ramesh whispered angrily through my headphones. "This time I mean it."

My phone buzzed to break me out of my video trance.

Fancy a cuppa?

Chapter Twelve

I ran to the ladies' to sting my face with cold water.

I had to slow down. Ramesh Khatri was just about the kindest person I'd ever met. Nothing I'd found proved definitively that he was guilty. Wanting your boss dead wasn't the same thing as actually murdering him. He wasn't a killer, or at least I hoped he wasn't because we had a lunch date.

Of course, if he was guilty and I hadn't told the police everything I knew, I could get in trouble. It sounded unlikely but then this whole situation was crazy in the first place. And besides, Miss Marple always seems to know who the killer is from the beginning and yet she waits for the most dramatic moment to reveal it, even if it means three other people get murdered first.

"Izzy, are you all right?" Amara appeared from one of the stalls and came to stand next to me.

I don't know if I've mentioned it, but I love Amara. She makes me feel grown up because she's so grown up. Sadly, the worried look she wore right then only made me feel more worried.

"Yeah, fine." Even paler and more ghostly than normal, I grabbed a paper towel to dry my dripping-wet face. "Actually I'm lying. I feel dreadful."

"I'm so sorry, Izzy." Why had Bob been my supervisor for the last four years? Why couldn't it have been lovely Amara? "Is there anything I can do to help?"

"Honestly, I'm fine." I tried to keep my voice under control. "Just got a lot of stuff going on at the moment."

"Tell you what, why don't we go for a drink sometime? Out of the office, I mean."

I subsequently lost control of my voice. "Urrrr... I... aggggg, are you sure?"

She smiled, all mature and professional as ever. "Of course I am. I'd be happy to lend an ear."

I couldn't believe my luck. "Tomorrow after work?"

She paused, perhaps to check my pupils weren't too dilated.

"Tomorrow, sure. We can go to the pub down by the station." Public place, plenty of people around; very clever of her.

"Great." Though still reeling from the shock of identifying my best friend as a likely murderer, at least I'd have the chance to quiz Amara on what she knew about it.

And maybe we'll become best friends!

There was an awkward moment as she shuffled round me to wash her hands and I hung around waiting for her to finish. When she was gone, I went back to staring at myself in the mirror. Call it mindfulness or the power of quiet thought but, after about thirty seconds standing there, I knew just what I had to do.

Until someone presented me with the video tape of Ramesh cutting up Bob, I couldn't accept that he was the killer. The only way I was going to know for sure what had happened was by continuing the investigation. I'd give myself forty-eight hours and, if I couldn't prove Ramesh's innocence by then, I'd hand everything I had on him over to the police.

I sent him a message from the toilet before going back to my desk.

**No tea for me, mate. I've got a murder
to solve.**

By the time lunch came round, I'd checked that there were no fruit knives left in the breakroom, drawn up plan of the crime scene and drunk about six hot chocolates. Like a proper detective!

At one, I met up with Ramesh by the server room, which was hidden away behind the photocopiers. We were always sneaking off there to get away from our lovely colleagues, so no one looked twice at us. I was a bit wary going into a small, dark space with a man who was probably a murderer. But then, who was I to judge? I once stole a bar of Dairy Milk from a WH Smith. Ramesh had his reasons to kill Bob just like twelve-year-old Izzy really needed that chocolate. I couldn't see either of us repeating our crimes.

"Did you keep the message vague like I told you?" I sat down in front of his workstation, with my Moroccan salad and mango juice, to wait for the action. I always told people that I brought food from home because I cared about healthy eating. In truth it was because my mum still made me a packed lunch.

"I wrote, *We know what happened with Bob.*" He put a scary voice on for the message bit. *"Go to the seventh floor at this time if you don't want anyone to find out..."*

"And you're sure it's anonymous?" I tossed a carrot baton into my mouth. "There's no way anyone can trace them?"

Ramesh managed to look both mysterious and cocky. "I sent them through a free online SMS service, used a VPN and did it all from your mate Suzie's computer."

I had no idea what he was saying but it sounded impressive.

On the screen in front of us was a live feed from the vacated premises of CodeBox a startup that had recently finished up. Beyond a black swivel chair in the centre of the image, we could see an identical office space to our own, cut up by abandoned cubicles.

At 1:05, Wendy appeared.

"What do you want in return for not talking?" Plonking herself down on the chair, her black and white hairdo was stacked up even higher than normal. She was clearly in an adventurous mood as her cardigan was a light salmon colour and her skirt bore tiny palm tree icons.

Ramesh pushed a button to cut our microphone. "Oops. I thought she'd just spill her guts. What do we say now?"

I wasn't so easily fazed and turned it back on. "We want the truth. If you tell us how it happened, we'll keep it to ourselves." There was an echo at the other end as my heavily disguised voice came back to us. I sounded like a gloomy alien.

She ran the nail of her thumb along the tips of her fingers as she looked into the webcam that Ramesh had hooked up to an old P&P laptop. "Yeah, all right. Me and Bob did it a couple of times."

My accomplice and I stared at each other with the exact same expression on our faces because neither of us could believe what we'd just heard.

Ramesh apparently felt the need to check. "Just to be clear. When you say 'did it,' you are talking about *doing it*?"

I gave him a slap for being an idiot. Wendy didn't seem to notice. "That's right. I thought you knew that already."

I attempted to smooth things over. "We did. And now we have it on tape." Ramesh gave me an over the top wink so I continued. "What we want to know is when it started and why it finished."

"I bet that cow Pauline in accounts told you, didn't she? I knew I couldn't trust 'er."

"Concentrate. Our patience will only last so long. If you don't tell us what we want to know, I'm sure the police would be interested in talking to you."

She sat up straighter in the chair, like a schoolchild scared of her teacher. "I didn't kill 'im if that's what you think."

"Concentrate." My moody Martian voice had got all serious. Ramesh put his hand up for a silent high five.

"All right." She huffed out a breath like she wished she was smoking a cigarette. "It started at the office Christmas party. Bob was really wild that night. He must have been drinking because he challenged Jack to a fight and ended up running around the office topless screaming, 'Nothing can kill me. I'm invincible!'"

"We know all that." Ramesh was copying my resolute tone. "Everyone knows that. Tell us what happened next."

Wendy shuffled her ample bottom around in her seat. "I ended up taking 'im downstairs to get a taxi because no one else wanted anything to do with 'im. Before we could find one though, he grabbed hold of me. There we were, out in the street, kissing like kids. It's not every day something like that happens to me. Before I knew it, we were back at mine with our shoes and socks off, about to tumble into bed."

She cast her eyes to the ceiling and chuckled like she wasn't currently being blackmailed. "Course, we'd only got about quarter of the way through when he was sick all over my leopard-skin bedspread. He cleaned it up and apologised. He actually seemed quite sad about it, but then he headed home and nothing went on between us for about a month.

"The second time it happened, he actually called me up and invited me out. I knew he was married and everything but that was none of my business. He took me to dinner, quite a fancy place down on Purley Way. We had tagliatelle and–"

She was starting to ramble so I decided to rein her in. "Concentrate."

"All right, all right." She rolled her eyes at the camera. "After dinner we went back to mine again and before he got frisky, he asked me all about the flat and my stamp collection and what I did in my free time. I thought he was just being attentive, but, when I woke up the

92

next morning, he'd gone and so had my Two Penny Blue from 1840."
She paused for a moment then explained. "That's a stamp."

"Why did he take a stamp?" Ramesh got in ahead of me again.

Wendy looked put out. Well, a bit more put out than she normally
did. "It was an unused, first plate pressing with its original gum." She
spoke as if everything she was saying was incredibly obvious. "I paid
eight grand for it."

"For a stamp!?" It was lucky Ramesh wasn't drinking his coffee at
that moment or he would have spat it all over the computer. "Was it
for sending letters to the moon?"

"It was mint condition, an absolute bargain. Course, I never slept
with Bob again after that. I have my standards you know. But I have to
say, he was a very sensitive lover. For a big man he certainly knew–"

"Urmmm, thank you." I really didn't need the details.

"The next time I saw 'im I gave 'im hell, I can tell you. He said
he'd taken it without thinking, but when I asked for it, he said he
didn't have it no more. Said he'd lost it. I've been trying to get my
money back ever since. Told 'im I'd call the police if he didn't sort it
out by the summer."

My turn for a question. "So why didn't you tell them all this after
Bob was killed?"

Her habitual frown scrunched up tighter. "And have 'em finger me
as the murderer? Not likely, mate." She yawned and stretched out one
arm. "Now if there's nothing else you want me for, there's a yoghurt
with my name on it in the breakroom fridge."

When we didn't reply, she stood up with a huff and disappeared
from our screen as if the whole thing was just another meeting or a
personal performance review.

"I reckon she did it." Ramesh's assertion immediately made me
think that he was trying to shift the blame. "If you ask me, eight
thousand pounds is a pretty big reason to do someone in. Maybe she
killed him to get the money back. Or maybe it was a classic broken
heart. She was in love with Bob and couldn't stand the rejection."

I didn't reply. I was enjoying Mum's salad and the chance to put my
thoughts in order before Jack came to see us. He turned up at 1:20 as
instructed. His bushy red eyebrows were twitching nervously and his
moustache was all pursed together, ready for whatever he'd come to say.

"Yes, it's true that Bob and I never got along. And yes, it came to blows once, but I didn't kill him." He'd pushed the chair out of the way and stood pointing into the webcam. "He thought he had some dirt on me, but he was the one doing coke in the office at all hours. And how many times did he turn up wasted to meetings?"

Ramesh and I glanced at each other once more but Jack wasn't done.

"The truth is that Bob was a thug. He was handsy with the girls in the office and treated the rest of us like scum. Worst of all though, he had a putrid core that would spill out whenever he was angry. I wasn't the one who turned his lights out, but he deserved what he got and that's all I'm going to say on the matter."

There was power to his words that I'd never imagined from Jack and with that, he was gone. Off to sit in his cupboard to sign for parcels and watch baby giraffe videos on his computer.

"Well, that was easy." Ramesh opened a bag of Cinema Style popcorn and began to hoover up the contents.

"I never imagined Bob as a coke fiend. Didn't seem his style." I continued picking at my salad. "Though that might explain his anger issues. Hey, maybe that's why he was so short-tempered in his e-mails this year. Perhaps he was an addict."

"Goes to show that you can never really know a person." He threw a piece of popcorn in the air but missed badly when he tried to catch it in his mouth.

How true, I thought but I stuck to the subject at hand.

"What do you reckon Jack meant by 'dirt'? We need to know what Bob had on him."

"Maybe he was stealing office supplies."

I thought about what else it could be. "I suppose so. Hardly worth killing someone over though. Do you reckon he could have done it?"

"Totally," he said between handfuls. "I'm coming round to the idea that every single one of them killed him."

"Everyone but Amara, right? In Christie's stories, practically all the suspects have a good reason to want the victim dead, but we haven't found anything on Amara. I don't see her murdering Bob just because he got the same promotion as her, no matter how much of a baby he was about it."

Ramesh raised one finger like he'd had a great idea. "Maybe she was in love with Bob, then found out about him and Wendy!"

I wasn't impressed. "Really? Young, pretty, happily married Amara was in love with horrid old Bob? Do you think that women all over the office were dropping their knickers for him?"

He went back to eating his popcorn because he didn't have an answer. It wasn't long before our final interviewee showed up.

"What do you want?" Will sat down in the repositioned chair. He was wearing that half-vulnerable expression I'd seen on him the day Bob died and a neatly tailored suit with a light-green shirt. He seemed to have a different coloured shirt each day but his suits were always silver and snugly fitted.

"We know what you did." Winking over at me, Ramesh sounded unconvincing even through the voice disguiser, which he'd now set to angry phantom mode.

Will smiled and his sheen of pure smugness returned. "You must be kidding." He full on laughed at us. "What were you expecting? That I'd come up here and confess to my terrible crime? I'd have to be pretty stupid to fall for that."

Sh...ugar. It wasn't going to plan. I turned the mic on to see what would come out of my mouth. "We know you argued with Bob in the weeks before he died. Tell us what it was about and we won't have to talk to the police." My heart was beating in double time. I was beginning to see what a mistake this whole thing could become.

Staring at us through Ramesh's widescreen monitor, Will remained silent. He put one hand on his plain black tie and smoothed it down from top to bottom. "We? I don't suppose that would be Ramesh and Izzy would it? Nice try, losers."

"You're wrong. We–" Ramesh was too nervous for a scary-voiced blackmailer. He really wasn't great at this subterfuge stuff.

"I tell you what, how about I let David know that you've been running around playing Scooby Doo? Or that you're using P&P equipment to harass your colleagues?"

If we were the plucky teenage detectives, then he was the cartoon villain, complete with a scowling lip and hard stare. I signalled to Ramesh to keep his mouth shut and turned off the ghostly disguise so that my own voice crackled through the airways.

"He was your mate. Why would you care if we try to help the police work out who did it? I mean… if you weren't involved?" It wasn't exactly table turning stuff but at least I'd wiped the smile off his face.

He looked about the empty office before replying. "You said it yourself, he was my mate. What nobody gets about Bob is that he was a good laugh. You all wanted to believe that he was some kind of monster when really he just loved trolling you. It gave him a kick but deep down he was a good bloke. And sure, we argued, like all friends do, but I didn't have some long-burning grudge against him if that's what you think. Now piss off and let me eat my lunch in peace or I'll get you both fired."

He grabbed the webcam and the feed went dead.

Ramesh was smiling for some reason. "You know what? That went better than I'd expected."

Chapter Thirteen

My brilliant investigative gamble had turned up more questions than answers and I was beginning to think I might never understand who Robert H. Thomas really was. To be honest, I didn't even know what the H. in his name stood for. Our supposedly anonymous interviews had done nothing to prove Ramesh was the killer, and there were still so many threads to tie up.

I hated the idea of the police getting there before me. I constantly imagined them walking into the office to reveal that they'd caught the culprit and that it was someone I'd never even considered – Pauline from accounts maybe, or Len the building security guard.

At the same time, I really had to wonder how they'd manage it without me. I'd been to Croydon police station. If their tea making facilities were any reflection on the standard of their murder investigations, I very much doubted their resources were up to scratch. Would they really have accessed all the suspects' computers and been able to find out what we had? Wouldn't there be issues with privacy and data protection?

I liked to think I was following in the imaginary footsteps of Christie's detectives but there was one big difference between us. More often than not, the police share what they know with Poirot and rarely object to the presence of interfering old maid Jane Marple at the crime scene. D.I. Brabazon, meanwhile, had sneered at me when I'd offered to help and yet, even without all the forensic evidence and witness statements they could access, I was hot on the heels of Bob's killer. Not that I was getting cocky or anything.

At the end of lunch, Amara and David made another announcement. Well, David did the speaking. Amara stood next to him looking respectful.

"Good afternoon, everyone."

He was wearing a sexy navy suit with a checked tie. Well, the suit itself wasn't particularly sexy but the man inside it was. His bright blue eyes were like torch beams in the already floodlit office.

I'd like to unbutton his shirt.

All right, brain. Take it easy.

"I've heard from Bob's family that, as per his instructions, they'll be holding a memorial service on Thursday morning at the Addington Hills viewpoint. I'll definitely be attending and if any of you would like to say goodbye to a long-standing member of our team, I'm sure he would have appreciated your presence."

Trust Bob to leave instructions for how he wanted his funeral to go. No doubt he couldn't stand the thought of missing out on one last shot at relevance in our lives. It still seemed strange for him to plan something like that in his fifties though.

David mouthed his thanks and everyone went back to work. Well, everyone except me. I was still looking through the data dump that Ramesh and Dean had hacked. With Bob not around to complain, I really could get away with doing very little. I suppose my deskmate Suzie should have been the one checking up on me but she had an aversion to words and rarely squeaked more than a few syllables in my direction per day.

As co-deputy director of the whole company, Bob wasn't officially my supervisor. But being the self-inflated, micro-managing Fagin that he was, he loved taking us waifs and strays under his wing. This was not because he had any desire to impart his wisdom or guide us through the labyrinth of the working world, he simply enjoyed having people around to shout at.

I had another look through Jack's files in case there was something I'd missed. From what I could tell based on his internet history, he had a serious thing for videos of baby donkeys. He must have watched hundreds of them. Which made me feel slightly less lazy after doing so little work that day.

It was surprising how singular he was in his browsing habits. There was no sign of any work-related topics – and there were definitely elements of his job that would have needed a bit of online research. He wasn't supposed to just sit in his cupboard watching animal videos all day, he had reports to write and systems to check. There was a bunch of word documents in a folder on his desktop but the only one that stood out was a list of about three thousand names and addresses from across London. They mainly appeared to be individuals, rather than businesses, but I could find no other clear connection between them.

I left behind his personal files and looked through the apps he used most on his computer. YouTube was number one, of course, but after that was a weird looking web browser that I'd never heard of, so I noted down the name to ask someone cleverer than me. By the end of the day, I'd found nothing particularly useful on Jack and was coming to the conclusion that he was just as harmless as he seemed.

Immersed in my investigation, the afternoon had passed in a flash and I realised I was the last one in the office. The tippy-tapping of computer keys had been replaced by the sound of a vacuum and I could see a couple of cleaners hard at work in the conference room and another going from desk to desk emptying the bins. I shut my computer down and went to collect my coat from the hooks by the photocopiers.

There were always discarded bits and pieces left behind there; like hats, scarves and forgotten shopping bags. A host of umbrellas rested against the wall and a few summery jackets that no one had removed since an unexpected two-day heatwave a month earlier hung limply. There were only two coats remaining. My shabby, blue woollen one that I'd had forever and couldn't bear to part with and Bob's black rain mac.

I might have emitted a yelp of excitement as I put on a pair of men's leather gloves from a pile of unclaimed items and carefully prised one side of his coat from against the wall. The stale scent of Bob's cigarettes instantly attacked my nostrils. In the inside, right breast pocket, I found absolutely nothing of any interest. There were a couple of two pence coins and a very sticky mint humbug but no wallet, no phone.

Wishful thinking. The police would have noticed that kind of thing was missing and scoured the office for them.

I didn't give up. The other inside pocket was more promising. I found a fiver in change and the receipt for Bob's lunch on the day he died. He'd spent sixty quid and appeared to have consumed half the food in Croydon. There was more still to find though. His outside pockets held a treasure trove of receipts and scraps of paper, bundled with a blister pack of medicine and all tied together with an elastic band. I had a quick flick through them and, besides more evidence of Bob's unhealthy appetite, there was a business card for someone renting audio-visual equipment and the address of Croydon Animal Experts. The pills were the same kind I'd seen splashed with blood on

Bob's desk. They had tiny white logos printed all over them but, not speaking Russian, it was impossible to say what Тымудак might cure. It wasn't even as if I could type it into a search engine.

I thought that my great haul of evidence might not be so great after all until I put my hand into the last pocket and came out with a single train ticket from Norbury to East Croydon. It had been bought on the Wednesday that Bob was murdered but the most interesting thing about it was written in thick black letters on the back.

OKAY, LET'S DO IT.
TONIGHT AT EIGHT.
B.

Nothing about the ticket made sense. Bob lived in Norbury but, to my knowledge, never took the train. And, if he'd written the note to give to someone, why was it still in his possession? At the very least, it told me that he'd planned to meet somebody on the night he was killed. It had always struck me as odd that there was only one wine glass on Bob's desk. Perhaps the killer removed the second glass.

Sadly I wasn't the only person who'd want to know about it so I put everything back in the pockets of the raincoat and called the police.

If they make me late for the date with David, I will not be a happy bunny.

I had to wait about twenty minutes but Irons and Brabazon soon showed up with evidence bags and surgical gloves.

"I told you not to interfere." He wasn't happy with me.

"And I told you, I could be helpful."

Irons stepped in before we could get into a fight. "We appreciate your assistance, Miss Palmer. We'll be in touch if we have any further questions."

I couldn't believe it. If I hadn't had somewhere far more interesting to get to, I would have stuck around for an argument. Talk about ungrateful. Any chance they had of solving the crime was surely down to the evidence that I'd uncovered.

It took me the whole tram ride and most of the walk home to get over my bad mood. I almost turned back to the office to tell them what I really thought of their detective skills.

100

When I got home, I didn't have time to share the new evidence with my family so I went straight upstairs to get changed. Just in case I'd got the wrong end of the stick and, instead of a date, David wanted me to help paint the ceiling or install a bird house, I didn't dress up too flashy. My blue sequin-infested mini-dress was out and some sensible black trousers and a white blouse took its place.

"You look like a proper grown up," Mum told me as she, Danny and Greg came to see me off in the hall.

"I am a proper grown up." I shuffled through them like a bride greeting her guests. This was hardly standard practice when I went on a date. I imagine they were desperate to discover what I would find out about their prime suspect.

"Try to make sure he's not the murderer." Greg had a posh voice which made everything sound incredibly simple.

Danny had no words for me. He held his hands out and sized up my outfit then pulled me in for an excessively long hug.

"Thanks, mate," I said, once I'd recovered.

"Am I too late?" Just in time, my father peered in through the front door. "Good, I've caught you. I thought I'd give you a lift over."

I'd always imagined David living in the residential equivalent of the Porter & Porter office. I saw him in a completely white apartment with no decoration of any kind and a confusingly located bathroom. In reality, he had a maisonette in Shirley that was more of a post-war family housing unit than a chic, executive shag pad. It had a little front garden with a cherry tree in and there was a sunburst stained glass window above the door.

I made sure my dad had driven off before I rang the doorbell but then felt nervous and wished he'd stayed to hold my hand.

We lied! We're not a grown up at all. Who on earth thought it was a good idea to send us off into the night to meet an actual man?

Brain, for once I agree with you.

"Hi Izzy. Thanks for coming." David opened the door and his lovely smooth voice and lightly stubbled charm made everything okay again. And yes, he still sounded like he was welcoming me into a meeting and I was even less sure if this was a date or not, but I no longer minded. As long as I got to enjoy the sparkly blue of his eyes – like twin photographs of a distant solar system – nothing else mattered.

Oi. You're doing that thing again where you forget to speak. Say something!

"You look lovely."

Not that!

David smiled despite the fact that my opening line had been stolen from my dad in the car. "Oh... thanks very much."

At least I hadn't called him darling.

He guided me into the house and I walked through a corridor lined with photos of wild-looking beaches; all green hills and jagged cliffs. I came to a stop beside one.

"Is that Wales?"

"Yep, it's the Gower. I like to make sure that anyone who steps into this house gets a healthy dose of Welshness right off the bat." His smile became a grin. "I considered painting a huge red dragon up there but decided it would be a bit obvious."

I let out a laugh that turned into a snort. "I've only been to Wales once. It was when I was a kid, but I remember it being very pretty."

"I'm not going to argue with you. It's the greatest country on earth. If only Mr Porter would open an office in Swansea, all my dreams could come true." He stopped and looked guilty. "Sorry, I could talk about Wales all night but I probably shouldn't."

He showed me into the front room which was divided up into a lounge and dining area. The dinner table was laid with two place settings, proper serviettes, red wine and even candles. That's right, people; candles! Okay, they were just tea lights on a tasteful glass platter, but they were real, physical candles and that could only mean one thing. I wasn't there to replace the batteries in his fire alarm or get something down from a high shelf. I was on a date!

"I've got a couple of things to do in the kitchen, why don't you make yourself at home for a minute?"

Woohoo! Perfect chance to nose about.

The main thing that possible boyfriends and possible murderers have in common is that they both need looking into extremely carefully. Once David had gone, I did a circuit of the room. It was very homely with big puffy sofas that had tartan blankets draped over the arms. In one corner was a flashy set of golf clubs which, if you ask me, lowered his boyfriend potential but massively increased the likelihood that he'd recently killed someone.

On top of a chest of drawers in the bay window, there were several framed photos. David by the sea with two people who – thanks to their matching jumpers – I had to assume were his parents, David in front of a castle by the sea, David surfing on the sea, David with his whole family in front of an NCP car park (weird location for a photo but they all looked very happy.)

I scanned the smiling faces, looking for any family similarity. He was the spitting image of his mother and aunt. They had the same light brown hair and striking eyes, the same permanent smile to their faces. The woman who I skilfully deduced was his older sister looked more like the father, their features harder and darker but their faces still jolly and bright.

Clinging on to this central group were two grandchildren aged around fifteen and twenty. The young boy was wrapped around David's sister while the twenty-year-old leaned casually against her grandfather. She was horrifically pretty, with the perfect mix of her grandmother's soft features and her grandfather's dark hair. She was the kind of person who was impossible to forget which is why I instantly recognised her as one of a gaggle of giggling interns who'd spent the summer at P&P two years earlier. Her name was Chloe.

There was one more person in the photo who looked quite different from the others, with a high forehead and a pale, freckled face. There was half a width between her and the rest of the group but her smile was just as huge.

"Were you married?" I asked when David returned with a chopping board covered in cut meats. No beating about the bush with me you'll notice.

He put the board down and walked over to see the photo. "Yes, that's Luned. Most people at work don't know about us. It's a bit weird to keep her photo there, but it was such a happy moment."

"On a family daytrip to a carpark?"

He gave me a playful shove. "Not exactly. That carpark is in front of the office where we signed our divorce papers. Everyone in my family adores Luned, so we went out for lunch and made a day of it. Sadly, she and I were no longer quite so in love."

His cheerful tone faded out and it made me want to smack myself for being an idiot. "Sorry if I sounded pushy." I searched for something to change the topic. "That's Chloe, right? I didn't know you were related."

"Yes, my niece. That's another secret I've kept. I suppose I didn't want to be accused of nepotism." He picked the photo up and let his eyes explore it like he hadn't noticed it there in years. "It's odd being the boss, you know? I've always kept so much distance from my staff. It's like, David Hughes is a totally different person to the Dai I am back home." He put the photo down and rushed back across the room as if it had given him an electric shock. "How about a drink, eh?"

"David, there's something I have to ask you." I finished my tour and joined him at the table. "Why did you invite me over?"

He immediately launched into a defence. "Oh no. You *would* have preferred to go to a restaurant. I thought this might be too much."

"No, that's not what I mean. I mean, why ask me out now? We've been working together for years and, be honest, right after a colleague gets murdered isn't the obvious moment for it."

"Fair question." He uncorked the bottle of wine and took a deep breath before continuing. "I've tried not to show it at work, but I really haven't taken Bob's death well. It's not that he was such a great guy, I think we all know that's not the case. But no matter what sort of person he was, nobody deserves what he went through."

It was my turn not to grasp what he was getting at.

"I'm probably not making much sense." He made a brief, melancholy laugh and motioned for me to sit down. "When I went in that morning and you'd found the body, I felt immensely guilty for never being anything but cold and impersonal to him and everyone at the office really. If I hadn't been so quick to criticise and condemn Bob, I wonder whether he could have become a better person. Perhaps none of this had to happen in the first place."

I sat down at the table and he passed me a glass of wine. "That's a lot of blame to take on yourself. You don't really think it's your fault, do you?"

He cleared his throat softly before speaking. "I'm not trying to play the martyr. I just mean that the whole thing got to me. Bob's life was over just like that and it made me see how much of my own time I'd been wasting. That photo you were looking at was taken five years ago and I've done nothing but work and sleep ever since."

"So, basically what you're saying is you're on the rebound?" I smiled. He smiled. It was sweet. "That still doesn't explain why you asked me. After all, we've got some very pretty colleagues at work. Wendy's still single for one and she's got a great sense of humour."

He leaned back in his chair and sipped his drink. I guess I'd been too nervous at first to notice how nervous he was.

"You're pretty," he said and I think my stomach might have eaten itself. "And you're ridiculously funny – funnier than Wendy even."

I raised my glass to him. "Well that is quite a compliment, thank you."

"Plus you're just about the ballsiest person around."

I let out one of my trademark cynical laughs. "Shows how little you know me. I'm about as brave as–" It was good that he interrupted me because I hadn't actually come up with a comparison.

"You're wrong. You're not afraid to be yourself and that takes courage."

"So, you're saying I'm weird?"

He twisted the stem of his wine glass back and forth between his thumb and forefinger. "Fine, if you want to put it like that. But I'm tired of boring people. And anyway, I've always thought you were kind of great."

"I didn't think you even knew my name until last week."

We fell silent for a moment but, for once, it wasn't uncomfortable. It was as if we'd finished the opening notes of that evening's conversation and needed a moment to process the fact that this was just the beginning. There was more still to come.

"Nice touch with the charcuterie board by the way," I said when the silence had lingered too long and I was worried my brain might tell me off again. "It's the kind of thing I'd make if I ever had a dinner party; fancy looking, but no effort whatsoever."

"That's just what I was going for." Another half silence was filled with more reciprocal smiling. "All right. Enough small talk. I will trade you facts that no one in the office knows about you for ones about me."

Nothing about that evening was how I'd expected it to be. I was nervous but in a good way, talking nonsense as ever but it seemed like he was enjoying it. I was already having fun and now we had a game to play.

"You go first."

"Okay." He tucked his lip in between his teeth to consider. "Right, got one. When I was at school, kids called me Squiddy for my long, gangly arms."

"No way. You're just saying that to make me feel better."

"Better about what?"

I threw a piece of chorizo at him. "Fine, my turn. My whole life people have told me that I must be good at basketball but the one time I played I scored in the wrong net."

I'd made him laugh. In all truth, he was howling away at my teenage misfortune.

"Hey, easy there." My phone was buzzing in my pocket but I ignored it. "This is bringing back a lot of childhood trauma. It's not funny."

"It is actually. Are you saying you took a shot at the wrong basket? That's practically impossible."

"Well, first up, I knew nothing about the game and I wasn't paying attention. My psycho P.E. teacher Mr Bath subbed me in as some sort of deranged punishment. So, when I got the ball, I just ran to the closest net. Everyone was shouting my name and for a second I thought I must be amazing. I tuned out all that noise, focussed on the basket and let the ball fly. I was so pleased with myself when it went in but, then I turned around to celebrate with my team and they were staring at me like I was the worst human in history."

My phone started buzzing again, but I was hardly going to spoil our wonderful conversation by whipping it out like a pervert in a subway.

"My turn." I could tell that he'd already got his next story cued up. "I once went to the bathroom on a packed train. I thought it had a self-locking electric door until some bloke came along and pressed the button. There I was, sitting on the toilet with my trousers round my ankles as fifteen people peered in on me, and that still wasn't the worst of it. The guy kept trying to close the door but it wouldn't go. He was really hitting the button, getting more and more worked up. In the end all I could do was finish my business and apologise to the poor fella for what I'd put him through it."

"Wow." The buzzing in my pocket had started again and I took a quick peek under the table. It was only Ramesh so I rejected the call. "You know I thought this was your idea to get to know me but this has quickly escalated into a competition to see who can tell the most embarrassing story. I'm sorry to tell you, that is one area where I am world champion."

We scoffed down all the sausagesy stuff as we talked. The chorizo was a bit spicy for me.

"Try this one. In my very first job, working in a fried chicken take away, I spent a whole day flirting with my new colleague Adam. At the end of our shift, as we walked home together and I thought it was super romantic and sweet, he said, "I'm really flattered and everything but I'm afraid I'm not gay.""

David accidentally dribbled his wine as he laughed at me. I found it insanely cute.

"Hold on a moment, I'm not finished. Though I blame the misunderstanding on Chick 'o' Mansion's poor-fitting uniforms and the dreadful haircut my mother had given me, I was so horrified that, rather than telling him I wasn't a boy, I quit my job and never went back."

I'd left my mobile face down on the table but it hadn't stopped vibrating so I finally decided to deal with it.

"I'm so sorry," I said. "I'd better get this. If Ramesh watched Glitter with Mariah Carey again, he might be having daymares. He won't leave me alone until I tell him that everything is okay." I walked over to the front window and accepted the call. "What is it, Ramesh? You know I can't talk now."

His voice was faint and he was breathing really heavily. "Yeah, sorry about that. I just didn't know who else to call. The police are at my house and they're going to break the door down if I don't open it."

"What are you talking about, Ramesh?"

"No biggie, but I think they're here to arrest me."

Chapter Fourteen

Ramesh's whole family lived up north (Watford) and his girlfriend was in Scotland so, killer or not, I couldn't just leave him to rot in the police station. Inevitably, David was really nice and insisted he drive me down.

"You really didn't have to do this." I'd already said these words about six times before we got into Croydon.

"Continue not worrying about it, please."

We were sitting in his car outside the station. What I hadn't considered before we got there was the fact that police stations aren't like hospitals. You can't just hang about there waiting for news. So when I'd run nervously up to the front desk and explained that my friend had been arrested, the officer on duty had fixed me with a definite look of *what do you want me to do about it?* on her face.

Two hours had gone by since then and the easy, relaxed atmosphere between us had long since dissipated. It was my fault. David had tried to continue the conversation to help keep my mind off things but that's not really my style. Mum likes to say I'm a thinker, which is a polite way of saying I massively overthink everything I do.

It's not always a bad thing. Take solving Bob's murder for example. I'd been brooding over the details for almost a week and I could feel the links steadily forming, a clearer picture coming together. What I'm not so great at is decision making.

I wasn't sure whether I should go back to the police station and let them in on what I'd discovered on Ramesh. I thought it might be a good idea to talk it over with David or ring Mum for advice first though. The problem with that was that I didn't know whether to stay where I was or head home. I couldn't even be sure whether I was desperate for the loo or not.

So it was a relief in more ways than one when Ramesh walked out of the police station with a big smile on his face.

"What the hell happened?" I'd bolted from the car with David just behind. Standing in the road in front of the police station, I hadn't brought a jacket so I shivered through every word I spoke.

"It's fine." Ramesh seemed amused by the whole thing.

"I'm glad they let you go." Having sounded a bit fed up in the car, David was just as energised as I was by Ramesh's unexpected appearance.

"It's nothing. They thought I'd killed Bob but I told them it wasn't me."

I gave him a slap around the arm. It was a perfect expression of my love and anger. "And they believed you?"

"Course they did. Wait, don't you?"

Ramesh and David were looking at me like I was the one who'd done something wrong. Which I suppose, in a way, I had.

"Urmmm…" I couldn't think of an excuse. "Well… I might have come across the webcasts you did."

"You thought I'd killed Bob just because I had a cry about him on the internet? Really, Izzy, if every fanboy who'd shed a tear online went out and committed a murder, there'd be no one left on earth."

David listened but wisely stayed out of our psychodrama. I kept going all the same.

"But I saw the video you recorded a few days before he was killed. You said you wished he was dead and that you were going to do something about him 'once and for all.'"

Ramesh laughed at me then. He threw his head back and really went for it. "I did do something about it. Just after we ate Amara's birthday cake, I fired off fourteen different e-mails saying what I thought of him in excruciating detail. I explained how he'd made my life hell and the number of times I'd gone home feeling worthless and defeated. On the very last day of Bob's existence, I told him that I could finally see what a petty man he was."

"I had no idea he upset you like that, Ramesh." David put his hand on my friend's shoulder. "You could have to come to me. I would have done what I could to make it stop."

"I appreciate you saying that, David, but I didn't have the strength. If I'd thought for a second that–"

"Wait a minute." As they spoke, several new pieces of the puzzle fitted together but there were still so many gaps I needed to fill. "Why did the police let you go? How could you prove to them that you hadn't murdered him?"

Ramesh stopped what he was saying and the smile on his face ironed itself flat. "On the night that Bob was killed, I was livestreaming from my bedroom. There were about thirty people watching me describe how I'd finally stood up to him. It's a little support group we put together. The police have got the video on a USB drive I gave them along with the names and e-mail addresses of some of my online friends."

"I can't believe that you didn't tell me any of this." It still stung a little.

"I'm sorry, Iz. But, to be honest, I was embarrassed. You never let Bob get to you and I always wished I could be strong like that."

The proof of Ramesh's innocence hit me almost as strongly as the idea that he was a murderer had. It was like someone slapping me back and forth across the face.

It was David's turn to ask questions. "So why did they arrest you in the first place? What did they think they had on you?"

"It was my fault. I couldn't tell anyone my alibi without making it look like I had a massive grudge against Bob. I was scared people would think I was the killer, so, on the morning that Izzy found the body, I deleted his e-mails from the previous afternoon. It was a stupid idea and I panicked and did a messy job. It didn't take much for the police to work out there was a bunch of messages missing. They're not very happy with me about any of it."

I gave him another whack. "You're an idiot, but I'm really glad you're not going to jail." We exchanged goofy grins.

"Come on, you two. I'll drive you home."

We followed David across the road to his rather nice Audi saloon which I hadn't been in a frame of mind to admire before. Sleek but sensible, a bit like him.

"Oh, no. I ruined your date, didn't I?" Ramesh said as he opened the back door.

David and I looked at one another over the roof of the car and he replied for the both of us. "No, you didn't ruin anything."

After we'd dropped Ramesh off, David drove me back home. He pulled to a stop outside and we sat there in awkward silence.

"I'm really sorry." I'd already said it fifty times so I figured once more wouldn't hurt.

He swivelled in his seat to look at me. "There's nothing to be sorry

110

for. I'm glad I could be here for you tonight. It can't have been easy."

I almost kissed him then. His voice was so warm and kind, his eyes were like tropical lagoons in the moonlight and I was just about to lean forward and plant my lips on his when my seatbelt held me back.

Seriously?

The moment had passed. "I hope we can do it again soon."

He looked all expectant then. "How about tomorrow?"

"Maybe we could have a night off." I took a deep breath. "In the last week I've been on four dates with three different people. I've been insulted numerous times, stood up once and tonight my best friend was arrested. I think I might need a little time to get over all that."

"Of course."

Moron, you made him look sad. Do something!

Under the glow of the illuminated dashboard, my brain and I couldn't stand seeing David so blue, so I unclicked my belt and leaned across to him. My lips were only centimetres from his when a thought popped into my head and I couldn't let it go.

"David, I hate to ask but, where were you on the night that Bob was killed?"

He put his hand on one side of my face and looked at me up close like he was trying to memorise the details of my face. "I was having dinner with my aunt like every Wednesday. The police have already spoken to her."

I kissed him and it felt like someone had rubbed tiger balm over my entire body. A warm buzz travelled across my skin from my toes to the tips of every hair. Our lips pressed together and it was as if they'd been anatomically engineered to one day be united in a passionate embrace in a mid-sized car.

"I'll see you in the morning," he said when I finally pulled away.

How I longed to stay in that car. If I could have paused our relationship right at that moment, I'd never have to discover anything bad about him. I'd never get to know his irritating habits that would come to annoy me. We wouldn't have to have our first argument or any of the ones that followed. We could have lived like that forever, a nascent couple preserved in a magic bubble of time.

I opened the door and ducked out. My smartwatch buzzed aggressively to inform me that, as ever, I hadn't met my step count and that time had not stood still. As I opened the garden gate, I looked over my shoulder to watch him drive away.

I'd already been through far too many disappointing romances in my life to start thinking I was in love. Sadly, my brain hadn't told my body not to get over excited and that tingling sensation was once more phasing through me.

I suppose I shouldn't blame my brain. After all, she was too busy going, *Weeeeeeeeeeeeeeeeeeeeeeeeeeeee!* to worry about any future disappointment.

Chapter Fifteen

"Without you guys I'm not sure I'd be here and I know I wouldn't have managed to stand up to my boss today. I have to say a special thanks to Sally4EVA, Daemon1 and TheScarletPimp, because you've taught me so much."

Ramesh was back in his bedroom, staring into the camera lens, but this time he was all smiles. Stars, hearts and rainbows flashed up on the screen as he said his friends' names.

"I think back to everyone that Bob has hurt over the years. My first assistant Zoe wouldn't even talk to me about what happened and there was an intern a couple of summers back who just stopped coming in one day. If I could speak to all the people who he's wronged, I'd tell them this…"

He paused and swept his floppy, brown fringe from his eyes. "We don't need to be afraid of bullies like Bob Thomas. The only power he has, is the power we give him. Without that he's a sad little man with a hollow heart and nothing he can do will ever hurt us."

It was a long video. Ramesh went into all sorts of detail about how he wasn't going to take Bob's bullying anymore. I didn't get to read the e-mails that he sent, and we'll never know if they'd have shown Bob the error of his ways, but I could see from his expression how much better Ramesh felt just by writing them.

The videos in his folder were arranged alphabetically rather than by date. If I'd noticed that and watched the most recent file, I could have avoided all that suspicion and saved my friend from having his door bashed in by the police. That lucky old biddy Miss Marple never needed a degree in computer science to solve her cases.

And so, Ramesh was not the killer. That left me with five suspects, one of whom I'd recently kissed and whose alibi the police had confirmed. The fact David and I were dating meant there was all the more reason to make sure he hadn't done it, but every time I spotted him in the office, I couldn't help but imagine how good he must be with puppies and what a great Dad he'd make.

Which is exactly why we mustn't let his too cute for school, sweetie-pie act fool us!

David, Amara, Wendy, Will and Jack. I recited my shortened mantra as I sat at my desk the following morning. I knew that one of these people would be the key to getting at the truth of what happened the night Bob was killed. I thought about the names one by one and it suddenly occurred to me that there was someone missing from the list.

David, Amara, Wendy, Will, Jack and Bob. I'd spent so long focussing on who could have killed him that I'd failed to concentrate on the man who'd been killed. There were millions of reasons why someone would have wanted him dead but I'd become fixated on what a bully he was and completely ignored any other motive.

It was obvious that Bob had really lost it in the six months before his death. When he bothered turning up at work he was always in a state, coughing his guts out and stinking of cigarettes. He'd done coke in the toilets, quaffed champagne in his office, fired off rude e-mails to clients, punched Jack and seduced then robbed Wendy. He'd stopped caring about his job and no longer gave a damn what his colleagues thought of him. It would be easy to dismiss his transformation as a midlife crisis but there must have been something driving it. By alienating the people around him, Bob hadn't just burnt his bridges, he'd called in an airstrike.

Though I couldn't look through the files on his computer or interrogate him from beyond the grave, there was one place he lived on. A quick search online provided me with Bob's complete CV. He'd been at P&P since the eighties and listed Mr Aldrich Porter himself as a reference. I found newspaper stories from a decade earlier about the company's move to Croydon, discussing the investment they were making into the consulting wing of the company which was already being led by a Robert H. Thomas. I learnt everything and nothing about a man I'd known for years. So with no new light shed on him, I returned to more speculative chains of thought.

Bob must have bought the drugs from someone, perhaps he'd got involved with the wrong kind of people and stolen from Wendy to pay them back. Or perhaps Wendy was in debt to the same gang and helped them kill Bob to wipe her own slate clean. Such theories came

114

to me as much from TV dramas as anything I knew about my dead boss and I didn't hold out much hope for their success.

I wish I'd had the resolve to be able to pick a suspect and stick with my hypothesis to the end. While I still couldn't imagine squeaky clean Amara or David being the killers, it was hard to choose a favourite between Jack, Will and Wendy. I just hoped that my drink with Amara that evening would make things clearer.

Not wanting to lose my job before I'd worked out who'd filleted my supervisor like a fish, I spent most of Wednesday doing the work he'd have been shouting at me to get on with. David was busy in meetings all morning and was out of the office in the afternoon so I didn't have him there to distract me and the day dragged by.

At five thirty, I met Amara at the Station Hotel down by the abandoned post office sorting depot. I couldn't imagine anyone wanting to stay there – with its view of the East Croydon railway tracks and the noisy taxi rank out front – which was lucky as it had stopped being anything but a greasy watering hole about fifty years earlier.

"I'm so sorry," she said as we sat down in a rather soggy booth. "I'd forgotten how grimy this place is. I used to come here when I was a kid because it was the only pub around that didn't ask for I.D.s."

She looked out of place ordering a sweet white wine, so I'd gone for a pint of nice cold camouflage to try to fit in. The bar was largely populated by old men with very few teeth and plenty of tattoos. The barman kept glancing at the door like he was scared who would come in next.

"I'll tell you what, we'll go to a pub I know in the centre next time."

As much as I loved the idea of drinks with Amara becoming a regular thing, I was playing the part of a troubled colleague and didn't want to appear too cheerful.

"That'd be nice." I stuck with my maudlin expression to push the conversation along.

She took a sip from her wine then made a face to show how bad it was. "Izzy, why don't you tell me what got you so upset at work yesterday?"

I cast my eyes to the sticky carpet and began. "I'm really sorry to take up your time but, ever since Bob died, I've been struggling. I can't get the image of his body out of my head."

Amara looked as sympathetic as ever. "I can only imagine. Have you considered going to talk to someone? A professional, I mean."

"I don't think that's necessary." I swallowed a gulp of beer and wished I'd gone for a kids' drink. "I'm not depressed, I just need to understand why anyone would do something so brutal. You and Bob didn't get on, but you wouldn't have slit him open, right?"

She didn't answer immediately and I was worried that I'd laid it on too thick. She took another sip of her drink and I anticipated her answer.

"Bob had this unique way of getting under people's skin. Whoever killed him must have truly hated him and, I'm sorry to say, I can understand why they'd feel that way."

She paused again to look around her old haunt. Her eyes traced the 1980s football scarves and car number plates fixed to the wall above the bar. "Bob was jealous and controlling from the time I started at P&P. When I got the promotion over him, he made my life hell. It wasn't just that he thought he deserved the job more than I did, he came to take pleasure in telling me how worthless I was. He was always trying to show me up in important meetings and did everything he could to take over the projects we worked on together. But as cruel as he was in public, he was ten times worse when there were no witnesses around."

Her words were so intense and the look in her eyes so hateful that, for the briefest of moments, I thought she was about to confess to killing him. She clearly needed to talk about what had happened just as much as I did.

"I'm pretty sure we all have it in us to kill someone, but I wasn't the one to do it." She stared down into her wine glass like it was a wishing well. "I can't stop thinking that one of our colleagues must know what happened. Whoever it was, Bob must have done something appalling to end up the way he did."

She faded out again but I needed her to keep talking. "He was pretty wild over the last few months. I heard he'd been doing drugs in the office and we all know what happened at the Christmas party. Do you think that could be it?"

She smiled then. She was too clever for me.

"You're a bit of a Hercule Poirot, aren't you, Izzy?" Woah, got it in one. "That's all right, I don't blame you. But I think that the way Bob was acting was a symptom more than a cause. You see, back in

116

January, Bob's wife Selina came to see David and I. She told us that he had lung cancer and was refusing treatment. She thought we might be able to talk sense into him for the sake of their kids."

She looked down into her drink, as if searching for sense in the story. "David did what he could and offered Bob early retirement but he was having none of it. He thought he knew better than the doctors. He told us we should mind our own business and said he could sort it out himself."

More pieces clicked into place. The medicine in his coat, his unconvincing claim of invincibility. My brain whirred with the possibilities.

"But he was a mess, surely you could have forced him out. He was losing the business money."

She looked at me again in that warm but critical way of hers and I knew she was sizing me up. I had to be careful not to overplay my hand.

"David took most of Bob's big clients away from him. The ones he had left were ancient friends of Mr Porter; pernickety old men who wanted everything done the way it had been forty years ago. They were more trouble than they were worth. And you have to understand..."

Her eyes flicked about the Station Hotel, searching for spies. "I shouldn't be telling you this stuff. David would kill me, but you're a clever girl. You'd work it out eventually. You have to understand that Bob was untouchable. He'd done things that no one else would have got away with. David has spent the last five years dealing with problems that Bob created but he couldn't fire him because Mr Porter wouldn't allow it."

This was what I needed to hear. "Do you know why?"

"At first I thought it was a typical old boys club, but it was more than that. Bob had worked his way up from the bottom. He'd been Mr Porter's pet for years and would probably have been director if he'd had an ounce of charm. Porter wanted to keep him around but cared too much about his business to put Bob in charge. Which is why he hired David as MD and why I was made deputy."

Something had changed in the way she spoke. I'd dropped the pretence that I was there for her support but so had she. Amara clearly wanted to tell me this stuff and I couldn't be quite sure why.

"Do the police know all this?"

"Of course. I went into the station the day after he died. They didn't seem very interested. Brabazon told me that with all the knife crime going on in London, they'll be lucky if they have the resources to pursue half the leads they've got. I hate the idea that we won't find out who the murderer is. If we never know why someone killed him, Bob will always be the victim."

"How do you mean?" I fiddled with a beermat as I listened to her explanation.

She knocked back half a glass of wine in one go. "Oh, yuck. That's awful." Her tongue sticking out, she used the muscles in her neck to express just how bad her drink was. "I mean until we know the exact reason Bob was killed, it's as if he's the only one who suffered. He was never a victim when he was alive so what right has he got to be one now?"

I let her words sink in before replying. "The truth is that I was crying in the bathroom yesterday because I thought that Ramesh was the killer. It turns out I was wrong but the idea that he'd be punished for years and Bob's pain was over in seconds just didn't seem fair."

She smiled. "I heard about your adventure last night. I'm glad that it wasn't Ramesh. He's a nice guy. Bit of a pain sometimes, but a nice guy."

"You can tell me to mind my own business if you like, but can I ask where you were last Wednesday night?"

She hesitated for a moment. "Well, why not? I was with my husband, tucking our kids in and reading The Gruffalo for the seven millionth time when Bob was offed." She served up a truly wicked smile. "I'd love to have been on the scene to lend a hand but it's hard for working mothers to find the time these days."

It was kind of refreshing to hear one of our suspects admit that they were happy that Bob was dead. I'd never imagined it would be careful, considerate Amara though. We finished our drinks and turned to safer topics – our friends, office gossip, TV shows. I was glad she could trust me enough to confide all she had, but it still felt weird to be the least important woman in the company sitting in a dive bar with the most senior one.

When it was time to leave, we walked up to the station to say goodbye.

"Izzy, as far as I'm concerned, you can look into this as much as you like. Maybe you'll find out something that the police don't know. But please don't do anything that could get you fired. I'd miss having lovely weirdoes like you and Ramesh around the office. It would be boring there without you."

"Okay, Amara." I smiled and waved her off through the barrier thinking, *Oops! Too late.*

Chapter Sixteen

By the time I got home that night, I was furious at myself.
We should have worked it out.
We *should* have worked it out.
All the evidence was there that Bob was sick. His reckless, carpe diem behaviour. The unbranded Russian pharmaceuticals. His sickly appearance and regular absences. Plus everyone knows that characters with unexplained coughs are almost always dying of some terrible illness. How could I have missed it?

"Nothing can kill me. I'm invincible!" Bob already knew that he was dying when he screamed those unconvincing words at the office Christmas party. I see that as the beginning of the end for him. As it turned out, he didn't know how he was going to die, or when, but he knew he didn't have long to go.

I scrolled back through old phone messages from that sordid Friday night in December and sat on my bed watching the videos one by one. It was a choice between that and lying there cuddling my pillow, dreaming of David.

The moment that people talked about for months after was Bob and Jack's punch up in the breakroom. It was Will who'd originally filmed it but I'd got the video from Ramesh, who'd had it from Suzie, who'd been sent it by Pauline from accounts and I haven't a clue how she came across it.

It was a sorry sight really. Two overweight men in their fifties, circling one another like kids in a playground. Their *dukes* feebly raised, it was as if they were actively trying to imitate olden time boxers.

"You're a fake!" Bob threw his words at Jack before despatching any jabs. "Acting like butter wouldn't melt. I can see right through you."

Jack sent a right hook into the air between them. "What you see is what you get with Bob Thomas, right? You look like a bastard, you act like a bastard; you are a bastard."

I could hear Will laughing from behind his mobile. "Get on with it and smack him one!"

A few of his finance bros took up the chant. "Smack him one, smack him one!" They didn't specify who should smack whom.

Wendy wasn't so impartial and was screaming Bob's name over and over with her own fists eagerly balled up. Bob took a comedy pause to down a glass of water from the sink so that Jack had to wait for him, still bobbing from foot to foot.

"Bob is wasted." Will turned the camera around to address his audience. "What a legend!"

Back in the ring, P&P's long-serving security guard beckoned his opponent forward. "Get on with it. Or are you scared I might hurt you?"

His face dripping wet like a slobbering dog, big Bob Thomas lunged forward. His left arm circled through the air to make contact with the top of his opponent's head and Jack threw himself theatrically to the floor. The video cut off to the sound of Bob's fan club cheering.

There were plenty of accompanying videos but that was the one that would be discussed and shared and mythologised. There was one of Wendy letting her hair down on the dance floor as her colleagues sang along to 'Stayin' Alive'. David made a speech in a Santa hat before wishing everyone a merry Christmas. Bob challenged Amara to a limbo contest and, for some reason, she accepted. I did not make an appearance because Ramesh and I were hiding in the server room, getting merry on supermarket brand Bucks Fizz.

We were the opposite of Bob in two ways that evening. He appeared in practically every video and, as far as I could tell, consumed no alcohol whatsoever. He must have known he was sick by then and started in on his medication. What else could account for the sudden belief in his immortality and the violent reaction his stomach had to Wendy's bedspread later that night?

Watching Bob's sad, macho display again made me wonder whether he could have been responsible for his own death. Did Bob Thomas subscribe to the credo that it was better to burn out than fade away? He'd already turned down cancer treatment, perhaps he'd paid someone to off him. I didn't dwell on the theory for long. Bob would never have clocked out when he was still having so much fun.

On Thursday morning, I met David to walk up to the Addington Hills viewpoint for Bob's memorial. It was a little odd seeing him again outside work. It felt like years had gone by since we'd kissed in his car and, instead of spending every waking moment thinking about

121

him, I'd been wasting my time trying to work out who killed a man that no one liked in the first place.

I met him by the park entrance. I'm afraid I have to say it; he looked dang sexy in mourning attire. He wore a well-fitted black suit with rather traditional styling to it, the cuffs to his shirt long, the collar high. I had a brief *David as a sexy 19th century baron-type* fantasy flash through my head.

God, Izzy. Stop being such a perv. We're on our way to a funeral.

You can talk, mate.

"It's nice to see you." He was back to the formal tone that we'd done so well to get beyond two nights before.

"You too." Personally, I fancied pashing him again but there were other people near and I didn't know how he felt about our colleagues seeing us together. We worked our way up the uneven path and, at one point, David had to take my hand when I stumbled over a rock. It was super romantic – well, except for all the funeralyness.

When we got to the plateau at the top of the hill, Ramesh rushed towards me. In an all-white suit with matching Stetson, he was not happy.

I couldn't resist the obvious question. "Why are you dressed like R. Kelly?"

"Will came to my house after work, gave me these clothes and told me I had to do a reading today at the memorial."

"Seriously, Ramesh? Why didn't you say no?"

His eyes wild, he looked like he hadn't slept all night. "Because I'm too polite, Izzy. I'm too bloody polite!"

Three rows of chairs had been set out to face the viewpoint that looked right across London. In front of them, there was a small platform with a large PA. To its right, a string quartet in eveningwear were elegantly sawing.

"How did Will even know what size suit you take?"

"It wasn't him. Bob set this whole thing up. He's trolling us from beyond the grave."

I had about forty other questions I'd like to have asked but, just then, Will got up on the podium to speak. He was dressed in an identical outfit to Ramesh's and stood before an ornate silver lectern.

"Ladies and gentlemen, if you could all find a seat, the Robert Harold Thomas memorial service is about to begin."

Oh. So H is for Harold apparently.

Pulling free from Ramesh's desperate grip, I followed David over to some free chairs at the back. The portion of the office who'd come to pay their respects/have a morning off had already occupied the front section. The only empty seats in the first row were **Reserved for Mr A. Porter +1** but our illustrious patron had refrained from attending. I was surprised to see Amara's family mixed in with Bobs'. All four children were dressed in neat black blazers, ready to be bundled off to the same posh school once the service was over.

"We are gathered here this morning to celebrate the life of one we held so dearly in our hearts." The grin on Will's face showed that he knew exactly what he was there to do and would enjoy every moment of it.

As he started in on his spiel, I looked around the crowd. I recognised the majority of the people there from work so, either Bob had very few friends, or he'd planned this whole thing for our benefit. There was no sign of Jack, but Wendy was already making her presence felt. Her head rested despondently on Pauline from accounts' shoulder, she let out a rhythmic high-pitch whine, like an over-emotional car alarm.

Loitering by the bushes at the back of the audience, D.I.s Irons and Brabazon were observing the ceremony. I couldn't help but wonder where they'd got to in their investigation.

"Philanthropist, humanitarian, amateur poet and Croydon-based financial expert, the kind-hearted chap we all knew as 'Bob' was a man of many talents." Will continued to recite from the pre-prepared text. "Taken from us so prematurely, it is a terrible sadness that he will never get to fulfil his true potential. His close friend and colleague Ramesh Khatri, is going to start the service by reading one of Bob's own compositions."

From his seat at the back of the stage, Ramesh looked over at me pleadingly before rising. His head bowed, he went to join Will at the microphone. Standing together, the brothers in white looked like a bad R&B duo.

"This poem is called 'The Loneliness of the Middle Manager.'" He sought me out in the crowd for encouragement, then put his eyes down and began to read.

"We have left behind the daylight.
We have walked towards the night.
We have lost our sense of wonder,
Though we know it isn't right."

It turned out that my friend was not a natural public speaker. I can't imagine Bob would have cared. He'd only chosen Ramesh for the reading because he knew it would upset him. He cantered through the lines, and, though I hated the fact that my best friend in the world was suffering up on that stage, I really wished he'd put a bit more expressiveness in his voice. Is there anything quite so jarring as bad poetry being read out badly?

"The abyss in which we enter,
Like a cold, and cruel November,
Is the absence of all heart.
It's the place from which we start.
But as we must all learn,
It's to there we will return."

There was some polite applause as Ramesh made a troubled sigh but the poem wasn't over. His anger at having to read out Bob's self-indulgent musings could easily be mistaken for sorrow at our old boss's departure.

"Greatness isn't chosen,
It's thrust upon those most beholden,
To the burden of responsibility,
The ones who look out for you and me.
Who strive towards another day,
And always do it their own way."

As Ramesh read the final line, twelve doves, all as white as his suit, launched into the sky from behind the stage. It was too much for Bob's wife Selina who, breaking down in tears at the spectacle her dead husband had provided, pulled her daughters up to standing and disappeared stage right. Amara and her children followed out soon after, waving apologetically to the people they passed.

Beside me, David did not look happy to be a witness to any of this. His jaw was fixed in a permanent clench and his tightly closed fists had scrunched up his trousers. At least he wouldn't have to sit there much longer.

Will returned to the lectern to introduce the next speaker. "We're lucky to have Mr David Hughes with us today. David is the director of the firm where Bob worked for the last three decades. I think if we give him a nice round of applause, he might just come up here to share his remembrances of the great man."

David didn't hesitate as Ramesh had. He walked straight to the front and mounted the stage. Will held out a white card to him before stepping aside with a smile. He was having a great time, and was no doubt eager to discover where David's speech would lead.

Standing in front of the lectern, David looked at his prompts for a moment then smiled almost nostalgically. "It says here that Bob was a unique, capable and intelligent man and I think we can all agree with that." There was a determination to his voice that was at odds with his usual relaxed tone. He paused and looked around the faces of those present then tore the card in two. "But I think I'd prefer to describe him in my own words."

There was a murmur of surprise from the mourners around me.

"I'm very sorry that Bob died in such a violent fashion. I'm sorry that his kids lost their father and for everything that his wife must be going through. At the same time, I'm not going to stand here and make out that Bob Thomas was a saint.

"If Selina and the children had been able to tolerate more than a few minutes of this sick display, I might have held my tongue. But I think there's been enough politeness for one morning so I'd prefer to tell the truth."

David's eyes scanned around slowly from one side of the audience to the other. "I've been working in the financial sector for over fifteen years and I've met some really nasty people in that time. Only a tiny minority, of course, but I've had bosses who ruled through intimidation, colleagues who liked to pick on the weakest to boost their egos and met plenty of guys who thought that putting on an expensive suit was a licence to harass and objectify the women they worked with. Bob Thomas was worse than all of them."

That was the line that really got the crowd going. The attentive silence was shattered as the forty or so attendees responded with a collective gasp. Whispered comments spread along the rows of chairs like leaves blowing in the wind and Wendy's wailing alarm fired up once more.

"The fact that he put his own family through this morbid spectacle says a lot about Bob. He only ever thought of himself. The whole reason we're here today is because he decided that it was more important to have one last dig at his colleagues than for his loved ones to have the dignified send-off they deserve.

"Bob had been sick for some months before he died and instead of spending that time with the people who loved him, he wrote out this awful script that I'm supposed to be reading, searched for a company that could provide doves for special occasions, pre-booked a PA system and no doubt auditioned the string quartet down by there."

Facing the audience in his seat on the stage, Ramesh's face was sketched over with a mix of shock, respect and immense joy.

And still David hadn't finished. "I can agree that Bob was unique because he's the only person I've ever met who instinctively knew how to get under the skin of everyone around him. He was capable too, of cruelty, selfishness, bigotry and arrogance. And, yes, he was intelligent but he never used that great big brain that he was so proud of to help anyone but himself."

The only thing in my head right then was how proud I was of David. Boyfriend or boss, he was doing the right thing. He took a deep breath and I could see that he was about to deliver his parting blow.

"Bob was a bully. Countless people suffered because of his actions. The only thing I should be coming up here to say is how sorry I am that I didn't do more to protect you from him."

With his piece said, he got down from the stage. Will watched him go with genuine wonder in his eyes and started to applaud. About half the audience joined in, the rest sat stunned, still trying to process what had just occurred. As David went to commiserate with Ramesh, Will took to the mic once more.

"I'd like to thank everyone for coming. I think this spectacular occasion would have surpassed even Bob's expectations."

The awkward hush that followed was interrupted by Bob's string quartet. The four musicians looked just as unnerved as their audience. Like their counterparts on the Titanic, they battled on regardless. A windswept rendition of Pachelbel's Canon soared around me as the congregation rose.

It was time for Wendy to burst out in tears again. "None of you knew him. Not like I did!" She shuffled to a spot in front of the stage and looked around the congregation accusingly. I noticed that the two inspectors at the back were watching her with interest. "Sure, he wasn't perfect, none of us are. But Bob had heart. Bob was an original. I don't care what you thought of him. He was a bigger man than anyone here."

Will couldn't let that one go and stepped back up to the microphone.

"A fact that no one can deny and yet another stirring tribute to our fallen comrade."

David shot Will a look which I could see meant *I'll see you in my office this afternoon.*

I walked over to join him and Ramesh led the two of us back down the path towards town. The rest of the mourners trailed along behind chattering loudly, any pretence of funereal discretion was long since abandoned. Taking his cowboy hat from his head, Ramesh sent it spinning through the air over the heath. For about fifteen seconds, the sun peeped out from its home behind the clouds to make my heart smile. It was true what Amara had said about Bob. In death he'd become a victim but David had put that right.

"How about we get a drink tonight?" he asked me.

I didn't have to think long. "I'd love to."

I'd been nervous that the relationship we were embarking upon could only exist outside the office. I was dreading the conversation we'd have and the ultimatum I'd make to get him to acknowledge me in front of our friends and co-workers. And I was pretty much resigned to the fact that such pressure would most likely backfire and lead to him breaking up with me. Except that wasn't how it happened.

David took my hand to swing our arms like we were on holiday together. Right there, fifteen metres in front of Wendy and Pauline and their bitchy buddies, he confirmed our new loved-up status.

Bob's fake-funeral trap had failed. Walking along with my best friend and my bossfriend, the world seemed like a good place to be. With the sound of the classical music floating down to us, it was like the shiny, happy ending to a movie.

Sadly though, it wasn't. We were only about two thirds of the way through and things were about to go a whole new shade of dark. Of course, I didn't know that then and, for a few moments, – before it started raining and we had to bomb it back down to the car park, dripping wet – I was full to the brim with happiness.

"Actually, I should probably get my hat back." Ramesh's own cheesy grin was replaced with an uncertain look. "It might be bad for the environment or something."

Chapter Seventeen

The mood in the office that afternoon was predictably subdued. Those who hadn't attended the memorial would have heard all about it and, whenever David stepped from his office, fifty pairs of eyes flicked across at him curiously.

Will got the telling off that he was due for. After a bit of muffled shouting from David's room, the lead consultant emerged looking chastened. Whatever had been said, he managed to keep his job at least. Apparently there's nothing in the Porter & Porter rulebook against facilitating a member of senior management's dying wish to humiliate his colleagues in an elaborate memorial service.

Wendy didn't come back in that day, whereas Jack seemed pretty upbeat, sitting in his cupboard giggling along to YouTube. It was Amara's behaviour that I found strangest. When we'd had our chat, she hadn't mentioned any connection to Bob's family, yet she was clearly close to Selina and their kids all knew one another. Perhaps she'd helped Bob's wife do him in. There was nothing to say that the hard drives were taken at the same time as Bob was murdered. If Selina had done the deed, Amara could have popped by after bedtime to cover her tracks. It was yet another hypothesis to add to Mum's list.

When my gruelling 9-5:30 was over, David and I walked down to the Boxpark – *Croydon's premiere leisure and dining complex* – to have a drink in the Cronx Brewery. Most people there looked far too cool for me to be in the same bar as. It was just the kind of place I normally avoided out of fear that everyone would point and laugh at me for ordering the wrong drink. With David beside me, I didn't care what they thought.

He ordered a pint of IPA and didn't give me a hard time when I told him I wanted a lemonade.

"So, we've gone through all the typical first stages of a relationship." His eyes glowed like neon under the retro-industrial lighting. "A trip to the police station to ensure your friend wasn't done for murder…"

I was already laughing before we'd found a table. "Yep and the denouncement of a co-worker at his own memorial service."

"That's right. I wonder what we've got to look forward to next."

There were no tables free, so we sat on some stools beside what basically amounted to a plank fixed to the wall. It felt like we were being punished at school for being naughty.

"Perhaps we should do something a bit wilder and go for dinner and a movie?"

David sipped from his proper grownup drink. "Go easy. I had no idea you were so adventurous."

Smile smile smile, laugh laugh laugh. Sorry if this is making anyone nauseous. We clearly made an astoundingly cute couple though. David, with his traditionally handsome looks, and me, with my eyes and a face.

I've never been the type to get all worked up about a bloke so soon but I'd already liked David – at least in a casual, *ahhh, isn't he nice* way – for years and we seemed to click for some reason. For example, and here's a rare thing for a date, I actually agreed with his opinions on stuff. He was funny without being super show-offy and genuinely kind-hearted, not just acting that way to get into my pants.

As we sat chatting beside our beautiful wall plank, we found out we had things in common that I never would have expected. Both David and I played the accordion as children, (how cool were we?) Neither of us had ever broken a bone and we'd both always planned to eventually at some point visit Scotland when we got round to it in the future one day. But most importantly of all – and please stop me if this sounds like a shockingly high expectation in a relationship – we both enjoyed one another's company.

The bar was so packed that we were squished up close together – and against the beardy bloke sitting next to me – so David got to do a fair bit of flirty shoulder touching. I responded by playing with my long hair seductively, until I realised that it looked like I was trying to untangle a knot and stopped.

When we'd finished a second drink, the weather was… well… not raining, so we decided we'd avoid a busy tram journey and walk. Out in the Boxpark, Croydon's thriving social hub was busier than ever with big groups of teenagers crowding in for a grime gig. As I stood waiting for David to reappear from the bathroom, I watched the distinct groups mixing in the central concourse. Over in the Blue

Orchid Bar, the town's only official gay night was getting started and its early attendees were filling up the gaps between businessmen and locals on the tables outside. A Crystal Palace match would soon be projected on the big screen and half of the rest of the crowd were dressed in red and blue. All Croydon life was there and seeing the diversity my birthplace had to offer gave me a warm feeling inside.

It didn't last long as, just then, I saw Porter & Porter's very own rabid pooch stalking about the lower concourse. We caught sight of one another at the same moment and he looked even less happy to see me than normal.

"Is that Will over there?" David asked as he rejoined me but our colleague had already blended into a throbbing crowd of teens. "I wonder where he's off to. I never imagined him as a grime fan."

I took David's hand and we started towards the exit. "What kind of music do sadistic yuppies normally listen to?"

"Oh come on, he's not that bad. When I spoke to him this afternoon, he promised that he didn't think anyone would be upset by Bob's last joke. He said he was just trying to honour his friend's dying wishes."

We'd emerged back out on George Street and I looked at him to see if he was being serious. "How did you ever get anywhere in business when you're so trusting?"

He didn't reply. He put his arm around me and we began the journey home.

The Croydon suburbs didn't exactly sparkle in the fading light, but they were prettier than you might imagine. We peeked into the big houses along Addiscombe Road and (sorry, I know I'm dreadful) I wondered if David was wealthy enough to buy one. We spotted a little family all playing together in their front lounge and he smiled at me as if to say, *yeah, this is obviously ridiculous and we know very little about one another except for that accordion thing, but still, it would be nice, wouldn't it?*

When we got to the turn for David's house, I didn't want the evening to end so I walked one block out of my way in order to stay with him a bit longer.

"I like you more each time I'm with you." That swine! How could he say something like that? He'd ruined all other men for me. What if we broke up after a couple of weeks and I had to find someone else?

My life might as well be over.

Instead of replying, I did that weird laugh that made me sound like I was choking. Standing on the corner of his street, with our eyes locked together and our hands entwined, I didn't need words. I bent down really not very far at all and kissed him. Kiss number two blew kiss number one out of the ocean. Kiss number two made kiss number one seem like a peck on the cheek from my great uncle. Kiss number two told kiss number one that she was going solo and, in that very same moment, became a world famous rock star.

I opened my eyes half way through, to make sure that I wasn't overestimating the power of that kiss, but he was just as into it as I was. His hands were all over my back – not like he was checking me for a concealed weapon – he was soft and confident at the same time. I discovered new muscles in my tongue that I'm pretty sure I'd never used before and my head fizzed like I was getting a full body massage from eight different pairs of hands.

"I think you're amazing," I told him, when we came up for air.

He gave me another little kiss and kiss number three was the perfect follow up to numbers one and two. You'll be glad to know I stopped counting after that.

And, afterwards, he didn't pressure me to follow him into a public toilet for a quickie or give a negative critique of my kissing technique. He didn't burp or whip out his phone to check the football scores and, for this alone, he made it onto my list of top ten greatest ever kisses.

Who are we kidding? He was number one with a bullet.

"Let's do this again soon." He was still holding my hand.

I let out a far too romantic sigh. "I may be able to fit you in."

"Night, Izzy."

"Night, David." I gave him one last kiss and a playful shove towards his house.

My heart was still playing a jazz drumbeat as we walked off in opposite directions. He clearly couldn't stand to be alone though as it was only about twenty seconds later that I heard him running after me. Instead of turning round to receive his embrace, I thought I'd play it cool. I put my arm over my shoulder so that I could take his hand in mine when he caught up with me. Of course, Izzy being Izzy, I made a complete mess of it and ended up smacking him in the face.

"Oh, David. I am so sorry." I turned round feeling like a massive idiot – just to make a change.

The man holding his nose in front of me was about three times the width of my (I think it's fair at this point to call him) boyfriend. He looked like he was an extra in a documentary about rhinos and wore a balaclava pulled halfway down his face.

"You're not David. Why did... oh shiiiii–" It wasn't his size, or even his choice of knitwear that made me cry out. It was the large knife he was carrying in his right hand.

"You punched me, you overgrown freak!"

I don't know if it was down to the impending danger or his sizeist comment, but the only thing I remembered from a self-defence class I'd once taken popped into my head. Before he could lunge the knife at me, my knee went shooting forward at just the right angle to do the maximum possible damage. I threw my bag to the floor and sprinted away. He could have my £20 in cash and the Alcatel phone I'd got free with points from the supermarket, I just didn't want to get stabbed.

"Police!" I shouted, like I was in a period drama and then tried, "Fire!" which also sounded ridiculous so I finally settled on, "There's a huge bloke with a knife." I saw some twitching at curtains and an old man stuck his head out of his window but, seeing as the rhino was up on his feet and chasing after me, I could understand why no one came to help.

You may recall that I'm quite a tall person, so covering distances isn't normally a problem for me. Sadly, the beast on my tail was about three times faster than me and I'd have been in stab range in seconds if it hadn't been for David appearing at that moment to rugby tackle him to the ground.

Thank God for the Welsh!

"David, he's got a knife," I said, but the large blade had spilled along the pavement out of reach.

There was a pause as, laid out on the ground beside one another, the two men watched the weapon come to a stop ten metres from where I was cowering.

"Izzy, leave it," David yelled, but he was too late.

I had a head start on the mugger who was already up on his feet. In an odd mirroring of the romantic scene that had played out minutes before, my eyes locked onto his as we both willed ourselves towards the knife. David was still on the ground, winded by his fall and could do nothing but watch the dramatic conclusion of the first ever attempt on my life.

I was no rugby player, I hadn't the skills to scoop up the blade and sidestep away from the oncoming defence. No, my toes weren't known for their twinkliness, so I switched to plan B. Arriving one second before the human-bulldozer hybrid, I kicked the knife under a parked car.

My foot swung determinedly through the air, but what I hadn't considered was where it would go after. Sadly for my attacker, that place was his crotch. This second blow was just too much for the poor guy and he immediately doubled over. Clutching himself and rolling about on the floor, he made a sound like a bouncy castle with a puncture.

"Whhhhhyyyyy?"

It was an odd question coming from someone who'd just tried to knife me.

"God, I'm so sorry!"

What are you apologising for? He just tried to kill us!

If he wasn't interested in my handbag, it must have been more personal, yet I felt oddly calm about the whole thing. I don't know what had got into me. Challenging armed men? Sprinting *towards* danger? It wasn't a side of my character that I recognised. If I hadn't been high from the buzz of my new relationship, I'd probably have chickened out and let him stab me.

You were incredible.

Thanks very much!

After I'd finished congratulating myself, David limped over with his hands to his ribs. We could hear sirens off in the distance but Rolly the rhino wouldn't be charging off anywhere soon.

"You're bloody lethal you are." His hands on his knees as he caught his breath, David peered up at me suspiciously. "I'm glad it wasn't you I had to bring down. I wouldn't stand a chance."

"Ouch, ow ow. I'm not so sure about that," I replied through searing pain that suddenly hit me. "I think I've broken my foot."

Chapter Eighteen

With several police cars and even a couple of ambulances, all with their lights a-flashing, we'd made quite a scene on the otherwise dozy residential street. The paramedic lovingly bandaged up my bossfriend (still funny) but, when I showed her my foot, she said it was just a bruise and gave me ibuprofen. I stuck my tongue out at her as soon as she wasn't looking. It turned out to be a surprisingly effective form of pain relief.

When the police arrested our scrotally afflicted friend and removed his balaclava, it felt like the unmasking of a comic-book supervillain. It wasn't as if I was expecting to find one of our suspects underneath – even that criminal mastermind Wendy couldn't disguise herself as a twenty-stone heavy with neck tattoos. Still, I thought that I might recognise the guy who'd gone to so much trouble to attack me, but nope; nothing.

D.I. Brabazon wasn't on duty that night – I guess the police occasionally get time off to sleep and that sort of thing – but his partner D.I. Irons was there to debrief us with her usual quiet competence.

"Looks like he was paid to do it. He's a local fella. Not the first time I've run into him."

I was biting my tongue to distract from the pain in my foot so speaking was a bit tricky. "That's good then, right? It means we'll find out who was behind it."

Perched on the garden wall of the old man who'd called the police, David sat with his arm around me, making sure to avoid all contact with his ribs. "Surely he'll tell you who paid him?"

"Nope. Bitcoin."

I'd heard the word before but assumed it was some kind of computer game. "Sorry. What-what?"

Irons looked at me as if I'd asked what a spoon was or how to open a book. "Whoever hired our guy found him on the dark web and paid with bitcoin. It's an anonymous digital currency; impossible to trace."

David seemed to be following the sounds she was making better than I was. "Why would he tell you this stuff?"

135

"The big chap currently having his testicles inspected in the ambulance knows that, as soon as we look at his computer, we'll see everything he's been up to. He's trying to show how willing he is to cooperate. Not that it'll do him much good. We knew that there was a hitman offering his services in London. It was only a matter of time before we came across him. We may not have his client but at least we stopped the hit."

With that one word, it struck me how much danger I'd been in. My foot throbbed again as if to highlight the point. "Hit? Someone put out a hit on me? Why would anyone want me dead? Did I eat their yoghurt from the breakroom fridge? Did they object to the potato-based re-enactments of classic romances Ramesh and I put on YouTube? I have so many questions."

"You'll be required to make a statement. My first thought would be that it's connected to the murder of Mr Thomas. Maybe you've stumbled across something that the killer doesn't want you sharing. I'd watch my back if I were you." She nodded efficiently and turned to go.

"Is that seriously your advice?" My voice went higher than the police sirens. "Isn't watching my back supposed to be your job?"

For the first time since I met her, she showed the slightest hint of a smile. "I think that Mr Hughes here will lend us a hand in that department." She walked back to the ambulance where the would-be assassin was still getting treatment.

David grinned proudly. "That's right. I'll be on hand twenty-four hours a day to launch myself at any man who comes near you."

"Sounds nice." I gave him a kiss that was made rather awkward by the fact that I couldn't touch him above the waist without causing pain. "How did you know to come to my rescue in the first place?"

He helped me to my very hurty feet. "I was almost home when I realised I'd left my keys in the office. I was heading to my aunt's to get my spare set when I heard you shouting."

We stood looking into each other's eyes again. "My hero."

To be honest there was another ten minutes of gooiness after that but let's skip to the bit where I got in a taxi and went home to bed.

The next morning I had a visit from two police officers who had come to take my statement. It was Brabazon in charge this time and the soap opera fan in me wondered if he'd had a lover's tiff with D.I. Irons.

Sat outside in the garden, with my legs up on Mum's wheelbarrow, I told him about the pain in my foot but he wasn't particularly sympathetic. "We just need the essential details of what happened last night, please, Miss Palmer."

Once his uniformed minion had written up the statement and I'd signed it off, he had one more question.

"So who wants you dead then?" He said it in a very matter of fact way, as if there were bound to be loads of people who wanted to kill me.

I gave it a long hard think but was too tired to come up with any serious suggestions. They informed me that I was now the key witness to yet another major incident, that it would be a long, drawn-out process and I'd have to make an appearance if the case went to trial. It made me question how many crimes I could get caught up in before the police came to suspect me of having shady underworld connections.

By the time the officers left, The Hawes Lane Morbid Curiosity Club had reassembled in our front lounge. Mum had been busy recruiting and it was getting out of control. In addition to the existing sleuths, our newsagent Mrs Dominski was there with her whole family, all of Greg's yoga friends had been invited and there was even the bloke who collects trolleys in our supermarket squashed into one corner. There was barely a foot of carpet free for me to squat on.

"Come on, Izzy. Get in here!" My father was standing beside the flipcharts, which were now overflowing with annotations. He was mid-discussion with my ex-neighbour/current lodger about whether or not we could reduce the suspect list. "You're being ridiculous, Danny."

"Admit it, Ted. Alibis aren't worth the paper they're written on."

Mum wasn't the type to stay out of an argument. "I disagree. I really do. We know that Amara was at home with her kids and David was with his aunt. I've no doubt the police would have checked their alibis. So that means, of the people who had access to the server room, we're only left with Wendy and Jack. We've practically cracked it."

The youngest Dominski girl, a student of about nineteen, was there to back Mum up. "That's right, Mrs Palmer. And don't forget that David basically stopped Izzy from being murdered last night. There's no way he could be involved." I have to say that she made a very good point and was evidently a wise and considerate young person.

"You're assuming of course that the same person who killed Bob also paid for the hit on Izzy." Greg was propped up in one corner, looking a bit put out at all the people in his makeshift studio. "We mustn't jump to conclusions."

"What about the train ticket Izzy found and the dodgy Russian pharmaceuticals?" Mrs 32 asked the group. "What about the e-mail from Bob that talked about a list? Where does any of that fit in?"

"Red herrings, beyond any doubt. Personally, I'm convinced that David hired the assassin to cover his guilt." Danny hadn't been involved in the investigation long but was really invested in it. "By saving Izzy, it threw everyone off the scent. He's still the obvious killer."

"You wouldn't say that if you'd been there last night." As I spoke, the room fell to a hush. One of Greg's yoga bros even let out an impressed *Ooh!* "The guy who came after me was dangerous. David was lucky to take him down for as long as he did. If the big thug hadn't dropped the knife we'd probably both be dead."

"Thank goodness you aren't." Ramesh beamed across at me. I have no idea why he wasn't at work.

Dad was still manning the evidence pads. "Okay then, just for the moment, let's say we cross off Amara, David and obviously Ramesh." He flipped the *Suspects* page over to reveal one he'd made earlier with just Jack and Wendy on. "Wendy was in north London so we didn't see any way for her to get back to kill Bob at nine o'clock. What we hadn't considered was that there is a direct train from Finsbury Park to East Croydon. She could have stashed her stamps and everything in her car, jumped on the train, done the deed and gone back later that evening."

"Thameslink!" the bloke from the supermarket shouted with pride.

"Exactly, Brian. The Thameslink train only takes thirty-five minutes station to station."

Yeah, Dad's detective work sounded impressive and, yeah, I should probably have checked that out myself, but I knew something he didn't.

"Nice theory, except that I once heard Wendy say that only tramps and idiots took public transport." I hated to disappoint my dad when he was clearly so passionate about his new hobby. "She wouldn't be caught dead on a train."

Mum made a frustrated click of her fingers. "So that means Jack is the only suspect we have without the hint of an alibi."

138

"He told me he was walking his dog, which is hardly an airtight cover story." Ramesh was scoffing down yet another chocolate hobnob that my mum had passed him. Whenever young men come to the house, she turns into the witch from Hansel and Gretel.

"Especially as I know for a fact that he doesn't like dogs." I got another *ooh* for my latest revelation. "I tried to show him my favourite golden retriever puppy live stream on YouTube once and he got really huffy about how they're the lowest of all animals and that he'd rather watch earthworms."

Dad expectantly peered around the group, waiting for some sort of response. When no one had any objections, his face filled with hope. "Does that mean we've cracked this case wide open?"

There was a murmur from his audience as this idea settled in. It wasn't long before the room erupted once more in disagreement.

"No way." This was about the angriest I'd ever seen Danny get. "What was the significance of that tiny knife?"

"Where's his motive?" Mum's hairdresser Fernando demanded.

"Why would he pay to have Izzy killed?" Mr Dominski screamed. "They share an affinity for animal videos. He wouldn't do that to her."

As the argument raged, I decided that I'd had enough and not very subtly snuck from the room.

"Izzy, wait." Danny came bounding after me, his tail wagging eagerly. "I meant what I said in there. David could be the murderer. You should be careful."

"Thanks for your concern, Danny. But the police will have done their job and checked out his alibi. If there was any chance it was him, they'd have found out by now."

He suddenly seemed agitated and grabbed hold of my arm. "I just hate seeing you get taken in by terrible blokes time after time."

"Really, Danny I'm fine." I smiled at him because I didn't know what else to do. "You're starting to sound jealous."

He released me and threw his hands in the air dramatically. "Of course I'm jealous. How obvious do I have to make it? All these years I've been trying to show you how much I like you and you don't even care."

I was speechless. Those things that normally come out of my mouth to help me express my thoughts had disappeared.

139

"I can't deal with this." He turned towards the kitchen and tossed these last words – words! That's what they're called! – over his shoulder. "I need some time for me right now."

Chapter Nineteen

Left alone in the hall, I couldn't quite process what had happened. I was pretty sure that Danny had professed his longstanding love for me, but that sounded very unlikely. He was practically perfect and could take his pick of any woman on the planet. What would he want with me?

You little heartbreaker.

Oh come off it. He must have been drinking. He'll soon sober up and forget all about us.

Up in my childhood bedroom, the world didn't look so scary. There were no muscly henchmen coming to stab me, my popstar posters were as smiley as ever and I planned to spend the rest of the day in my comfy old armchair, reading an Ian Rankin to help me forget about my week – see, I am aware that modern crime writers exist.

Well, that was the plan, but after twenty minutes hanging out with Inspector Rebus, Ramesh popped his head in and looked around my super cool room.

"Wow, it's like you're the precocious daughter from a sitcom. Does James Blunt know you're his number one stalker?"

"Shut your mouth and get in here. I'm hiding from everyone."

He stepped into the room. "Things really kicked off downstairs. Your mum started shouting at anyone who disagreed that Wendy was the killer. I was scared she would punch your stepdad."

"My mother is a woman of conviction." I allowed myself a moment's thought. "To be honest, I think I'm giving up on the whole thing. I mean, it's been fun trying to work out who killed Bob, but I'd rather not end up murdered if I can help it."

He sat down on my unmade bed. "Don't say that, Izzy. We've come so far."

"Have we though? Sure, we know more stuff. But I don't feel like we're any closer to identifying the murderer and I haven't the first idea who would shell out to kill me."

"Don't be so pessimistic." He looked miserable all of a sudden.

"I'm realistic, not pessimistic. We're not police officers, we're not private detectives, we're just two idiots who got carried away with a game."

"You're wrong. We're good at this… Well, you are."

I wasn't in the mood to argue and let out a long, tired huff. "Come off it, Ramesh."

"I mean it. You see things that I don't. I bet that you'll work out how everything fits together before anyone else does. The letter opener, the champagne, the drugs and the hitman. There's a thread that links them all up and I know you can find it."

I put my book back on the shelf. "I think you're overestimating me."

"You're wrong, Izzy." He made the face that told me he was about to go off on a rant about something (it was normally related to Cher). "I don't know if you know this, but I'm good at my job. Ever since I was a kid, I understood how computers worked without really trying. When I'm dealing with the networks in the office, it's like they're all laid out in my head and I can walk my way through them. I'm not that great with people and I'm not some amazing thinker but I'm a good head of I.T."

He put his hand on the arm of my chair. "You and I are different. You chose a job that demands nothing of you because it means you don't have anything to prove. The truth is that you found what you were good at years ago but I reckon you thought everyone would laugh at you so you let the idea die. This is what you should be doing, Izzy. Figuring out puzzles, putting together clues, deciding who's good and who's bad."

"That's really nice of you, Ramesh, but–"

He ploughed on regardless. "I remember when we first met and you told me why you loved crime fiction. I saw how passionate you were and I'll never forget what you said. You told me it wasn't just because they were fun to read but because you were good at solving the mystery. You weren't boasting, in fact you sounded pretty surprised yourself, but you said that nine out of ten times you could work out who the killer was."

"In books, Ra. Books – not the real world."

Ignoring my bad mood, Ramesh suddenly brightened. "Tell you what. How about I go through some of my ideas on the case and you say what you think of them?"

142

"How about you go away and let me read?"

"Number one: What if Wendy and Amara were in the midst of a secret love affair and Wendy had Bob killed so Amara could be the only deputy director."

"Please stop!"

"Then Wendy paid for the hit because she was jealous that you and Amara had gone for a drink?" He watched me, desperately hoping I might agree with him.

"That's absolute drivel."

"Ha ha! But I've got you interested now." He jumped to his feet and began to gesture about as he continued with his presentation. "Number two: What if Bob was trying to blackmail Jack?"

"Go on." I have to admit, he'd hooked me back in.

"Perhaps Jack was stealing from the company and Bob found out."

"It's plausible, I suppose. Except for the lack of any evidence. And it's not as if we keep piles of money at Porter & Porter. What was Jack stealing? Printer paper?"

"Fine, but I think you're going to like this next one. Number three." He held both hands up to make a box in the hope I'd picture whatever nonsense he was about to spout. "Imagine that Bob had a dark past none of us knew about. Let's say he was a messenger for the mob or he forged fine jewellery. He took a job in finance to escape but, three decades later, his criminal associates caught up with him."

The more he said, the more I wanted to hear. "Okay. Keep going."

"Right, so they track him down and say, 'If you don't come back to work for us, we'll kill someone close to you.' Bob's torn. He loves his family but he can't fall back into the shadowy world he'd escaped from. So what does he do?"

"I don't know but I really want to find out."

Ramesh was one giant emoji by this point, bobbing about as his tale unfolded. "He plots to take down the boss of the crime syndicate, but before he can tell the police, the mob get him and silence him for good."

"Yes!"

"Then you got too close and they decided they had to kill you too."

I jumped to my feet. "YES!"

"Really? Do you think I'm on to something?" He was rocking on his heels like a kid who'd drunk all the lemonade.

"No! It's absolute trash, but you made me think of something."

Unable to hold it in anymore, he jumped into the air with excitement. "Brilliant! That's just what I wanted."

"Okay, calm down. Sit down. It's my turn." We swapped places so that I could ponce about in front of my wardrobe and he could sit in the chair. "The only thing you got right was that you left the suspects to one side for a moment and focussed on Bob. I've been trying to do that but it's difficult. So, tell me this, what is the most important thing we know about Robert Harold Thomas?"

"He was the worst human being that we've ever met?"

"No. We keep getting hung up on that but I don't think it's very helpful. The most important thing about Bob was that he knew he was going to die. Not because of the murder, but the lung cancer. He'd known how bad it was since late last year. He didn't want to suffer through treatment – no doubt hating the thought of anyone pitying him – so he went on as if nothing had changed.

"But something had changed, something very important. He had no interest in his job anymore and said exactly what he thought of people so that – even by his standards – he became intolerable in the office. He was morose, self-indulgent, offensive and massively hedonistic. He didn't care about his health, kept a crate of champagne beneath his desk and do you remember the huge food deliveries he used to order in?"

"Urgh, it was disgusting. I saw him order the whole menu from Le Sheek once and scoff it all down in half an hour."

"There's something else as well. Remember those Russian pills Bob had in his coat? I managed to translate the name and find them online. They're an experimental cancer treatment, not licensed over here yet. I'm guessing Bob was self-medicating in the hope he might find a cure. Perhaps he started out buying illegal medicine and then thought, *well I might as well get some fun stuff while I'm shopping.*"

"The cocaine you mean?"

"Exactly. And tell me this; where does a middle-aged man who'd done nothing exciting or exceptional with his life go to buy illegal drugs?"

Ramesh thought for a second. "I dunno, some bloke in a pub?"

"I doubt some bloke in a pub would offer specialist cancer

144

medication along with the coke. Bob was on his own private quest of depravity. He'd upped his bullying game, he'd been sleeping around and he'd even tried his hand at theft. If he was going to get high, he'd want something secure and reliable. I reckon he bought them online."

My friend face palmed himself to show that he should have thought of it first. "Of course. That's exactly what he'd do. He was super lazy, he probably had them delivered straight up to the office."

"He had packages coming all the time this year. There's an email Wendy sent him where she complains about how much money he was spending, so she must have noticed them too. But no one's going to imagine that brown-suit/brown-tie, middle-management Bob is having coke delivered. Computer gadgets, sure. Office stationery, perhaps, but who'd have guessed they were class A drugs?"

"That sneaky old man."

I paused to consider where to go next. "Ra, how do we get onto the dark web?"

He looked at me like I'd just confessed to murdering Bob myself. "Izzy, in case the name isn't clear, that is not something you want to get involved with. Unless you're in the market for weapons, narcotics or illegal pornography, I'd recommend staying away. It's risky even taking a look."

I came to kneel next to him so that our eyes were at the same level. "We're not going to do anything illegal. All I want is to see how you do it. D.I. Irons said that the bloke who tried to kill me was advertising on the dark web and this is the only connection I can think of between Bob's death and the hit."

He thought about it for a few moments, his teeth chewing at the inside of his mouth and his eyes flicking nervously. "Fine, but not here. I'll show you at work on Monday."

It was right then that my mum burst into the room in a panic.

"Darling, what were you thinking?" I had no idea what she was talking about.

"I have no idea what you're talking about." See.

"Danny, darling! I'm talking about Danny. He's out in the garden in a right state, he can barely light his campfire for lunch."

"I didn't do anything to him." I tried to sound innocent but I knew Mum wouldn't believe me.

"Huh! 'I didn't do anything,' she says. Didn't break his heart no doubt. The poor little lamb is in tears. You know how he gets around you, darling. Couldn't you have let him down a little more gently?"

I didn't know what to say. Until about an hour before, I'd thought that handsome, charming, medically competent Danny Fields was in a different galaxy from sarcastic antelope Izzy Palmer. It turned out I was the harlot who'd been stringing him along for years.

"But I had no idea he liked me."

Mum looked at me like I'd just put a lampshade on my head and suck three fingers in a socket. "How could you not? He's been hanging on your every word since you were five years old. Why do you think he still comes to stay? It's not to visit your fathers, I can tell you that."

Hearing it out loud, it was pretty hard for me to get my head around.

"Izzy, you little minx." Until this point, Ramesh had been still and quiet, like he thought we might forget he was there – which I suppose I had. "Now you've got two sexy, scrumptious, yummy-yummy men to choose from."

"Really, Ramesh, and yet you wonder why people think you're gay?"

Mum hadn't finished telling me off. "Darling, you must be more careful with your feminine wiles. There's only so much that men can take." And with that, she was gone. Off to comfort the son she never had.

I ran after her and flung the door open. "If I ever had any feminine wiles, mother, I'm pretty sure I'd used them all up by high school."

I was beginning to wonder if I was on drugs myself because nothing I'd just heard made the slightest bit of sense.

Ramesh looked impressed and made a cat noise in my direction. "Miaow! You tiger."

Chapter Twenty

Though I'd promised to continue our amateur investigation, I couldn't think about any new leads because, wherever I went in the house, I could hear the sound of sobbing. Lunch was excruciating; Danny stayed out in the garden, Mum would no longer speak and even Greg looked at me like I was a heartless wench.

There was nothing else for it. I couldn't spend the whole weekend at home, so I rang David to beg him to save me from my family.

"I know we didn't plan to hang out. I don't want to be pushy or demanding or anything and I respect that, sometimes, you might want time to yourself to do what–"

"Izzy?" His voice was calm, confident, reassuring. "Just tell me what it is you want."

I took a deep breath. "I was wondering if we could hang out tomorrow."

I could hear him smile down the line. "That would be great."

"Really?"

"Yeah, really. I would have asked you before but I thought you might need some time to yourself after Thursday."

My heart skipped a little in my chest. "No, David. Thursday couldn't have been sweeter. It was genuinely one of the best dates I've ever been on."

"Someone tried to kill you."

Oops!

"Oh, yeah. Not that bit. That bit was horrible. But the part before – the part when it was just the two of us – that was perfect."

We fell silent for a moment and the muscles in my stomach got all tense from missing him.

"I'm afraid it won't be just the two of us tomorrow. We'll be taking my aunt for lunch and my niece will be there too. But you already know Chloe so you'll fit in fine."

I made a sound like I'd swallowed my tongue.

"Don't worry though. I've told her about us and she can't quite remember but she thinks she really liked you when she was at the office that time."

"Uhuh."

"We're going up to London as a special treat for Auntie Val's birthday."

"Uhuh."

"Shall we say twelve thirty at East Croydon?"

I didn't answer immediately. I couldn't think what to say, so I eventually went with, "Uhuh."

"Great. I'll see you then…"

He stayed on the line for a moment, presumably expecting a bit of lovey-dovey back and forth. Sadly I'd forgotten how to speak again so he hung up without me saying anything.

Izzy, you moron!

How had I ended up getting myself invited to a family outing on our third ever date? I'd been with my previous boyfriend for two years and never met so much as a second cousin from his family.

In general, I like to keep as far away from my partners' families as is geographically possible. The ideal scenario, was when I had a long distance boyfriend who lived in Leeds. We used to meet up at weekends in exotic places like Kettering and Wolverhampton. It only lasted a couple of months, but that time was spent safe in the knowledge that I'd never bump into his mum in the supermarket.

Ramesh was really good with other people's parents. He wooed his girlfriend Patricia's folks before she was even particularly interested in him. I was the opposite. I'd get all nervous when I knew I had to make a good impression. On the one occasion I'd agreed to go to an ex's house, I ended up accidentally flirting with his mother and trying to convince his dad I knew everything about football. It was a proper car-crash, so-painful-you-can't-look-away, don't-know-whether-to-laugh-or-vomit moment.

I didn't want to make David's aunt think that I was only using her nephew for his body, or challenge Chloe to an arm-wrestling match, but that was exactly the kind of stupid thing I'd do as soon as I met them.

At half past twelve the next day I was standing in East Croydon Station, dressed in my most conservative summer dress (it looked like a tablecloth from the seventies, which I guess made me look like a table from the seventies.)

"Auntie Valerie, I'd like you to meet my friend Isobel."

David's aunt looked a lot older than she had in his family photo. She was small and grey, but had the smile of a cheeky teenager.

"Ooh, *fancy*. Isobel," I said, inappropriately loudly as if I thought she was hard of hearing. "No one's called me Isobel since my German teacher Frau Schmidt caught me and Gary Flint behind the north block with his hand down my top."

David looked at me like I'd just tried to bite her. I didn't blame him.

For some reason, Auntie Val started laughing. "You told me she was funny, Dai. That's brilliant." She took my arm, as is the right of anyone over the age of sixty-five. "You know, darling. I've always been a bit of an eccentric myself. Life's too short to be bored or boring, that's what I say."

We went through the ticket barriers and she chatted with me the whole way to the platform. She borrowed my wrist after that to see how long there was before the train arrived and then snuck off to buy herself a treat.

"I've never put much stock in clocks and watches, my lovely," she called down the platform to me. "But I do love a nice bar of chocolate."

"I knew she'd like you," David told me while she was busy charming the shopkeeper. "And it was nice of you to speak so clearly. How did you know that she was hard of hearing?"

Once on board, Val gave me a full run down of Hughes-Lewis family history. She took me on a trip to the mining valleys of the Rhondda, along the coast to the golden beaches of Swansea and way up north to Snowdonia.

"Of course, I came down to London myself when I was still just a girl. I was a teacher you see and there wasn't much work back home in the valleys so a lot of my friends moved away."

"Oooooh, that must have been an adventure." I was still talk-shouting in a slightly camp manner. I'd failed to get it under control and a few people further along the carriage had craned their heads to see what was wrong with me.

If only we knew.

"I lived with Val when I first came to Croydon." David looked lovingly at his aunt. "It was the most fun I've ever had."

"You would say that. You're a charmer." Val beamed at her nephew before continuing with her story. "Then Chloe came to live with me a few years ago. She's moved up to the city now, but she still comes to see me most weeks. I'm lucky to have such a close family."

"Ahhh, that's nice. I'm pretty sure my mother's a nudist."

I continued to spout awful bilge like this all the way to Victoria Station and Val continued to find me amusing. We were meeting Chloe at a restaurant boat, moored opposite the London Eye. The sun had come out for Val's birthday and London looked beautiful as we walked along the river bank.

"Happy Birthday, Auntie Valerie!" Chloe shouted as soon as she spotted us, before running to embrace her great-aunt with all the bubbly charm I remembered her having. "I've got a little surprise for you inside."

She gave me a quick hug but was clearly desperate to get the birthday girl onto the boat.

"You're going to love this place." David led me down the gangway into the restaurant. "Beautiful views."

"I can't believe it," Val said when the waiter showed us over to a large table that appeared to already be occupied. "I can't believe you all came."

"I can't believe it either," I tried to sound excited as I looked around the faces of David's entire family. "There's lovely to see you all."

David shot me an apologetic look. "Chloe, you should have told me they were coming. Poor Izzy's been ambushed."

Chloe replied with a *not-sorry* smile and David's parents stood up to interrogate me.

"He's told us literally nothing about you," his mother explained. "But sit near us and we can get to know you."

"Leave off, Mam. You'll scare her."

"Izzy, is it?" His father had a deep, booming voice which made him sound like he was practicing for a male voice choir. He held his hand out and then – with the wine already flowing – said, "What am I doing? Get over here!" and gave me a rather large hug which his wife joined in on.

"Izzy, please don't feel like you have to talk to these people. I've yet to see any evidence we're related." I noticed David's Welsh accent coming out more strongly than normal. For some reason, so was mine.

"Don't be silly, Dai. It's lovely to meet your folks, like. Shall I sit

150

down by 'er'?" Sadly I've never been great at accents and ended up sounding more South Asian than Southwalian.

"That's right, love. Just by there." David's father already sounded a little concerned.

I ended up with Chloe and David on either side of me and his parents sitting opposite. Auntie Val went to chat to the rest of her large, extended family. There was still one seat free but, not to worry, that was soon filled by David's ex-wife Luned who turned up a few minutes later. I felt like closing my mouth and never opening it again. Alas, I was in an inexplicably chatty mood.

"So there I was, some bloody great gorilla trying to kill me, like, and I run towards the knife instead of away from it. I'm bloody mad me." I was regaling my future in-laws (too soon?) with the story of our brush with death. Just in case they thought I was a normal, sane person, I'd dropped my voice a couple of octaves to match David's dad's.

"That's a very distinctive accent you've got there, Izzy," he soon commented. "Let me guess… Carmarthen?"

"No, Croydon."

Somehow… SOMEHOW! I made it through lunch without anyone accusing me of being a racist, though Auntie Val had a good laugh whenever I spoke. I didn't feel so bad about not bringing a present considering all the joy I was giving her.

Despite the general hugginess of the Hughes clan, I came to think that I'd finally found my people. They were so open and friendly and I wondered if the land of Wales was full of weirdos like me.

When dessert arrived, and I'd calmed down a bit, I had the chance to chat to David's niece. Next to Chloe, I felt like a Christmas tree that someone had tried to take back to the shop the following June. Talking to her was like looking into a mirror that only shows you beautiful things.

"I'm sorry for not warning David that everyone would be here." She didn't sound it. "But I wanted to surprise him. He's had a tough couple of weeks."

"That's okay. He told me how low he's been."

"God knows why he'd waste a tear on that monster, Bob." A strain of anger suddenly cut through her voice. "I'm glad that disgusting man is dead."

I, the woman who had recently led the table in a particularly raucous version of 'Delilah', was taken aback. "Woah. Where did that come from?"

"You know what happened? To my friend Pippa I mean."

I retained my blank expression.

"No, course not. They hushed it up." She slammed her beer bottle down on the table, causing foam to splurge up out of it like a mini volcano. "Bob practically raped her. And I don't mean he held her hand inappropriately, I mean he forced her up against his desk and ripped her underwear off. If Amara hadn't walked in, he'd have managed it too."

"I had no idea." I took a slug of Rioja to process what she was telling me. "No wonder you hated him. There were rumours he'd upset one of the interns, but I didn't imagine anything like that."

"That's how people like him get away with it, right?" She spat the question from her mouth. "No one can imagine how depraved they are. To be fair, David did all he could to get rid of Bob, but Mr Porter was having none of it. They even paid Pippa off to keep her quiet. I tried to get her to go to the police but she was terrified. I don't think she's recovered, even now."

Chloe's hate fed my own and a thousand abusive memories sparked in my brain. Not just of Bob, but of every filthy bloke who touched girls up on the tube, or stood weirdly close to me in lifts. I couldn't imagine the fiery girl in front of me putting up with any of it and it soothed away that fizz of anger.

"Sorry to spoil the mood." She didn't sound sorry and she was right not to. "It still makes me furious to think about it."

I wanted to tell her that it wasn't okay and her friend should never have had to put up with our odious boss, but I hesitated and the conversation moved on.

"Here, Izzy," Auntie Val shouted from the other end of the table. "I don't suppose you know the words to 'It's Not Unusual?'"

Chapter Twenty-One

Auntie Val had reached the prodigious age of eighty-one and was fierce and funny throughout the party. At six o'clock, David whispered that it might be getting too much for her and suggested we head home.

She was just as sparky on the train journey as she had been in the morning but, as she grew more tired, she repeated stories I'd already heard and began mixing up people's names. To be fair, I get like that if I haven't had a proper night's sleep myself and her good humour and bright burning intelligence never dulled.

"It's been such a perfect day." She told me when we got back to Croydon, still grinning from cheek to cheek. "And you're a little marvel, Izzy. I'll make sure this lummocking nephew of mine doesn't let you slip through his fingers."

We dropped her off at home, round the corner from David's, and made sure she was well installed before leaving.

"Next time you come, we'll have to do some karaoke," she told me with a mischievous sparkle in her eyes.

David had looked embarrassed throughout the day as everyone told me stories of his childhood but he clearly adored his family.

"They're lovely." We were walking back to mine, with the very clear instructions that he would not be meeting my Mum. "I honestly thought they were brilliant."

"Well, that was apparent. I had no idea you were such an entertainer."

"I am so sorry." He took my hand and swung it between us again. "I should have warned you how I can be around boyfriends' families. If you want to break up with me and fire me and never talk to me again, I completely understand."

"And miss out on more Tom Jones singalongs? They're a rare event in London, I'd be a fool to get rid of you."

All right. Gooey gooey gooey. Kiss kiss kiss. We did the flirty talking most of the way home and, when we got to West Wickham High Street, I knew I had to change the topic.

"Chloe told me what happened to her friend Pippa."

Perhaps it wasn't the conversation to be having next to a Chick 'o'

Mansion but I needed to tell him. His face turned serious and at first I thought he wouldn't reply.

"I'll never forgive myself for what happened."

We stopped on the corner by the launderette. "You're not the one to blame. Chloe told me you did everything you could."

"Hardly." He looked back down the road from where we'd come. "I should have quit my job or convinced Pippa to go to the police. The fact that Bob could get away with something so evil will haunt me forever. And that's nothing compared to what Pippa went through."

An old man with a trolley bag gave us a guilty stare for getting in his way, so we walked on.

"You weren't responsible, David. You couldn't have known that Bob would do something so despicable."

Even though two years had passed, I could see it still upset him. "I was his boss. It was my job to keep an eye on him and protect my other employees. I'd always known he could be inappropriate with female staff, I shouldn't have let the interns anywhere near him."

I didn't know what to say to that because I basically agreed with him.

We turned into my road and he took my hand once more. "But I want you to know that it wasn't me who covered it up. I didn't stop anyone from talking about what Bob had done. It was Mr Porter who offered Pippa the money; he summoned her to his house down in Surrey. And she made Amara and I promise that we wouldn't say anything to anyone. She didn't want her dad finding out."

"Her dad?"

"Yeah, Pippa is Jack's daughter." He had a melancholy look on his face as he spoke. "Well, estranged daughter. I think he hoped that getting the internship for her at P&P would bring them closer together. It's sad, really."

A spark, a click and then threads started weaving together in my mind. "And you're sure that he never found out about the assault?" We'd stopped in front of my garden gate.

"Not as far as I know." His usual cheerful expression still hadn't returned. "Why?"

I didn't answer, I had too many questions of my own. "David, why do you think Bob was killed?"

"It's obvious, isn't it?" He looked at me as if this was true. "He pushed someone too far. You know what he was like. He took pleasure in other people's suffering. I thought that after he got sick he might find some humility, but if anything, he was worse. It was as if he wanted everyone to know just how despicable he could be. I'd go into my office sometimes and find notes confessing to all sorts of small barbarities."

I glanced into the front room, worried that The Hawes Lane Murder Appreciation Group could be watching us. Luckily there was only Greg there, his canvases restored to their rightful place. "Bob wrote notes specifically for you to find?"

"He knew that Porter wouldn't fire him, and that he could do what he liked, so he taunted me with his indiscretions. He was even worse to Amara. She found that stupid knife of his stabbed into her desk one day and a little message saying 'I stole your stapler. You won't be getting it back.' I got the impression he liked having her as an adversary best of all."

I kind of wished Bob was still alive right then so that I could give him a smack. "He was pathetic. If only I'd told him just that."

"He wouldn't have taken any notice. Bob thought he was the king of the office. He thought he had all the power."

"What I don't understand is why Mr Porter kept him around in the first place."

David sat down on the garden wall. "Aldrich Porter has been good to me. He gave me an opportunity to run the company, when I was still young to be a director. He put his faith in me and I'm pretty sure he did the same for Bob twenty years ago. But Porter doesn't like admitting his mistakes. Punishing Bob, would have meant conceding that he'd trusted the wrong person."

"That or he didn't want the last dinosaur in the office to be done away with."

David's face brightened a little. "Well, that is another possibility."

"David, darling?" A voice called from the doorstep. "Why don't you come in for a cup of tea?"

I pulled him up to standing before my mother could grab him. "Run, David. Run while you can."

He didn't seem worried. "Hello, Mrs Palmer. I'm afraid I'm meeting friends for a drink this evening but I look forward to it another time."

I gave him a quick peck and pushed him on his way.

Kiss number nine; the most perfunctory so far.

Shhhhh! We said we'd stopped counting.

With my mother suitably told off for scaring my boyfriend away, I entered the house, grabbed the flipcharts from the hall and headed to my bedroom.

I had to hand it to Mum and Dads, they'd done a good job of processing the evidence. There were pages laid out for all the suspects, with an explanation of how the evidence related to each of them. I turned to Jack's page.

JACK CAMPBELL

Alibi:
~~Walking dog.~~ Unlikely.

Motive:
Hated Bob.
Had been humiliated at office Christmas party.
Bob had dirt on him.

Evidence:
Jack knew about Bob's coke habit.
Had access to P&P offices out of hours.
Had full knowledge of security systems.
Had access to server room to remove hard drives.
Was reluctant to detain Izzy on the morning she discovered Bob's corpse.

Questions:
What dirt did Bob have on him?
Where did Bob's drugs come from?

Theory:
Jack killed Bob to settle their feud.

Of the six suspects they'd written up these crib sheets for, Jack's was the least substantial. If he'd found out what had happened to his daughter though, it would change everything. Maybe Bob had dangled the crime before him as he had with Amara and her stapler.

156

Jack Campbell. Just the sound of his name called up images of brown cardigans and walking holidays in Norfolk. Could there be something more sinister lurking behind his drab, Middle-Englander façade?

Chapter Twenty-Two

From feeling like I wanted to give up my amateur investigation, that weekend's revelations had reenergised me. There were theories to test out and a host of new avenues to explore. Even though our suspects had no idea I was watching them, I could feel how close I was finally getting.

But first, Sunday at home with the folks.

At least Danny had decided to spare me his tears by going to visit his real family, in their caravan in Hastings, not that it made Mum any less furious at me. Even Greg's sensationally delicious roast dinner couldn't make up for how slowly that day dragged by.

When Monday finally came I couldn't wait to get into the office and down to work – well, you know what I mean. As soon as I entered the Porter & Porter premises, I noticed that the police tape had been removed from Bob's room and his door was open. I took a peek inside on the way to see Ramesh, only to find a strangely fragmented version of the space I remembered.

The blood was gone but so were many other traces of Bob. A family photo had been removed from his desk, a painting was missing from the wall and all the clutter that normally marked the place as his had been boxed up. It was strange to be in there again for the first time since the murder. I could still picture his horribly vacant stare as he lay slumped there.

"Coming to see my new digs?" Will had turned up without me hearing. He pushed past me into the office, with a pile of folders in his arms.

"Really funny. Who even said you could come in here?"

"I had an e-mail from Mr Porter this morning telling me the good news." He stuck out that hound-like jaw of his and showed his teeth. "New office, a promotion. They'll probably get me a company car too. It'll save me taking the train with the plebs."

Talking to Will was never exactly a pleasure, but this was becoming a chore.

"Congratulations. There are few people who deserve to get to where Bob ended up as much as you do."

He offered his best wolf's grin and dumped the files on the table. I thought that our sparring was over so turned to go.

"Wait, Izzy. I want you to know that I'm going to be a fair boss to you. You and I may have a different sense of humour, and David warned me that the memorial service could have upset some people, but I'm not Bob."

I couldn't be sure what was happening. He'd lost the spiteful tone that he normally used and sounded oddly professional. It was as if I was a client he was schmoozing. It was confusing and I didn't know how to react.

"Actually, you're not my boss. Suzie is my boss, then Tim, then David. You don't have to bother yourself with little old me."

"True. That's absolutely true, but Bob liked to keep an eye on lower ranked members of staff and I think it would be a tribute to all the good work he's done for me to continue with that."

He pulled his teeth in self-consciously. "And so, as your superior, I'd like you to spend the morning writing a report on the status of your current projects and what sort of workload you are expecting over the next few months. Make sure it's really thorough, referencing the office calendar and anything that Tim and Suzie might be able to give you a heads up on. "

I'd almost believed that he was offering an olive branch. It was the same old Will Gibbons though. Well on his way to becoming the sadist he'd replaced.

"Sure, boss. I'll get right to it."

I sat at my desk, but not before checking that my chair was free of upturned drawing pins. As if having Will as my supervisor wasn't bad enough, the completely pointless task he'd given me would take up all my time and meant that I couldn't continue the investigation with Ramesh until our lunchbreak. I hated it when people made me do my job!

"All right," my techy friend said when we were huddled together in the server room a few hours later. "I've set up an old computer here with the Tor Browser, just about the best VPN around and a bunch of other safety protocols. Even if someone had hacked this very computer and was remotely spying on us, they'd have a hard time knowing what we were doing."

"Ra, I've told you not to use that kind of language around me. I have no idea what you're talking about and it makes me feel stupid."

He looked both put out and sarcastic at the same time. "I'm so sorry! What I'm trying to tell you is that I've made this computer secure so we can poke around in nasty places we wouldn't normally go anywhere near."

I put my hands under my chin and made a face like an angel. "Thank you!"

"Okay, this is the browser we have to use to access the dark web."

"Yeah, yeah. The dark web. I know all about it. I read the Wikipedia entry at home yesterday."

He hummed appreciatively. "Great. So then you'll remember that you can only access these sites if you know where they're hidden. Regular search engines can't find them. In reality it's not all that difficult to track down what you're looking for, but it's not as if they put ads on Facebook saying, click here for drugs and guns."

I nodded to suggest I really had remembered all that. In front of us was a blank browser window, waiting patiently for our submergence into the illicit tunnels of the internet.

"So is everything on the dark web illegal?"

"In theory, no. Some people use it for privacy or to get around censorship but I think they're in the minority. I can honestly say I have never had any need to install this software before and I will be getting rid of it as soon as we're done." He clicked on the address bar and typed in a link. "Okay, now I'm going to show you how easy it is to buy stuff."

A page called CrystalCage popped up on the screen. It looked just like any high street shop's website but, instead of selling clothes and homeware, there were listings for *psychedelics, stimulants* and *opioids.*

"All you have to do is choose your poison – in this case pretty much literally – then decide how much you want and they'll send it to any address you give them."

Picking through the Italian salad Mum had made me, I tossed a carrot baton into my mouth. "What about local deliveries? Can you get it brought round so that you don't have to wait?"

"I thought about that and had a look on some forums, but I couldn't find anything. I came across an exclusively British site…" He stopped speaking to type r78rtdjs92core58fg.onion into the browser and a few seconds later, a website called High Albion popped up. "On here, everything is coming to you from within the UK. The whole point of using the dark web, instead of selling in the street, is that it's anonymous. It's safer for the dealer and safer for the buyer. I imagine there's a way to have courier deliveries, but it would be more expensive and far riskier."

Ramesh sounded completely different when he was focussed on his job. His flamboyance and eccentricities were smoothed out by the technicality of the world he worked in.

It was a little bit scary looking at this stuff. The closest I'd come to illegal drugs was smoking a joint with Danny when we were sixteen. It turned out he'd been sold dried basil in place of marijuana and, anyway, I didn't inhale.

I figured we could go a bit further without getting into any trouble. "Click on the cocaine link. Show me how Bob would have done it."

"Okay, but we're not ordering anything." Ramesh's voice spiked louder. "Cocaine. Choose a variety. One gram. Enter address. Pay with bitcoin. Payment details. That's all it takes."

Still getting my head around the alarming simplicity of everything we'd done, a little bell finally went off in my brain. "Wait, press the browser's home button a second."

Ramesh did as instructed and a welcome message with a picture of an onion popped up on the screen as I'd been expecting.

"I've seen that before." I pointed at the icon.

"Instead of .com or .co.uk, the pages on the dark web all finish with the suffix .onion. I guess you have to peel the layers away to get to them."

"No, I mean, I've seen that specific page before. It was open on Bob's computer when I found him dead."

"Hardly surprising." Ramesh wasn't impressed. "We already figured that Bob was getting his stuff online. It doesn't help us work out who killed him."

"Let me finish." I imagine I sounded pretty smug saying that. "I saw it on Bob's screen but I also noticed that one of Jack's most used apps was a browser I'd never heard of before. A browser with a little onion logo."

Chapter Twenty-Three

Jack Campbell: Divorced. Mid to late fifties. Security guard at Porter & Porter for longer than I'd been on the planet and potential murderer.

The fact that two men in the office had installed the same piece of software for anonymously accessing unlawful services didn't mean that one of them was a killer but it certainly added some colour to our dull little company. If the gossip that Bob had unearthed was that Jack had been buying drugs, like him, I don't see why it would have led to a fight. If anything, they could have recommended each other websites and exchanged druggy anecdotes. No, it had to be something more.

The dark web isn't just for buying drugs. Jack could have been after weapons or credit card numbers or paying to have his ex-wife hacked. And there's nastier stuff on there too. Stuff that I didn't want to read or hear or even think about.

Back at my desk after lunch, I decided to text Ramesh my idea.

So, here's my new theory: Jack did something disgusting online that even Bob was appalled by. Bob tried to blackmail him over it, Jack gave in after their fight and for a while everything was okay. Eventually, Bob got greedy so Jack did away with him. Then, when we started looking into Bob's murder, Jack realised and put the hit out on me.

Hang on a second, Izzy. When you say 'Jack did something disgusting online,' do you mean that he was watching an altogether different kind of animal video?

Yuck, Ramesh. Don't be gross.

But actually, yeah. Something like that.

*I'm going to keep an eye on him and
see what he gets up to.*

Maybe there's another explanation.

**Nah. I'm pretty sure you just
cracked this case wide open.**

Thanks. Busy now. Bye.

Though I hadn't finished the completely bogus work that Will had cooked up for me, I spent most of that afternoon watching our new prime suspect.

Ooh, I like that phrase. It makes us sound like Helen Mirren.

Yeah, it does. Only sexier.

Than Helen Mirren? We wish.

When he wasn't on one of his trice-hourly toilet breaks, Jack spent eighty per cent of his time on his computer but only about a quarter of that laughing. This told me that the animal videos he watched were either a cover for something shady, or he'd become desensitised to the cuteness of a baby elephant on a trampoline or kittens falling off sofas. The very idea of which was laughable.

Jack's main responsibilities appeared to be signing packages in and out. There was always a receptionist on duty for that sort of thing but, as Jack's cubbyhole was the first thing anyone saw when they entered the office, such tasks had fallen to him over the years.

A cunning idea exploded into my brain like a firework and I decided to put it to the test. I grabbed my coat and headed towards the exit. As I walked past Jack, I could hear the unmistakeable sound of the Dramatic Chipmunk video clattering out of his tiny, tinny speakers. Instead of getting into the lift as he'd have been expecting, I hid out of sight around the corner and listened to what he was up to. For the next five minutes, no one entered or left the office and there wasn't a peep from Jack's computer. I could hear him busily clicking and typing away, but his speakers were silent.

"I hear you bought a dog." This was my opening gambit when I returned to the office. It was carefully designed to let Jack know that I was on to him without giving too much away about the investigation.

"That's right. His name's Baron." He pulled his phone out and

163

opened the photo app. I was in no way expecting what came next. "There's Baron when I first got him. Baron with me in the park. Baron on his own in the park. Baron by the sea. Baron and me by the sea…"

"I thought you hated dogs?" I probably let my surprise come out a tad too clearly in my voice.

"I used to. I once foolishly considered them the lowest of all animals, but that was before I met Baron. He's lovely, isn't he?"

I looked at the photo he was holding up. Baron was the biggest, meanest Rottweiler I'd ever seen. I was scared he would bite me through the phone. "Lovely! Have you had him long?"

Jack continued swiping through the pictures. "Only a couple of months, but he's changed my life." He paused on a photo of Baron with another dog in his mouth. "Such a joker he is. To be honest, I was a bit lonely until he came along. And now I don't have to worry about punk kids in the street giving me trouble."

"I bet you don't."

A beatific smile crossed his face. "My grandkids love him."

"I bet *he* loves them." I watched him scroll through the pictures and wondered once more whether he was putting on act. "I also heard that Pippa the intern is your daughter."

Somehow, his smile grew even wider. "That's right. She didn't want me to make a big thing out of it when she was working here, but I helped her get the placement."

"Ah, that's nice. How's she doing these days?"

He put the phone down and sat up in his chair, all proud. "Really well, thanks. The experience she gained here was invaluable. She's working in the city now at one of the big four." I watched for some sign that he knew what Bob had done to his daughter but there wasn't the slightest flicker.

"Make sure you send her my best wishes."

"Will do."

I left Jack to get back to whatever he did when he wasn't pretending to watch animal videos. If his alibi checked out, what did that mean for my whole Jack-as-killer theory?

So much for Helen Mirren.

Oh shut up, brain. No one can hear you and no one would want to listen if they could.

Perhaps Jack was paranoid about online security and that's why he'd downloaded the dark web browser. It would fit with him buying the world's biggest Rottweiler and the fact he's a *security* guard. Maybe the only dirt that Bob had on him was that he'd gone home with Suzie one night or made fun of Wendy's large selection of skirts. My grand theory suddenly felt a bit small.

I decided to switch off again and think about something other than Jack and his kindly beard. I returned to the work I was supposed to do for Will and tried to make my report sound both professional and insincere. Half an hour in and my mind had already been wandering for about twenty-nine minutes.

It didn't make sense. Jack was up to something on his computer, I just knew it. There was no way that he could be so innocent. *Butter wouldn't melt,* that's what Bob said and he was right. Jack's old duffer personality was a costume he put on each morning, along with his black jumper with the epaulettes and his mobile phone holster. No one else was going to work out what he was up to, so it was down to me (and possibly Ramesh).

***Fancy doing some real detective work
this evening?***

**You betcha!
Actually, can we go for Tapas too? I
have a hankering for patatas bravas.**

Unless there was a special meeting, or some kind of event, Jack normally locked up the office when the cleaners finished at seven every evening. We waited for him down in the street and he appeared ten minutes later, coming out of the underground car park on his particularly old-fashioned shopping bike.

"Wow, he's good," I said to Ramesh who was hiding his face behind an extra-large coffee cup. "He's got bicycle clips on his trousers and everything. No one would ever suspect a man wearing bicycle clips."

No one except us.

"Let's go, Iz." It was probably down to the vat of caffeine he'd imbibed but Ramesh was pumped. "Let's do this."

Following Jack wasn't particularly difficult. He literally pootled

165

along and at one point we had to slow down so that we didn't get ahead of him. He turned right towards Wellesley Road and the faded glamour of the Whitgift Shopping Centre with its vaguely nautical funnels. Buses and cars beeped and roared past as he, slow and steady, lost the race.

Jack lived in West Croydon – the wrong side of the wrong tracks – and we were soon transported to Broad Green Village, one of the epicentres of the 2011 riots. It had been years since I'd been there. When I was a kid it was... well, not that pretty either but there was a really good shoe shop that Mum used to take me to and then we'd have an ice cream on the high street or go to the Safari cinema for a matinee.

As we padded along behind Jack, pay-day loan sharks shouted at us from their shopfronts and the smell of kebabs and Halal meat filled our hungry nostrils. Eventually, we turned off the high street into a road of identical, two-story houses that looked like they would have once been very pretty. Jack turned in to number seventeen and chained his bike up outside without noticing us.

"Great." Ramesh had apparently deflated. "So now we have to hang around here for hours on the off chance he comes back out. If I miss 'Britain's Got Talent' because of this, I'm telling you now, I'll freak out."

"Seriously, Ramesh, you can see it online about thirty seconds after. Just relax."

"You know it's not the same, Izzy. BGT's only good when you watch it live."

I stared at him, unsure if he was serious, or even sane. Before I could find out, Jack had reappeared. He was dressed all in black, had a large rucksack on his back and was being tugged along by a monster on a chain. He and Baron were heading right for us.

We bolted round the corner and stood in the doorway of an abandoned shop. I could see Jack through the window, walking along the other side of the road. When he crossed over, I knew we'd have to take drastic action.

"Quick, pretend we're making out."

Ramesh looked shocked. "I have a girlfriend!"

"I said, *pretend*." I grabbed hold of him, buried my head in his shoulder and pulled him towards me.

"Ooooohhhhh…" he moaned seductively.

Once Jack had continued on past us, I pushed Ramesh away. "What was that noise?"

"What?"

"The moaning?"

"I was trying to make it authentic. More importantly, why didn't you tell me that Jack has a pet demon-hound? You know that dogs are racist, Izzy. If he sets that thing on us, I won't stand a chance."

"Shut up and move. He's getting away."

We crossed the high street but kept our distance. I wanted to make sure that Jack wouldn't spot us as Baron pulled him along another residential road. The dog was even more terrifying in the flesh, it was as if someone had taken a bull and shrunken it down to fit in a maisonette.

"If Jack turns round, he'll spot you immediately." My friend was fond of stating the obvious. "Where did you get the idea to be a detective, anyway? You stick out like a peacock at the north pole."

At least he didn't say giraffe.

I was about to punch him when I saw that Jack had come to a stop. I pulled Ramesh behind a parked car before Jack could notice us.

Standing on the corner of the street, he glanced nervously in our direction and swung his backpack to the floor. Baron was pulling at his lead, straining to escape along the road towards us.

"I think he can smell us, Iz. I swear that creature wants to eat me."

I held Ramesh's shoulder to stop him shaking. "I thought you loved dogs."

"And I thought Jack hated them. Looks like we were both wrong."

It was a gloomy evening and the streetlights had turned on to lend the scene a Victorian glow. Jack looked terrified and I remembered what he'd said about punk kids on his street. For the next few minutes, he was like a weather vane spinning in the wind. His attention constantly flicked between his phone, his watch and the four streets of the crossroad he was standing at.

"You're late," he shouted before we could see who he was talking to. Baron emitted a low growl.

"Yeah, well. That's the way things go sometimes." A boy of about sixteen had joined him on the corner. He dropped his bag to the floor and knelt down to stroke the beast under its dribbly jowls. "Who's a good boy, eh? Who's the best boy?"

Baron didn't answer.

"Any problems this week?" Jack was still looking back and forth along the road.

"Yeah. I got a paper cut and we ran out of envelopes."

"Don't be a prat." Jack's normally uncertain tone was gone. His voice had become blunt, aggressive, threatening even. "You know what I mean."

The boy wasn't scared and spoke back just as curtly. "Does it look like I had any problems?"

"Tell your brother I'll meet him here again on Wednesday. I'll see you next week. Same time, same place."

"Guess so." The boy walked off in the direction he'd come from. "Cya round, boss."

I was worried that Jack would turn straight back our way but he took a right instead and instantly disappeared from view. I figured he'd either got wind that someone was following him or Baron needed to stretch his legs.

"What just happened?" Ramesh asked when it was safe to stand back up.

"Didn't you see?" I was happy to have spotted what my friend had evidently failed to.

"See what?"

"Jack has broken bad!"

Ramesh wasn't amused. "Izzy, you know the only American shows I watch have the words Project, Chef or Race in the title. What just happened?"

"If you'd been paying more attention, you would have noticed that Jack and the boy exchanged bags."

"And?"

"And now we know what Bob must have discovered."

He let out a huff – okay, I was probably milking it. "Which is?"

"Jack isn't buying drugs on the dark web." Pause for effect. "He's selling them."

168

Chapter Twenty-Four

Both Ramesh and I got what we wanted that night. I found out what Jack had been up to and he got to choose the Tapas we ate.

We went to our favourite place in South Croydon and ordered (tiny) bowls full of exquisite food. There were Padron peppers, chorizo cooked in cider, Roman-style calamari, jamon and three big portions of patatas bravas smothered in garlic mayonnaise and nicely spicy tomato sauce.

"So do you get it now?" I tossed a carrot baton into my mouth.

Ramesh nodded. "Yeah... Not quite."

"Jack buys the drugs, passes them on to a bunch of kids to divide up and send out but presumably keeps most of the profit for himself. Then one day, let's just imagine, a package comes for Bob. Jack spots it, sees where it's come from and tells him off for having cocaine sent to the office."

"Only, Bob's smarter than Jack and realises what's going on. He says, 'How do you know what's in this envelope if I haven't even opened it?' Jack's no improviser. He can't come up with an answer and so Bob realises that our ever-faithful security guard has been using his job at P&P as a cover for his side enterprise... Or something along those lines anyway."

New ideas were bouncing about in my brain like pinballs. "It fits in with the list of addresses I found on Jack's computer. And I bet that's why he spends so much time in the toilet. He must be checking up on orders, calling suppliers. Jack's a damn gangster."

"Does that mean we've cracked this case wide—"

"That's starting to sound a bit naff."

"Does that mean that Jack killed Bob?"

I thought for a second. I'd got so caught up in working out what Jack was up to that I'd lost track of the bigger picture. "Maybe... I'm not sure yet. I mean, it would make total sense now if it was him. He's got a clear motive. And even if his dog is real, that's hardly a sound alibi for the night of the murder. My only problem is the hit on me."

"How come?" He was struggling to gnaw through a calamari ring and the words came out coated in breadcrumbs.

"We didn't have anything on Jack until this afternoon, right? So why would he have paid someone big money to go after me?"

"Maybe there's been something under your nose this whole time and he's scared you'll put it together."

"If that was the case, surely we'd have seen it by now. And, anyway, it still feels wrong. Just because someone's a drug dealer, it doesn't make them a heartless killing machine. And even if Jack knew what happened to his daughter and got his revenge on Bob, it would be a stretch to think he'd go after me too."

"Right." Chew, chew, chew. "So where does that leave us?"

I waited for our nattily dressed waiter to walk out of earshot. "Think about it. We always assume that whoever killed Bob also tried to kill me, but what if we're looking for two different people?"

Ramesh wiped his mouth on the cotton napkin that had already saved his shirt from a number of spills. "Ooh, two killers. Double the fun."

"I know it might sound unlikely that there are two killers at P&P. The question remains though, who wanted me dead and why?"

He didn't answer. He was too busy scoffing down our fried *patatas*.

Up until now, I'd tried not to take the assassination attempt too personally. It seemed natural to think that it was just our pesky office murderer, trying to cover their tracks. But perhaps Bob's death had planted a seed and now everybody was at it. Could murder be contagious?

I was starting to feel self-conscious about the whole thing. If someone wanted me dead, what did that say about me? Who did I know that hated me enough to want to erase me from existence? There was only one thing for it. While Ramesh was in the toilet, I made a list.

POTENTIAL MURDERERS

- **David's ex-wife? – Naaahhhh.**

- **Danny, after he found out about me and David – ha! Funny.**

- **17-year-old Gary Flint, who I got even with by sharing a picture of *his* micro-penis (that was actually copied off the internet) with every girl in the sixth-form? – I imagine he's recovered.**

- **My first stepdad? – Bit of a weirdo. Mum should never have**

170

married him, but I like to think I'd won him over by the time they got divorced.

- **My high school P.E. teacher, Mr Bath? – Yep, complete psycho. Nailed it! It was probably him.**

And yet, if it wasn't Mr Bath, – who could never remember my name, even when he taught me twice a week, and I hadn't seen for a decade – I couldn't imagine who would have paid thousands of pounds to have me killed. I'm not saying I was the easiest person to get along with, but I was no Bob. I didn't go out of my way to upset people and, though there were those at work who found me weird, there was no one I actively didn't get on with except–

"We need to go home right now," I told Ramesh when he got back to the table.

The look on his face was one of pure horror. "But I haven't finished my chorizo!"

Caring not one button for my bank balance (until I saw it at the end of the month and had a good cry) we jumped in a cab and rocketed towards West Wickham.

"You two, quick!" I overacted to Mum and Greg when we got there. "Dad's on his way. I need all of you in the front room immediately and it's going to be a late one."

My stepdad looked alarmed. "Can't I make a cup of tea first?"

I chewed it over for a moment. "Fine, make the tea, then get in there."

Mum was somewhat more jubilant. "How exciting, darling. This is what we've been waiting for. Tonight is the night that Izzy comes alive."

Five minutes later we were all sitting on the sofa having a lovely cup of red label. It really did the trick and then I was ready to–

Crack this case wide open?

Fine – that.

The evidence pads had been restored to their rightful place on Greg's easels and Mum was on hand with fresh markers. When everyone was ready, I got things started.

"I'm going to give you each a part to play this evening. There aren't enough of us to cover all the roles which is why I've brought Sir Hugalot down from the loft." I pointed at my oversized teddy bear who I still felt bad for deserting up there.

171

"Can I just ask," my father interrupted, "will there be questions at the end?"

"It's not a test, Dad. We're going to act out potential theories to see if we can settle on exactly what happened."

"Right. No questions. That is a weight off my mind."

"Here are your parts." As I spoke, I tore the relevant pages from the suspects pad and handed them out. My friend sat up very straight in his armchair and crossed his fingers. "Ramesh, you can be David."

He jumped up from where he was sitting and pumped his fists like he'd won a marathon. "Yes! I won't let you down. I've been practicing my Welsh accent and everything. *I'm going down the valleys. The vaaaaaaalleys...*"

"Thanks, but I'm afraid that, unless you're dating a Welshy, doing the accent could be considered offensive." I made a sad face for his sake. "Greg, you're going to be Jack."

My stepdad nodded as if that was exactly what he'd been expecting. "Mum, you're Amara."

"Marvellous. Now, a couple of things to help me get into character–"

"Not necessary, Mum. Just use what's written on the sheet."

"Okay, but–"

I could see that she was about to make things complicated so I moved on. "Dad, I'd like you to be Will."

"*Whatever*," he said sullenly before breaking out into a smile. "That's how young people talk, isn't it? *Whatever*."

"Sir Hugalot will have to stand in for Wendy. Are you happy with that, Huggy?" I looked at the ancient bear I'd won in the school summer raffle when I was seven, but he said nothing. "Good, no complaints. Now Mother and Ramesh have searched round the house and will be handing out accessories to give you a feel for who you're playing."

"Sir Hugalot, don't worry too much about holding the cigarette lighter, you haven't got any fingers." Ramesh balanced the lighter on the massive bear's shoulder and distributed a plastic truncheon (which could only have come from Mum's bedroom – yuck!) to Greg.

Mum had already put on a tasteful scarf and given her ex-ex-husband a very dated silver suit jacket.

"Are we all clear what we're doing?" I felt like a nursery school teacher.

"Yessssss, Misssssss," the children sang as one.

"Okay, we'll start with Amara. Mum, tell us what you've got."

I sat down on the carpet in the middle of the room and watched as my mother lolloped forward. I have no idea where she got the idea that Amara walked with a limp. She took some liberties with the text too.

"My name is Amara, I'm the deputy director of Poptart & Poptart–"

"Porter & Porter!"

"Sorry, haven't got my glasses on. I'm the deputy director of Porter & Porter and I had a falling out with that wicked man Bob Thomas when he tried to take my job away from me. I claim to have been at home with my family on the night that Bob was disembowelled, but I could easily have slipped away from my luxury apartment in the centre of town to do the deed."

"That was perfect, Mum, just what I was looking for. We don't have very much new to add about Amara, except that she concealed the fact she was friends with Bob's wife and that Bob had continued to humiliate and upstage her since their run-in."

"She sweet-talked you into investigating the case too." Ramesh was up on his feet, waving his felt daffodil around furiously. He was so riled up that his words launched out at me in one great burst. "And she told you about Bob's cancer, which set us off on a whole different track. What better way to hide her guilt than to nudge us towards another suspect?"

"Ra, we're going to be here a while. You need to pace yourself."

"I just love am-dram so much." Looking a bit guilty, he sat back down and it was my turn to speak.

"Everything that Ramesh said was true – not to mention the fact that Amara was the one who witnessed the attack on Jack's daughter. But remember that this is the same lovely lady who once bought pain au chocolat for the whole office and drove Ramesh to the hospital when he thought he'd broken his finger."

"Ahhh, I love Amara." He was smiling again.

"Ahhh, me too. She's basically the anti-Bob. So, unless anyone objects, I think we can rule her out for good."

The room remained silent so Mum took a bow before sitting back down.

"Ra, you're up."

Ramesh shot from the armchair like it was on fire. He shook his hands out and did a little sprint on the spot to loosen up before he started in on his vocal exercises.

"*Catherine* Zeta Jones. Catherine *Zeta* Jones." He stretched the words out and made his mouth into an O at the end of the name. "The Vale of Glamorgan can be boring in the morning but the isle of Anglesey is the place I love to be."

"Ramesh!" I barked. "Can we start?"

He proudly tossed aside the sheet of paper and started his monologue.

"I left the valleys when I was but a lad and moved to the metropolis of Croydon." He couldn't help sliding into an Anthony Hopkins lilt with the odd spike of Tom Jones' in his Vegas years. "Little did I know back then what awaited me in the big city. I was destined to become the director of Porter & Porter, a thriving financial services firm with its offices in the most spectacular building in the whole of Croydon."

"Skipping along to the part we're most interested in?"

"One day, my slothful and slithery deputy was slain in his office while I was at my elderly aunt's having dinner, as I do every Wednesday night because I am a very nice man indeed. I didn't think much of Bob, though I tolerated him as best I could. I wouldn't gain anything from his death and, like anyone with an ounce of human compassion, I long to see his murderer bought to justice."

With his big finish approaching, the daffodil was once more produced and he began to slash it around wildly through the air. "Yes, whichever bloodthirsty so and so would dare despatch a member of my managerial team should be strung up from the neck until dead!"

My three parents went wild. They whooped and yelped at Ramesh's performance. He passed Mum the daffodil so that she could throw it back at him adoringly.

"You sounded a bit Victorian at the end, but otherwise a very competent display," I told him. "You do realise that not everyone in Wales lives in a valley though?"

He stopped his bowing and crossed his arms. "Did David?"

"Well, yes."

"I rest my case." He took one last bow and sat down.

"Okay… Next, and hopefully more revealingly, we have Jack."

Greg pointed at himself, to check it was his turn, then rose to his

174

feet. "Here goes. Jack Campbell – Alibi: Walking dog. Motive: Hated Bob and had been–"

I had to stop him. "Sorry, Greg. Could you maybe personalise it a bit and not just read it out? The idea is that I get a feel for each of our suspects in relation to the case."

"First person?"

"First person would be great. Thanks."

He cleared his throat. "My name's Jack Campbell. I say I was out walking my dog on the night of the murder but, either way, I truly hated Bob Thomas. He humiliated me at the office Christmas party when he threw a lucky punch at me. That same night, he claimed I wasn't as innocent as I pretend to be. What's more, I knew all about the naughty things Bob had been up to. Drugs, drink and sex at all hours. I was familiar with the security systems more than anyone else in the office and could have come and gone that night as I pleased."

Greg had gone about it with his usual capable air and I nodded my approval. "Excellent. Now, don't get too excited, but Ramesh and I have made a major discovery this evening. We tailed Jack–"

"Woooop!" Mum let out a squeal.

"We tailed Jack and worked out that he's been selling drugs – which must be what Bob discovered. It gives Jack a very good reason to want Bob out of the picture. He doesn't have much of an alibi either and, as Greg highlighted, he would know how to get rid of the hard drives in the server room."

"So would I." Ramesh sounded rather disgruntled. "I don't understand why I'm not even considered a suspect anymore."

"Ra! We've been over this so many times." I shot him a stern look. "Your alibi has been confirmed by the police. And besides, you don't have the arm strength to knock someone unconscious and spill their guts across the office, let alone the killer instinct."

"I'm just feeling left out, that's all." Ramesh looked sadder than the time I said Lady Gaga's music was a bit derivative.

"Back to Jack. I really think he could be the killer."

"Especially after what Bob did to Jack's poor daughter." Mum tossed the scarf over her shoulder dramatically. "I reckon, all in all, we're onto a winner."

There was a murmur of agreement from the others but I cut them short. "I've been thinking about that a lot. I'm not sure that the situation with Pippa is as significant as we'd imagined."

"He practically raped the poor girl." My father suddenly looked horrified. He was such a caring man and I felt a surge of pride that he was my Dad.

"That's not what I mean. I mean that, after speaking to Jack this morning, I don't think he could have known about the attack. Pippa made David and Amara promise not to tell him. There's nothing we've seen in his behaviour towards Bob that would suggest he had that much bile and hatred boiling up inside him." I got a murmur of agreement of my own. "Let's move on to Will."

Dad stood up and waved to his audience. Getting into the role, he hunched his shoulders and hung his head. He'd apparently got the idea that Will was about fifteen.

"My name's Will Gibbons. I'm the bad boy of the office. I was best buds with Bob, yeah? But we didn't always get on and sometimes we argued." Dad's performance was part bratty teenager, part middle-class retiree. "I didn't have access to the server room to remove the hard drives so, if I was involved, I had an accomplice. I claim I was out with a lady… I mean *a bird* that night, but I can't prove it or nuffing."

Mum and Greg were very impressed and applauded enthusiastically.

"Did I do okay?" Dad was back in character as himself.

"Brilliantly, thank you." I stood up to fill everyone in on the new developments. "I've come to realise two important facts this evening which I think could be very significant to our investigation. But, first, I'd like to take this moment to thank my wonderful friend, Ramesh.

"In fact, I'll go so far as to say that, without his inane prattling, we wouldn't have got to where we are now." I looked over at the Watson to my Holmes, the Q to my Bond, and he smiled back at me like the sun in a children's drawing.

The moment lingered until my stepdad helped it along. "So what's this big reveal you're slowly building up to?"

I narrowed my eyes knowingly. "Ra suggested that there could be something right under our noses which had previously seemed insignificant. So I ran through the list of evidence in my head and the only thing that just flat out didn't make any sense was the note written on the train ticket that I found in Bob's coat. We always assumed that whoever it was written for never got it. But what if we were wrong?" I looked around their attentive faces. "What if that note wasn't from Bob but to him?"

"Who wrote it then?" Ramesh raised a puzzled eyebrow. "Barbara from HR? Brenda from reception?"

Another pause for them to stew. "Or good old Billy Gibbons from consulting?" My parents gave a theatrical gasp.

"So you think that Will was meeting Bob on the night of the murder." Dad sat back in his seat to think. "Yes, that's interesting that is."

"And what did they get up to?" Mum asked. "A bottle of champagne and brainstorming for Bob's memorial service?"

My selected loved ones were hanging on my reply. "No. Think about what I saw the morning after. Bob with no tie or socks and one missing shoe. Alcohol in the mix too, what does that all suggest?"

"A party?" Dad attempted.

"Wait. You're not saying..." Ramesh began. "But Will's not gay. He goes on about women the whole time."

"Yep and his Facebook is covered in beer and football posts. It's all fake. Since we started looking into him, Will's been acting weird and I knew that he had something to hide. What if it was nothing to do with the murder and everything to do with the double life he leads?"

I paused for questions but no one made a sound. "On Thursday, when I was out with David, I saw Will outside the gay night at the Blue Orchid Bar. He changed course when he saw me, but I'm sure that's where he was headed. When I started to think about it tonight, it all made sense. The way that he talks about women never sounded right to me. I know it's not impossible, but the casual, anonymous hook-ups he claims to have are far more common in the gay community. I'm almost certain that, just like Jack, Will is concealing a whole side to his personality. He's a sharp-suited, mouthy womaniser at work and someone completely different after hours."

"Wait." Greg put his hand up for clarification. "Are you saying that Bob was gay too?"

The question whirled around my head. "I've thought about Bob a lot over the last few days. I believe that he's the key to what happened, not our suspects. We know that he'd been living this wild lifestyle ever since he discovered he was dying. I think that he'd got it into

177

his head that he wanted to do everything. He wanted to tick off every thrill and peccadillo. He tried drugs, booze and petty crime, so why not dabble with his sexuality too? At the very least, it would explain why he was only half dressed."

My four fellow sleuths were computing this new theory so I kept talking.

"It always struck me as strange that Bob would write that note on a train ticket when he drove pretty much everywhere. Will on the other hand gets dropped off by his brother or comes in via East Croydon. He wouldn't have a season ticket because he doesn't always need one, so a single would suit him fine. He lives near Mitcham but that's a completely different train line and, looking on the map, I think it would be quicker for him to go from Norbury, where the ticket was purchased."

"So, Will met up with Bob that night." Dad shuffled in his seat. "Does that mean he's the killer?"

"Slow down a bit. We're not there yet. Imagine that Bob confided in Will over his diagnosis and, with their hearts open, Will revealed his own big secret. They spend some time together, one thing leads to another and before you know it, Bob's invited Will up to the office for champagne. Even if they'd argued after, even if Bob had been his usual cruel self, it's a big jump from kissing and cuddling to cutting someone's guts out."

"Will was acting weird that day in the office before Bob was killed." Ramesh pointed at me with the daffodil. "Perhaps Bob was messing with him the same way he messed with everyone else. So when Will realised, he slashed Bob to pieces."

"Then how did he get rid of the CCTV?" I asked and his felt flower drooped. "I think it's more likely that Will's oddly quiet behaviour and the arguments they had that week were because Bob was pressuring him into a relationship and it took a while for him to give in. That's why he wrote the note when he could just as easily have told Bob in person. Remember, it said, *okay, let's do it,* which always sounded kind of reluctant to me. Whatever was going on between them was new, unexpected, unsettling for him."

"But if Will didn't kill Bob, he might still have ordered the hit on you." Greg was a step ahead as usual. "Perhaps he blamed you for his lover's death. Or perhaps he was worried that you'd find out about his relationship and reveal his secret."

"I was thinking just the same thing." I turned the suspects pad back to the first page and circled Jack, Wendy and Will's names. "Whoever called the hit must really not have liked me. Okay, Jack's a part-time drug dealer and Wendy spouted off when she found me in Bob's office. But there's no personal connection between us. It came to me in the restaurant tonight that, with Will, it's different. He's never hidden his disdain for me and there's a side to him that can be full-on savage. It's still a stretch, I admit, but I think that Will is the most likely suspect to have ordered the hit."

The room was silent. I waited in case the others thought of something useful.

In the end it was Mum who spoke first. "I'm sorry darling, but it doesn't add up. There are too many what-ifs, too many conclusions we have to leap to."

I let out a long, exhausted sigh. The energy that had surged up within me an hour earlier had dissipated. "It's all got so complicated. Why couldn't Bob have been murdered in a nice normal office with nice normal people?"

"You're doing really well though, Iz." Ramesh stood up to put a sympathetic hand on my shoulder. "If you keep at it, you'll work it out."

I felt like lying down and giving up altogether. "I'd love to believe you." My trusty teddy was still on the sofa by dad, awaiting his call to action. "Sorry, Sir Hugalot. Do you mind if we skip Wendy? This isn't helping me the way I hoped it would." He bore the disappointment as well as could be expected.

"Maybe I'll be off," Ramesh said. "If I'm quick, I can skip through the 'Got Talent' highlights before bed."

"We'll leave you to it as well, darling." Mum took Greg's truncheon and moved to leave. "We're here if you need anything."

On command, my stepfather followed his wife out of the room. Even Dad was getting ready to go.

"Remember what Ramesh said. The answer will be right there in front of you. You just have to look at it the right way."

"Thanks, Dad." I gave him a hug and he squeezed me super tight like when I was a kid. "You've been great tonight."

Looking up at me, he held my gaze. "The last piece of a jigsaw is always the hardest to fit."

We both let go. "That's a terrible metaphor but thanks for your support."

He trundled out after the others, so then it was just me and Huggy and I had no idea what to do next.

Chapter Twenty-Five

Two hours later I was still sitting on the front lounge carpet, surrounded by the large sheets of paper that I'd torn down from the three pads. I'd read them all a hundred times. I'd crossed out clues and added new ones. I'd even tried throwing a marker at the list of suspects with my eyes closed but I kept getting Ramesh, so that wasn't much help.

The number of ideas that were running through my head was starting to freak me out. I knew there was a path through the mess of information we'd assembled, but it felt like I needed a map to find it.

So I gave up trying.

I lay on my back, with the Hawes Lane Fun Club's notes beneath me, and waited for inspiration. Instead of searching for the murderer, I thought about what I'd said to Ramesh on my first day at P&P. I'd instantly felt relaxed around him, which was weird because I'd been pant-wettingly nervous all day until then. We chatted about the TV shows we both watched, he told me about his love of Cher, Shania and Celine and then I told him about my friend Agatha. My best friend really and certainly the only one who'd stuck around since high school.

What Ramesh remembered me saying was true. I'd always been good at working out murder mysteries. It wasn't because I was some kind of genius. There was certainly no magical-structural formula I'd concocted or clever trick to it. The reason I normally ended up identifying the guilty party was because I could see through all the red herrings. When I set aside the false leads and focussed on the suspects, it just made sense to me who would have killed to get what they wanted.

It's not always the little things that give the game away. Bob's hands weren't pointing to anything in particular and the stamp on his desk really was just a second class stamp – so nothing to do with Wendy, or the money she was owed. What helped me get closer to the killer was coming to know the victim, spending time with the suspects and trying to put myself in their places.

The way I see it, except for the odd all-out maniac, people normally murder one another for personal gain or deep-rooted emotion. Love can drive someone to kill just as much as hate will. None of our suspects would gain enough financially from Bob's death, so who felt so strongly about him that they would contemplate snuffing him out? That was the most important question I could ask, but I'd let myself get distracted by convoluted theories.

If I wanted to work out what had really happened, I'd need to go back to the beginning, use my instincts and believe in my judgement. All of the suspects had lied to protect themselves, but only one had killed Bob. I didn't have to solve an uncrackable puzzle – that would come later. All I had to do was read a group of people who I'd known for years.

I wasn't possessed with Miss Marple's vast trove of character types to compare my suspects to but I could tell what each one wanted most in life. I didn't have Poirot's knack for observation or his phenomenal brain. I didn't even have the resources that the police could access and yet I had an advantage over all of them. I'd been there to watch the fallout of Bob's death, I'd witnessed things that they never could have.

I opened my eyes and pulled a now blank flipchart down to me. All of the evidence we had was irrelevant without knowing the motivation behind the murder. So I lay on the floor and planned out a whole new list for everyone involved. I'd start with the people I knew the most about and finish with Amara whose entry would probably only stretch to a few lines.

I wrote **Desires and Motivations** at the top of the page and started off by thinking about my best friend in the world, who I still couldn't believe for a second had wielded the knife.

RAMESH

- **Wanted to stop Bob's cruelty**
- **Needed equality and respect**
- **Wanted revenge for everything that Bob had put him through?**

I thought about the last two vlogs he'd livestreamed and the contrast in him. In the one a few days before the murder, he was filled with rage but, after he'd sent the e-mails telling Bob exactly what he thought of him, there was calm. He had healed his wounds.

- **Wanted closure**
- **Was searching for peace**
- **Needed to heal the hurt he had suffered**
- **Killing Bob could never have done that.**

I moved on to Bob next. In some ways he was the most distant, the only one I couldn't question or manipulate to reveal the truth. And yet, in his last months on earth, he'd been painting his motivations on his office door in thick red letters for all to read.

BOB

- **Drink**
- **Drugs**
- **Sex**
- **Adultery**
- **Theft**
- **Cruelty**

I read the words over and again. They were a bad bucket list; a last hurrah to cement Bob's reputation as a total scumbag. But they didn't tell me everything. They lacked the personal side of Bob's hatefulness. And so I wrote out the list again.

- **Hurt – Ramesh**
- **Rob – Wendy**
- **Fight – Jack**
- **Screw – Will**
- **Humiliate – Amara**
- **Torment – David**
- **Lie – His family**

Bob's death sentence from cancer, didn't turn him into a bad person; he'd always been one. He'd already taken advantage of Pippa, a young intern who he should have been looking out for. He'd victimised Ramesh, directing his bullying at the most sensitive person he could find. He'd made working at P&P torturous for everyone who had to deal with him.

No, Bob's diagnosis didn't spark his bad instincts, it magnified them. He knew he could do whatever he wanted and he embraced the hedonistic carnage full on.

I read the list I'd written in thick black marker and I could tell that it wasn't the first time it had been compiled. Bob had never done anything by accident. He'd planned it all out. First the elaborate memorial service, to make sure he'd have the last laugh, and then his careful targeting of each one of us.

It felt like a bomb had detonated inside me as a burst of frantic electricity buzzed through every nerve in my body. Something clicked in my brain and everything finally fitted together.

I took my phone and wallet from my bag and searched for the card D.I. Irons had given me after my assault. My hands were shaking so much that I could barely type in the number. My heart was going off like a siren in my ears.

I pressed call but immediately hung up again. The phone fell from my hand and I had to sit back down and think about what I was doing. Nothing seemed real. My mind was filled with doubts, not just about my detective work but whether revealing what I'd discovered was even the right thing to do. I found some resolve despite my fears and dialled again.

"This is Detective Inspector Victoria Irons speaking, I can't come to the phone right now but, if you leave a message, I'll make sure to get back to you." It was no wonder that she wasn't answering, it had gone twelve at night. "In an emergency, call nine nine nine or contact your local police station."

I spoke after the beep. "Sorry to bother you, detective, but I'm pretty sure I've worked out who murdered Bob. And I'm absolutely certain I know who paid to have me killed. Come to the office tomorrow morning at nine fifteen and bring two sets of handcuffs. If I'm wrong, you can always arrest me for wasting police time."

Not allowing myself time to question my actions again, I called Dean from Bromley next who was still awake, but grumpy that I'd interrupted him while he was playing Fortnite. He demanded yet another favour in return for the answer to the very simple question I had for him, which I should probably have just looked up online.

Then, finally, I called David. He was asleep but answered the phone anyway when he saw it was me.

Such a sweetheart.

I know, right?!

It took about an hour to explain everything that had happened since Ramesh and I had started investigating. I went through all our theories and even the mistakes we'd made along the way and he helped confirm some of the stuff about Bob I'd only been half sure of. I can imagine how shocked he was to get a call like that in the middle of the night, but he didn't let on. He told me he was proud that I'd worked everything out and, at the end of the conversation, he only had one question for me.

"Are you sure this is this is the best way to go about it, Izzy?"

I pictured a twelve-year-old girl reading 'The Murder of Roger Ackroyd' by torchlight for the third, fourth, thousandth time and I knew that, at the very least, it was what I wanted.

"Yeah. I think so."

"All right then. You can use the conference room and I'll make sure everyone's there." It was his business voice again. Our morning meeting was arranged.

"Thank you, David."

Now that he'd agreed to my plan, I was half relieved, half terrified. The immensity of what lay ahead would take a while to sink in, but I was glad that no one would come between me and my Poirot style finale – not even the hunkiest Welshman since Richard Burton in The Robe.

I tidied up the pages from the floor, set the pads back on their easels and, with one last swish of the marker, put a circle round the guilty parties.

It was done and now I could go to bed.

Chapter Twenty-Six

I know what you're thinking. *She's been bumbling along this whole time, what makes her so sure she's solved the case now?* Well, first, I prefer to regard my bumbling as a choreographed wander and, second, there's something you may not have realised about me. I'm actually quite good at this detective stuff. Okay, I admit it was a slow start but, as soon as I got my confidence up, it was plain sailing.

More or less.

Yeah, more or less.

When I woke up the next morning, and I'd showered and dressed and brushed my teeth, a numb reality had started to set in. I'd solved Bob's murder, but that didn't make what I had to do next any easier. Before I could think about how the morning would play out, I had to deal with an irate police officer complaining that I'd interfered in her investigation.

"I believe my partner already impressed upon you the importance of leaving us to do our jobs."

I felt a bit defensive. "I'm sorry, I really am. I don't think I've done anything very illegal. I just wanted a go at working out *who done it*."

She didn't sound reassured by my explanation. "It might surprise you to learn that *who done it* is not a term we often use in the Metropolitan Police."

"So you'll come then?" I was hoping my undying optimism would be too much for her to resist.

"I should make you go to the station so that we can verify your information and assess any risks."

"I knew you'd come!"

I confirmed the details then rang off before she could change her mind.

The office was quiet when I arrived. I thought I'd get in early to set things up before it got busy but, in the end, David was already there. We met in the conference room, the site of my future glory. My nerves started firing again as soon as I saw him. This was really happening.

Despite knowing everything I had planned, he spoke in his usual relaxed tone. "Are you still sure about this?"

It helped me calm down a bit. "Urmm… sixty to seventy per cent. And you?"

"Not so much. I think we should tell the police everything and let them do their jobs. But, if this is what you want, it's your choice."

"Thank you. I really mean it. Thanks for this."

He smiled and tentatively took my hand. "Who am I to disappoint?"

I'd only ever been in the conference room for staff functions before. It made me feel a bit special to be putting on my own presentation in there. Nine tall windows on the left-hand side of the room gave a clear view of East Croydon Station with its red and white masts and beyond it the Boxpark and the town centre.

To set the scene perfectly, I organised the room. I pulled chairs to the side of the long, rectangular space so that only six remained. One for me, one for each suspect, but David would have to stand as seven chairs just looked wrong somehow. I put glasses and water out in the middle of the table and then, as I still had time before everyone got there, I went for a wee.

When the others arrived, David ushered them into the conference room.

"What the hell is going on?" Will asked as I swung round to face him in the boss's chair at the end of the immense oval table. "Don't tell me you've given your freak girlfriend a promotion?" He glared at my bossfriend, (okay, last time. I promise.)

Amara, Wendy, Jack and Ramesh had already gone through these opening scenes – and, yes, I did the dramatic spinny chair thing for them too.

David pulled out a seat for Will to take his place at the table. "Izzy isn't getting a promotion. She just wants to talk to us."

Will was about to complain, but then spotted Irons, Brabazon and two uniformed officers walking over to us from the entrance. His arms folded across his chest, he sat down with the others.

"Detectives," I said when they arrived, sounding all cool and composed. "Thanks for joining us."

David sat casually on a coffee table by the door which was guarded by the two P.C.s. I exchanged a smile with the senior officers as they flanked the table. I could tell they were eager to see what would happen next. It was a big moment for me and I'd like to have run across to

David for one more kiss. Instead, I stood up from my chair and began.

"We're here today to talk about the death of Bob Thomas."

"Not more of your Nancy Drew nosing around?" Will's canine muzzle was practically growling.

Brabazon peered down at him warningly and David was just as quick to my defence. "Let her talk, Will, or I'll have to tell to Mr Porter to rethink your promotion."

I tried again. "I didn't like Bob. Not many of us did."

"Speak for yourself, love." Wendy was still playing the doting mistress for some reason. "He was a gentleman. A true gentleman."

I didn't let her break my stride. "I wanted to find out who killed him because it's the right thing to do. David told me recently that, even if Bob wasn't a good man, he didn't deserve what he went through and I believe that's true."

Ramesh looked at me, and I could tell that he was as surprised to see me up there as anyone.

"It's taken me a long time, but last night I found the evidence I needed to identify Bob's killer. Not only do they work here at P&P–"

"It better not be Pauline from accounts!" Wendy mumbled over me.

"–but they're in this room right now." I was hoping for a gasp of surprise. Presumably most of them had worked this much out already. "It was only the people in this room who had access to the CCTV footage of that night's fatal events."

"I didn't have access back then, so perhaps I can go," Will said, so Brabazon put one hand on his shoulder to keep him in place.

"You might not have realised but, over the last two weeks, I've been watching every one of you in order to find the culprit."

"I realised." At least Will could enjoy this small revenge.

"Me too," Jack added.

"It was you on the other end of that video-call whatsit, weren't it?" Wendy asked.

Amara just shrugged an apology as she'd also figured it out.

Busted. Ha!

"Fine, you all knew that I'd been watching you. But I doubt any of you really considered I'd be the one to solve Bob's murder." I'd got them there. "Anyway… where was I?"

"For the last two weeks you've been–"

188

"Right. Thanks, Ramesh." I took a deep breath. This wasn't going as I'd hoped. "I came to understand that whoever killed Bob felt true hatred for the man."

Will started clapping. "Genius. Bravo. What a mind!"

"I mean to say that the murderer literally *despised* Bob Thomas. Hated him with every ounce of their being and did what was necessary to get rid of him." I looked across at the lead detective. "D.I. Irons, please correct me if I'm wrong but three weapons were used in the murder. First a blunt object across the head, which I assume was the champagne bottle that the killer removed from the scene. Next a small kitchen knife that had been on Bob's desk. And finally his prized medieval-sword letter opener, plunged into his back almost like a calling card from the murderer."

Seizing a biro from the table, I stabbed Ramesh and he kindly faked his own death. "What does this tell us?"

"That Ramesh isn't a very good actor?" Will kept destroying all the tension I'd built up. I'd have to stop asking so many rhetorical questions.

Walking behind them around the table, I locked eyes on each suspect as I went. "It tells us a number of things. First, the weapons were already at the scene, which suggests that the attack wasn't pre-meditated but the killer snapped for some reason.

"Second, it's clear that, what started out as a crime of anger, perhaps even passion, was finished off in a cold, calculating way. The murderer didn't regret what they had done with the champagne bottle. They didn't call for an ambulance or, most likely, even check for a pulse, they took the knife and finished the job."

I jumped forward again and, holding his head in one hand, pretended to slit Jack's stomach open with the ballpoint pen. He didn't play along. "And third, whoever killed Bob wanted us to know that this was personal." With one final blow, I lodged the pen between my fingers, with my hand laid flat upon Amara's back.

She let out a little eek and a guilty smile. "Ooh, that sent shivers through me." Will and Wendy frowned at her. "Oh… sorry."

"The murderer removed various items from the room. The knife and bottle of course that, covered in blood, would have been hard to clean the fingerprints from. There were also several pieces of Bob's clothing missing – a tie, his shoes, and one sock. For a long time, I couldn't imagine why they'd been taken." I glanced at Will to see if he'd react to this but he maintained his surly expression.

I'd probably already gone round the table three times by this point. I decided that my ominous stroll had turned into a cheery jog so stopped, back in my place once more. "The murderer escaped the way they'd come in. Through the fire exit which, as anyone who's ever wanted a quiet cigarette knows, has no alarm or even video cameras and can be easily jimmied open with a credit card.

"The following morning, I, Izzy Palmer, came into work, planning to leave Bob a folder full of documents that he'd spent the previous day demanding. I peeked inside to find the lights all blazing and Bob Thomas dead. Being of an inquisitive nature and perhaps, deep down, having always thought of myself as a potential detective, I went in for a closer look which is when Wendy burst in on me to kick up a stink."

She didn't like the spotlight of suspicion being turned on her and immediately started shouting. "And who's to say that you haven't concocted this whole thing to hide the truth. Who's to say you weren't the one what killed 'im?"

She'd gone along nicely with my plan. "Just like that. You screamed and yelled and spat your words across the office so that everyone knew what had happened. You accused me of murdering Bob without any evidence or the hint of a motive. You were loud and public and emotional, just as you were at Bob's memorial service a week later. Despite the fact his own wife was present, you made a scene, crying on your frenemy's shoulder. And why was that?"

She didn't speak this time. She gathered up the folds in her floral skirt and gripped them tightly.

"The truth is that you and Bob had enjoyed a short and underwhelming affair that culminated not in him taking you as his mistress or leaving his wife. No, Bob concluded your romance by stealing one of your most prized possessions. A stamp worth eight thousand pounds which you wanted so desperately that you put yourself in debt to add it to your collection. You may have acted the grieving mistress, but there was little love left between you when Bob died, isn't that right?"

Wendy was still short of words as her bottom lip began to tremble. I saw Brabazon's eyes flick across the room to his partner. Irons responded with a *no hurry* hand gesture.

"In fact, you were furious with him. You saw the endless deliveries coming to the office and realised all the money he was spending – expensive champagne, the best food Croydon had to offer, not to mention the fancy letter opener that he loved to show off around the office. So you demanded that he pay you back for what he'd taken. Bob made his excuses, but your patience eventually ran out."

No longer looking at me, but staring straight forward out of the window, she pursed her lips so that the folds in her chin came together like the pleats of her skirt.

"One night, when you knew he'd be in the office late, you snuck inside. Perhaps you tried to seduce him, slowly removing articles of his clothing before he told you to stop. When that didn't work, you gave him an ultimatum; the money now or he'd suffer the consequences. But instead of the eight thousand pounds he owed you, he offered you the sixty-one pence stamp from his desk and you saw red.

"You grabbed the champagne bottle from in front of you and, with all the strength you could call up, smashed him across the head with it. You took the knife to make sure he was dead and then, as a final revenge, stabbed him in the back with the expensive silver letter-opener that he'd bought with the money he owed you. It was the easiest thing in the world to post some old photos to the stamp collecting group on Facebook that you yourself run. Anyone would think you were in north London at the time you were actually disembowelling your ex-lover!"

The room fell silent for a second before, her voice hoarse and close to breaking, Wendy said, "I'm not a murderer. I did nothing of the sort."

Feeling about twenty per cent guilty for being so cruel, I let her suffer a moment longer. "No, that's right, you didn't. And nor did you accuse me of being the murderer and make a big scene at the funeral to hide your guilt. You did all that to show off to your workmates. Being Bob's bit on the side was a real boon in your ongoing war with Pauline from accounts and the other ladies in your morning tea circle. You had something you could laud over them and, even after he was gone, you wanted to make the most of it."

There was a short burst of heavy sighs as everyone in the room caught their breath. Even David over by the door seemed tense and it was the second time he'd heard this.

"No, Wendy's not the murderer. So that only leaves five of you.

There were five little piggies but only one had roast beef."

"Oh get on with it," Will snapped again. "This is ridiculous."

I enjoyed seeing how each of them reacted. Though Will fumed and complained, Jack hadn't made a sound. Ramesh and Amara meanwhile seemed thoroughly entertained.

"So if not Wendy, who? Sometimes in these sorts of mysteries, the last person you'd ever expect is the very one who turns out to be the killer. There's somebody in this room who I trusted more than anyone. Who I truly believed could never do such a thing as cut the life from another human being."

Ramesh smiled even more. "Oh, goody. My turn!"

"I wouldn't be so smug if I were you, buddy. I saw through your alibi." He suddenly didn't look so chirpy. "If there's anyone here today who wanted to see Bob dead it was you. You were the one he'd bullied and victimised for years. You were the one who went home every night and cried about it. It was Bob's mission in life to make you suffer and wow did he fulfil his goal. It didn't take much for me to find the hundreds of videos, documents, and even dreadful songs that depicted your obsession with the man who'd made your life hell."

I paused, my gaze fixed hard on him. "But there were two things in particular that gave you away. The same week that Bob was murdered, you shared a video online telling the world that you wished he were dead and that you were going to do something about him *once and for all*."

Ramesh's smile had gone into hiding. Gripping the side of the dark wooden table with both hands, tiny droplets of sweat abseiled down his face despite the cold waves of conditioned air that were cutting through the room.

"The morning after he died, you came to the office and deleted all the nasty e-mails you'd sent him. I can only imagine the wicked threats you'd made, but it was that hasty cover-up that got the police suspicious.

"You weren't afraid though. You had a backup plan, a foolproof alibi in fact. You explained to the detectives that, at the moment of the crime, you were online, counselling your followers on how to deal with a bully. And not only that, you had the video and witnesses to prove that poor, innocent little Ramesh had nothing to do with his boss's bloodthirsty slaying."

Pushing his chair back, Ramesh shot up to standing but Brabazon shouted at him to stay put.

"It was a clever trick. Pre-recording your message and then setting it to broadcast at just the right moment. You even gave a shout out to the specific users who were watching you, which wasn't too difficult to organise considering that the same sad devotees always tuned in. Inspector Tweedle Dumb and Tweedle Dumber here couldn't–"

"Hey, go easy!" Irons barked. I might have been getting a bit carried away with my role.

"Sorry… The good officers of the Metropolitan Police force may not have had the resources to fully check whether there was a technological solution that could account for you being in two places at once, but one phone call to a techy friend of mine helped clear it up."

"No, Izzy. You've got it all wrong… I…" This time, Ramesh couldn't control his urge to run. He jumped to his feet, dived past D.I. Irons and was at the door in a flash. The two constables outside wouldn't be so easily got around and dragged him back into the room.

He was practically crying as he hung from their arms. It was quite painful to see my best friend in the world reduced to such a pathetic state.

"Please," he begged. "I'm too pretty to go to jail. They'll eat me alive!"

"You know, I'd feel an ounce of sympathy for you if you hadn't strung me along all this time."

His tears finally broke and he gave up struggling. "I'm sorry, Iz. I really am."

"You're not sorry." My words were coated with disdain. "You're a killer and, the next time I see you, will be in court."

The atmosphere was shattered and the five other suspects let out a relieved sigh, knowing that it was finally over for them.

Chapter Twenty-Seven

A silence lingered. Even the police seemed taken aback by the way things had unfolded. Ramesh had stopped short of outright confessing but it wouldn't take much to break him.

Will let out a high-pitch whistle. "Bloody hell, was it really him?"

"I did not see that coming," Jack pronounced with a laugh.

"Never the ones you expect," Wendy said. "Though I knew from the beginning he'd done it."

D.I. Irons stepped forwards to read out her detainee's rights. "Ramesh Khatri, I'm arresting you for the murder of…"

Irons' big moment was interrupted by my so-called friend bursting into laughter.

"And I thought you said I was a bad actor, Will?"

Irons herself couldn't resist a smirk. I was surprised how far she'd gone along with the act.

Supporting his weight once more, Ramesh stepped free of the constable's grip. "You fell for it, Will. You totally fell for it." He took a step forward to foppishly bow at the end of the conference table.

"You absolute git." Will wasn't happy to have been tricked.

"Izzy," David said, leaving his perch to deliver a critical stare across the room at me. "No more messing around."

"That wasn't me." My voice got all squeaky as I tried to defend myself. "He was improvising. I knew he'd do something like that."

Ramesh sat back down and the four officers returned to their posts. When the room was still again, I was ready to continue.

"Nope, sorry everyone. It wasn't Ramesh. Though he had every reason to kill Bob after the cruel and bigoted comments he'd had to put up with on a daily basis. He really was at home on the night of the murder. If you watch the video of his live stream, the things he says fit too perfectly with his follower's interaction for it to be pre-recorded. Which is lucky for him as he really is too pretty for jail."

"Ahh, thanks, Iz." We BFF-thumbs-upped at one another across the table.

"And there's someone else here today who couldn't have killed

Bob." I paused, scanning the faces of the remaining suspects before pointing to the end of the room. "Though he knew full well what a wretched person Bob was, and he'd had to deal with his bad behaviour for years, our beloved boss David cannot be the killer. He was having dinner at his Auntie Val's house that night, as he does every Wednesday. I've met her and she's lovely."

David smiled at me kind of shyly which, I must say, I found incredibly cute. If it hadn't been for all those people there, and the fact I was building up to my big moment, I might have had to ravish him on the conference table.

Go on. Do it anyway!

Shhhh!

"So what about the final remaining member of upper management?" I turned to Amara, who was still smiling like this was all just a game. "The woman who Bob had forced to sit through a tribunal hearing after he falsely claimed she'd been promoted over him due to ageism. The same woman who had been a long-term friend of the Thomas family, their kids going to school together and the two mothers maintaining close links despite countless obstacles. The very woman who urged me to investigate Bob's killing, hoping, no doubt, that I would pick another suspect, any other suspect, as the murderer. What about Amara Donovan?"

I leant over the table, my eyes fixed on hers. "No. She didn't do it either. And from everything I've seen, she really is the friendly person she comes across as."

She looked a little uncomfortable but remained cheerful all the same. "Thanks very much, Izzy. That's kind of you to say."

I thought about asking if we could still be friends but decided it would sound a bit desperate. "Four down. Two to go." I started walking again, slower this time, gradually working my way around the room. Sitting on either side of the table, Jack and Will glanced at one another, then back at me.

"So who will it be? Will Gibbons, Bob's partner in cruelty? Or Jack Campbell, our trusted security guard who Bob insulted and humiliated in front of the whole office?"

Jack let out an indignant huff.

"Will who admired Bob so much that he rose up the ranks to be like him? Or Jack who was very familiar with the security systems, not just in P&P but this whole building. Jack who Bob was blackmailing and had already announced at the Christmas party wasn't the whiter than white protector he appeared to be. Jack who had used his poorly paid job to hide the drug dealing ring he ran from his cupboard at work. Jack, who killed Bob when he threatened to uncover that dark secret."

"That's ridiculous."

I stopped in front of him and leaned in close so that my face was nearly up against his. "That's how you got away with it for so long, isn't it Jack? No one would take you for a gangster in a million years. International drug dealing? Not our Jack. Murder? Not a chance. Old Jack Campbell with his silly animal videos and his knitted sweaters? Security Jack, who could always be relied on to sign for a parcel and have a chat over a nice cup of tea?" I was shouting now, really screaming in his face to get him to spill. "Surely it wasn't Jack."

"You've got it all wrong," he finally snapped. "Yes, Bob was blackmailing me but he spent everything I gave him ordering off us anyway. It was no skin off my nose."

"Oh, okay. So you think we're going to believe that the self-confessed drug dealer in our midst let the man who'd crossed him get off scot-free and that there's another deranged criminal lurking in the office?"

"It's the truth!" Jack gave back just as good as he was getting. "I'm not really a drug dealer. I'm only doing it for a bit of extra cash. Do you have any idea what sort of pension I'll get from this place when they kick me out?"

"Oh, poor Jack. Tell that to the families of the addicts you've been selling to."

"It's not as if I've been slinging heroin. We only sell weed and coke."

"I'm tired of listening to your excuses."

D.I. Irons moved towards him but Jack wasn't finished. "If it wasn't us, someone else would be doing it. Plus all the packaging we use is recycled, we only deal to London addresses to reduce our carbon footprint and we support our local post office. We're an ethical business and, I promise, I had nothing to do with Bob's death."

Jack looked desperate, his eyes bloodshot, his whiskers suddenly greyer; he'd aged ten years in two minutes. I actually felt sorry for him. I mean, his criminal enterprise aside, I'd always liked the guy.

"I know you didn't, Jack. And so do the police. You see, I had to give my colleague D.I. Irons some of the details so that she'd agree to this meeting. The only reason she's letting me talk to you is because she knows that, when I finish speaking, she's going to make her arrests."

I walked back to my place and sat down in the black leather swivel chair. I'd moved way past the point of subtlety so decided to keep going. I put my feet up on the table and my hands together meditatively. "The problem is that we've already ruled out five people in this room and I certainly didn't kill Bob." Wendy still looked sceptical on that point. "Which only leaves one person. A man, in fact, with no concrete alibi. A man who adored Robert Thomas and would have done anything for him. A man with vicious streak who could be just as malicious and vindictive as his mentor." I swivelled in my chair to point at Will. "A man sitting right over there."

Despite my impressive theatrics, there was no reaction from my audience. I guess they were smart enough to take five from six and come up with a slimy yuppie in a grey suit.

Will didn't look quite so calm anymore and his anger surged out of him. "You said it yourself, I couldn't have taken the hard drives. There's no way I killed Bob."

"We'll come to that in time but first, tell me, have you ever seen this before?" I held up a train ticket, which I'd scribbled out a note on and shoved in a plastic freezer bag from my kitchen. D.I. Irons refused to bring the real one. "It's dated from the day Bob died and, in neat black capitals on the back it says, 'Okay, let's do it. Tonight at eight. B.' When I found it in Bob's coat after he died, I assumed he'd written it and never had the chance to hand it over. But I was wrong, wasn't I, Billy?"

This time there were a couple of gasps from our colleagues as they realised that I was homing in on my suspect. Will raised his eyebrows but kept his Doberman mouth tightly closed.

"Billy and Bob had become good friends. They hung out at the Boxpark, watched football matches over a beer and hatched plots to annoy Ramesh together. They even liked to come to the office sometimes and muck around up here. Isn't that right, Will?"

"Fine, you're right." He looked down at his nails like he had far more important things to be doing than sitting there. "It's hardly a secret."

"No, that's not the secret, but there's worse to come. At first it was great fun. You looked up to Bob and he trusted you. He even told you about his diagnosis."

Will was getting nervous, his hands shaking, his eyes flitting about.

"But then, you and Bob started to argue. You told us it was nothing. Just friends having a row, but there was more to it than that. He wanted you to do something that you didn't think was right. He pushed and manipulated you until you went along with his plans. What was it? The memorial service? The two of you organised the whole thing, but you're not so emotionally bankrupt that you couldn't see what an impact it would have on his family after he was gone. Bob didn't give a damn what his wife and kids felt, so long as he could have one last dig at Ramesh and David and all of his pet enemies."

Will was rocking fractionally back and forth now, in time with his jangling nerves.

"In the end, you gave in. Or at least, that was the plan. You came up here to see him but nothing was good enough for Bob. He thought up savage new ideas for how to punish all those that had crossed him. You didn't want to go along with it but he broke you down, didn't he? He beat you up with his words, bent you to his will. He defeated you and you promised to go along with his plans on one condition; that he removed the CCTV footage of your humiliation."

Ramesh looked across at me, surprised at this unexpected fork in the story.

Suddenly resolute, Will locked his gaze onto mine. "That's right."

"But that was just an excuse, wasn't it?"

"No."

"Why would anyone have bothered looking at the footage from that specific time if something terrible hadn't occurred just after? With the hard drives removed, you knew that you could turn the tables. You hit Bob across the head with the champagne he'd been downing. It wasn't supposed to be hard, just a warning maybe, but you lost your temper and really belted him. There was blood, he was unconscious and you panicked. You knew that, if he woke up, he'd report you to the police and you would lose everything. Business lunches with the boys, smart suits, fancy holidays on the Italian Riviera. So you took the knife from his desk and you cut the life from him."

I wielded the biro one last time and slit my own stomach open like a shamed samurai. "To cover your tracks, you programmed the air conditioning to blast on full power for a couple of hours to mess up the coroner's estimated time of death. Then, finally, you plunged the letter opener into Bob's back to make it seem as if his murder was a crime of passion.

"With that simple action, you shifted the blame onto Bob's enemies. Everyone in the office would say *Will couldn't possibly have done it, he was Bob's best friend.* Helped along by your own accusations, we thought of Ramesh and Jack and his other rivals but not Will Gibbons."

"You're talking rubbish." As Will's anger flared, Brabazon took a step closer.

"You played the devoted friend to the man you'd murdered."

"Enough."

"You lied to the police, who quickly found the building security footage of you leaving while Bob was apparently still alive. They didn't think you could be the killer anyway because you'd never have got into the server room. You lied to your colleagues, inventing an alibi that no one could prove or disprove with a mystery woman who didn't exist."

"It's not a crime to prank a bunch of idiots." With his typical arrogance still controlling every movement, his eyes flicked away to the view out of the window.

"Admit what you did."

"Watch your mouth."

All eyes were on Will and, in three quick steps, I was right beside him. I spun him round in his chair so that we were face to face. "You killed Bob Thomas."

"No."

"You killed your best friend."

"No, I didn't."

"You murdered him!"

Chapter Twenty-Eight

Will's eyes were locked on mine, but he gave nothing away. There was no trace of guilt. He was no longer shaking and no tears came to his eyes. He wasn't going to break.

As I stood there, gripping the armrests tight, the room was practically silent. There was a soft rustle of clothes as Jack shuffled about in his seat and, at the door, I heard one of the uniformed officers' radios crackle and her chunky soles scrape against one another.

I stood up straight and looked around the room. "I'm sorry for putting you through all that." I took a deep breath for the first time in what felt like days and allowed the tension to drain out of me. "You see, I had to imagine all these different possibilities before I could be sure of what happened on the night Bob died."

"Wait, is Will the killer or not?" Trying to make sense of what he'd just heard, Ramesh's gaze was bouncing around the room like a squash ball.

"Stop messing with us," Wendy said. "You're sick you are. Playing with people's feelings. It's not right."

Jack was the angriest of the lot, pointing across the room at me and spitting the words out. "She hasn't got a clue who the murderer is. She was hoping one of us would confess."

I slammed my fist down on the table. It hurt more than I was expecting. "Don't be so high and mighty. Every one of you has lied at some point to cover your backs. If you'd told the truth in the first place, none of this would've been necessary."

I looked over at D.I. Irons who gave an infinitesimal nod. Still standing very straight against the wall behind Jack and Amara, she seemed content just to observe. David was in the corner by the door, there in a supervisory role, but leaving the hard work to me.

Typical boss.

"You see, when we started our investigation, I made a mistake. I focussed on the wrong people. I was so fixated on identifying the murderer, I forgot about Bob himself. In my head, he was a cartoon monster that everyone would be glad to get rid of. I didn't think about the person he really was."

I wandered back to my place at the head of the table but remained standing. "Bob was a bully, yes. But he was also clever. He'd come up through the company from the lowest level; starting work as a junior office boy, back when such jobs existed. Mr Porter saw something in him that he thought deserved kindling and promoted him through the ranks.

"But Bob's success went to his head. He took pleasure in his newfound power. He tortured his subordinates and treated every woman at this firm like we were his possessions. When he took it too far and assaulted an intern, Mr Porter had to deal with it."

I was pleased to see that Jack showed no sign of knowing what I was talking about. For all that I had to reveal that morning, there were still a few secrets I wanted to keep. "I can only imagine how little Bob must have cared for the poor girl he tried to rape in his office. And I can't begin to describe the anger that subsequently drove him. He knew that he'd used up all his favours with Porter, but seeing first David and then Amara promoted above him, pushed him over the edge."

I paused, looked at my audience. The grilling I'd previously delivered had turned into a business presentation and they'd all got too comfortable. It was time to turn the screw. For the final time, I started walking around the table. I went slowly, gradually ratcheting up the tension as I delivered the last chapter of the story.

"He threatened to sue the company and began the proceedings that would cause poor Amara so much suffering. It must have been terrible to be put through that by someone you'd previously called a friend." I tried to look cheerful and Amara reflected back a weak smile of her own. "Even when Mr Porter caved in and made him deputy director, the initial slight was too much for Bob to forgive.

"Another thing that I'd failed to consider was just how hard done by he could be. He wallowed in rejection and, when he found out he had cancer, it was just something else for him to feel sorry about. He dismissed the idea of treatment, not caring in the least what his wife and children might want. If anything, it gave him fuel for his pity and the revenge he now so desperately desired."

As I crossed from one side of the room to the other, I passed in and

201

out of my colleagues' vision. Their eyes clicked onto me like magnets whenever I was in view.

"Bob set out to make working at P&P the nightmare that he now found it to be. He upped the ferocity of his invectives, became crueller and more bigoted. Staring down certain death, he was convinced that he could get away with whatever he wanted, so he taunted his colleagues over each fresh indiscretion. He left notes around the office, boasting of petty cruelties and, like a rotten child who no one pays attention to, he came to crave our contempt even more than our approval."

I caught Will's eyes as I walked past. He looked different, calmer. He'd lost the arrogance and aggression that normally boiled beneath his paper-thin exterior.

"It wasn't enough. Nothing Bob did gave him the satisfaction he sought, so he looked for new ways to shock and upset. His crimes escalated. He raised the bar of his own depravity and his hunger for the extreme increased. He lied, insulted, screwed and stole, but it's taken me until now to make out a pattern to his behaviour. Sometime at the end of last year, without fear of repercussions, Bob wrote down all the things he wanted to do in the world. It was a bad bucket list for his final months on earth. Each item on it was directed at one of us, but he was doing it for himself."

Her smile long gone, Amara let out a short, sharp breath. Sitting opposite her, Ramesh looked just as upset, but I knew that he wanted me to keep going.

"I've never seen the list but I know what was on it. He bullied Ramesh, fought and then blackmailed Jack, humiliated Amara, stole from Wendy and lied to his family. I could find examples of almost every sin and debauchery, every type of malice and indulgence to attribute to him. But there was a single missing entry that told me everything I needed to know.

"It took me a long time to realise that there wasn't just one mystery to solve, there were two. Bob's death and mine. His occurred in his office two weeks ago, and mine was foiled in the street last Thursday by blind luck. Bob thought he could get away with murder, so it's hardly surprising that he tried to do just that. I don't know why I was the lucky staff member who he wanted dead. But I know that he ordered the hit."

Finally, a proper, everyone-at-once, full-on gasp of surprise. Even D.I. Brabazon looked impressed.

"The same day that he died, Bob found an assassin online. Just one hour before he was murdered, he wrote an e-mail to say that his dark wish list was complete. Adultery, theft, greed, cruelty, dishonesty and finally murder. Bob ticked them off one by one and might have lived long enough to see his plan completed if he hadn't got cocky. You see, Bob wasn't just smart and vindictive, he was a show off. He hungered for the thrill of an audience or else all his achievements would be empty. He needed someone to be shocked by the depravity he'd stoop to. Someone to live on as a witness after he'd gone; someone pure to corrupt."

I came to a stop at the end of the table closest to the door. Knowing that my story was almost at an end, David stepped forward to stand alongside me. Without looking at him, our hands fell together naturally.

"Bob pictured himself dying in a hospital bed as the shockwaves from his terrible deeds reverberated through the town, but there was something he hadn't planned for. They say that the only thing necessary for the triumph of evil is for good men to do nothing and the opposite must also be true. In the end it was a good man who stopped Bob Thomas."

My loyal, kind-hearted boyfriend kissed me on the cheek, walked over to the constables and put his hands out.

"Bob loved to cause us pain but none of us here suffered the way David did. He watched Bob's crimes go unpunished, saw them increase in savagery and vindictiveness and he tried to put things right. David tried to convince Bob to stop and Bob loved it. He found great joy in taunting his superior. He told him the things he had done and promised that there was worse to look forward to until, finally, David could take no more."

Every pair of eyes in the room were on the murderer. I knew what they were thinking, because I'd had the very same thoughts. *He was supposed to be the good one.* And just like me, they were trying to work out if perhaps, somehow, he still was.

"I don't know exactly what happened on the night of the murder, but I think I can fill in the gaps. David had an early dinner with his elderly Aunt. But, as Auntie Val proudly told me when we met, she never put much stock in clocks and watches and wouldn't have noticed a shift from their normal dinner time.

"After they'd eaten their takeaway, David went back to the office and in through the fire escape, so as not to be observed as he crept inside. Bob didn't know he was coming, didn't know anyone was there to watch the last great cruelty to Will but he probably didn't care. When Bob returned to his office, he found his boss sitting at his desk. Determined to put the odious man in his place, David threatened to reveal every last dark secret but Bob just laughed at him."

The female P.C. had secured the handcuffs and D.I. Brabazon came to stand by their detainee. Around the table, no one made a sound. Ramesh's eyes were as wide as Frisbees as he processed the final revelations that even he didn't know. Amara was drained of life, Jack still disgruntled at his own misfortune. Wendy's expression had turned to stone, but Will kept that peaceful look on his face – oddly zen in the midst of all that darkness.

"Mocking and conceited, Bob poured himself one final drink and offered the bottle to David who used it as best he could. It was a split-second decision, a moment of madness which would trigger several more. David killed the man who had been tormenting him with the boasts of his own wickedness. Bob Thomas was a thief, a potential rapist and very nearly a murderer but he's gone now. His list will never be completed, his despicable desires never entirely fulfilled and he won't hurt anyone, ever again."

The story was complete so I sat back down in my place and watched as first David, then Jack were read their rights. I watched as the police led my boyfriend away.

I had solved Bob's murder. My goal was achieved; my heart smashed to pieces.

As the two suspects stepped from the conference room in cuffs, a wave of shock passed across the office. I could hear my deskmate Suzie's high pitch squeal and Pauline from accounts' unmistakable grunt mixed into a chorus of shouts and gasps. Amara followed on with D.I. Irons and then Wendy went out to greet the mob.

In the end, only Ramesh, Will and I stayed behind. I poured us each a glass of water from the jug in the middle of the table and handed them out. We drank in silence, with our thoughts for company.

Wendy had shut the door after her and the world beyond that room seemed very far away. I didn't have to hear what the bitchy secretaries would say about David or how Wendy would repaint every last detail to impress her friends. For another few minutes I could sit there in peace.

It was Will who finally broke the silence. "Thank you..." He struggled to find the right words. "I know it will come out eventually, but I appreciate what you did for me."

Ramesh looked over at him but said nothing.

"I can't explain what happened with Bob because I don't understand it myself." This wasn't the Will we knew. His anger had been wiped clean away and I could see that he needed to talk. "He had a weird hold over me that I've never experienced with anyone else. I didn't want to go along with his plans but I was in awe of him. I could never say no and he used that against me. It took me until the night he died to see who he really was."

I suppose I felt bad for Will. I could understand him pretending to be someone he wasn't in order to fit in. I could even understand the influence Bob held over him. The one thing that didn't make sense to me, though, was the way he'd treated us for years. No matter what he'd been going through, that didn't excuse his cruelty.

He turned to look at me. "I'm sorry for what I did to you. It was all part of the act. When they found out I was gay in the last place I worked, the blokes in my team treated me like a traitor. People who I thought of as friends turned their backs on me completely. I didn't want that happening here, so I created a character – I played a part. But it took too much out of me and it's over now. I just hope you forgive me."

When our silence refused to break, he stood up from his seat. He cast one last look at us from the door before a burst of noise floated in from outside. I heard someone crying, several men shouting in disbelief and Amara trying to quieten everyone down. The door swung closed again and calm returned to the conference room.

Ramesh put his hand out across the table and his tears triggered mine.

Chapter Twenty-Nine

I didn't get to visit David at the police station. His family took precedence of course and he had to be processed and interviewed and all sorts of other things before being formally charged. I didn't go to the magistrate's court for his initial hearing either. Chloe called to say that David thought it was better if he did it on his own.

It probably goes without saying that I'd never visited anyone in prison before. I mean, I'd seen it on TV and in movies and stuff. In fact I've watched every season of Orange is The New Black and Oz, and even saw a few episodes of Prisoner Cell Block H when I was a kid, but it's hardly the same.

I had to take two buses to get there and I hate buses, but that obviously pales in comparison to David's experience there. I'll skip the details of the long, dehumanising process I had to go through to gain entry. Signing in, bag searches, stern looks and security doors all featured heavily before I was allowed to sit at a small table in a large room with the murderer I'd recently started the process of falling in love with.

Once we were finally there together, I struggled to form a whole sentence. I finally went with, "I don't think I've seen you in anything but a suit before."

In his black jogging bottoms and grey sweatshirt, he looked like an entirely different person. "That's not true. Team-building day last October, I wore some nice comfortable chinos." More than anything, he looked tired. Not older, or thinner, just tired.

"I stand corrected."

There we were, David and I and a big silence between us. I'd been longing to see him. I hadn't thought about anything else for days but now that my wish was a reality, it was hard to know what to talk about.

"Thanks for coming," he eventually tried. "I wasn't sure you'd want to."

"Thanks for having me." I always know just the wrong thing to say.

I put my hand on the table for him to take but he shook his head and after a brief moment of agony, I realised that he meant it wasn't allowed.

"I'm so happy to see you," he said instead and it was almost as good. "If I try really hard, I can imagine we're in a bar together and, after this, we can go to mine and I'll make something easy to eat that looks impressive."

"Sounds delicious." I laughed a little. "May I recommend homemade guacamole? If you've ever accidentally sat on an avocado, then you're already halfway there."

He smiled and I wanted to kiss him. "Have you ever sat on an avocado?"

Don't tell him the truth! He might still think we have an ounce of sophistication.

"Urmm… once or twice. But only because my favourite bag has a hole in it and, for some reason, Mum always makes me buy avocados on my way home from work."

I smiled. He smiled. It was sweet.

"I don't think you came here to give me recipe advice."

"And I doubt you get many avocados in here anyway."

Silence. Silence. Silence. Pain. Pain. Excruciating pain.

"How did you know it was me?" Why did he have to ask that? As long as we were being sweet and flirty, we could pretend that everything was okay with the world. "I mean, I know about the evidence you found, but what convinced you deep down that I could have done it?"

I swallowed hard, my throat suddenly dry. There was a café area over by the entrance but I didn't want to waste a second of my time with him – even if it meant having to live through this conversation.

"It might sound weird but you were the only one who cared enough. Ramesh was hurt, sure, but he had no idea how evil Bob really was. Wendy, Amara and Jack didn't give a damn about him and Will somehow still liked him. So that only left one person."

"Right. I figured it was something like that."

"Every time you spoke about Bob after he died, it sounded like you were in pain. I thought at first that you felt sorry for the guy, but when I found out what he'd done to Jack's daughter, I started to understand what you'd gone through. Right up there on the list with all his other crimes, Bob was trying to destroy you."

"Sounds about right." He breathed in sad and slowly and I wished that I could whisk him off to pretty much anywhere else on earth. "Bob loved to see the effect he could have on me. The nastier he became, the more I suffered. He knew the guilt I carried and he took advantage of it. If I'd called the police when he assaulted Pippa, none of this would have happened."

"There was something else as well." The only other people I'd explained everything to were Irons and Brabazon. It felt odd to be saying it so openly. "No matter how many times I ran through the evidence, I couldn't find anyone who'd want me dead except Bob. He was the only one cruel enough to pay for the hit. When I realised that, it didn't take much for me to guess what was on the list he talked about in his final e-mail."

The silence between us returned for a moment and, when David finally spoke, his voice was hurried, nervous. "I want you to know that I had no idea he was planning to kill anyone. I would have gone to the police immediately if I'd thought that was possible. He told me each time he crossed something off his 'bad bucket list' – that's exactly what he called it – but he never showed me what was on it. I knew about Wendy, Ramesh, bits and pieces about Jack – there'd be notes on my desk each morning or e-mails and texts if he couldn't be bothered to leave his office. But even on that last night, all he said was that he had something big planned. His grand swansong.

"He said he'd been a good man all his life and got nowhere so it was time for a change. Said he'd had his punishment, but there was still time to commit the crime. He used to laugh and call me soft whenever I tried to reason with him. He was right of course, I didn't want to upset Mr Porter, or lose my job, so I did the minimum to soothe my conscience. I told myself that there was no other option, but the truth was killing me. I wasn't just his witness; he'd turned me into an accomplice. That's why I went there that night. Bob kept dropping hints about what he was up to and I thought, if I caught him together with Will, I could blackmail him into giving up on his plan."

There were other conversations going on at the tables all around us, but I tuned them out and focused on our own. "It wouldn't have made any difference. D.I. Irons told me that Bob had already paid the assassin on the morning before he died."

David shook his head wearily. "You might not want to hear exactly what happened that night, but you're going to have to one day and I'd rather it came from me." He looked around at the couples and families we were surrounded by as if he hadn't noticed them before. "I need you to know that I wasn't planning to kill him. I went into the office through the fire escape, but that was only to be able to catch them at it.

"When I got inside, they were together in the main office. Bob was standing over Will, shouting out boasts and insults as Will quietly sobbed. It made me sick to see Bob's cruelty first hand but I didn't have time to stop him because, a few seconds after I arrived, Bob was doing his trousers up and it was all over. Will begged him to get the hard drives from the server room and Bob eventually gave in. Now that his goal was achieved, I could see how little he cared about his so-called friend. He barely glanced at the poor man as Will walked out still in tears."

He looked away for a moment, no longer able to hold my gaze. "You worked out most of the rest. Bob went off to have a shower. He was gone for ages, so I waited for him in his room. He was furious when he found me there and demanded that I leave, but I stayed firm. I told him to sit down and shut up and he plonked himself in the free chair.

"He took his time, poured himself a drink and said, 'What are you going to do? Tell on me? I'd wait a bit longer if I were you, there's so much worse still to come.'

"That was when I hit him." David swallowed hard, like he wanted to take the words back and never utter them again. "I could see there was no sense in arguing. My hand shot out to grab the bottle and I smashed it across his face. Even as he felt the blow, he was smiling and it made me wonder if that was what he'd wanted all along. Perhaps that was on his bloody list; making me just as bad as he was."

"He fell unconscious, but it wasn't enough. The knife was on the table and I knew what I had to do if I wanted to stop him."

It was more painful to listen to his story than I'd imagined. I thought that, after everything I'd already discovered, I'd have become hardened to it. I was way off and it felt like every cell in my body was rebelling against me.

I didn't want to dwell on all those emotions – I could deal with them at home – so I kept talking. "What about the letter opener? It probably ruins any defence of seeing red and losing it. It makes the whole thing seem more deliberate."

His luminous blue eyes looked so sad right then and I had to resist reaching out to him.

"I guess some stupid part of me worried that it would be mistaken for a suicide and I couldn't stand that. I wanted the world to know that someone truly hated the man. And I did; I despised him."

He looked away, out through the high windows that showed nothing but chalk-white skies, so I nudged him on. "Keep going. Tell me what happened after."

"I never thought I'd get away with it, but I did what I could to hide my guilt. I took the bottle, the knife and Will's champagne glass. I rubbed the door handle clean, just in case. Then out in the office there were bits of Bob's clothing strewn about. I didn't want to leave anything that might incriminate Will."

"The missing clothes confused me at first. Wendy said that Bob took his socks off when they did it and I eventually put three and three together and came up with sex." I can never resist a bad joke.

He didn't smile. I could see how badly he wanted the story to be over. "I was laden with stuff. It was ridiculous. I should have found a bag or something but, after I went downstairs with my hands full, I tried to wipe my fingerprints off the exit and dropped the bottle. I picked up the big pieces and stashed them in my coat pockets then emptied them in a bin a mile from the office.

"I slept better that night than I had in months. And when I woke up the next morning, I decided that I wouldn't do anything more to cover up my crime. I made a silent promise that, if anyone else was arrested, I'd turn myself in to the police. That's why I insisted on going to the station with you to see Ramesh. I spent the whole time we were in the car wondering if I should confess but I couldn't until it was absolutely necessary."

"Why not?" My voice came out colder than I'd intended. "If you thought it was inevitable I mean."

"I had something worth being free for."

I let his words hang in the air about between us. I'd gone to see him to be the loving and supportive girlfriend he needed, but now that I was with him, other feelings were rearing up. There was a question I hadn't been willing to ask myself before and it was about to jump out into the world. "David, why did you start a relationship with me after everything you knew?"

Another breath, another pause. "Selfishness, first and foremost. I guess I wanted to enjoy my last days of freedom the best I could –

210

a bit like Bob really. But there was more to it than that. The night that I saw you in the supermarket, you were so bright and full of energy."

"Me?"

"In your shiny blue dress you were like a meteorite streaking across East Croydon." A hush descended as David attempted to put his thoughts in order. "I meant what I said, Izzy. I've always known you were wonderful, seeing you out in the street that night, you were effervescent. I dreamed of another life. I even kidded myself that it might still be possible."

Tell him it is. Tell him it's not too late.

I wanted to comfort him, but I couldn't. I cared for him but the words wouldn't come so I changed the subject.

"I'm probably just as much to blame. You were my very first suspect. I couldn't imagine who else Bob would have given up his chair for and, you were so weird on the phone the next day, I immediately thought it was you. I could have asked you about the e-mail Bob sent at any time, about the list, but I never did. I didn't want to believe you were capable of murder. And even after I'd worked it out, when I rang you at home, I prayed that you'd run away and never look back but I knew you were too good for that. So here we are."

His face became one big smile like he was opening his door to me on our first date. "Here we are."

I couldn't do the same. I couldn't pretend that everything was okay. I put my hands on the table in front of us and linked them together. With physical interaction forbidden, it was our eyes that made contact. Neither of us said anything as the sounds of the prison swelled around us – chairs scraping, the low murmur from neighbouring desks, metal gates clanging shut.

It was too painful to listen to and I forced myself to speak.

"So… What now?"

Get your **Free** Izzy Palmer Novellas…

If you'd like to hear about forthcoming releases and download my free novellas, sign up to the Izzy Palmer readers' club via my website. I'll never spam you or inundate you with stuff you're not interested in, but I'd love to keep in contact. There will be one free novella for every novel I release, so sign up at...

www.benedictbrown.net

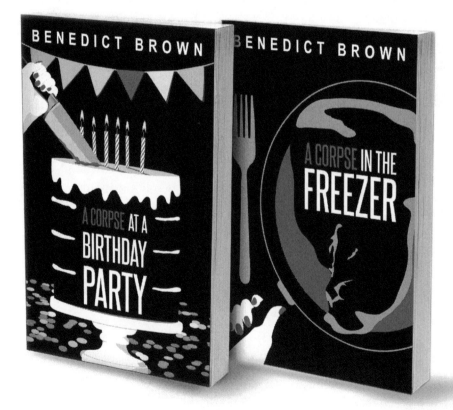

Buy the next **Izzy Palmer Mystery**
now at amazon

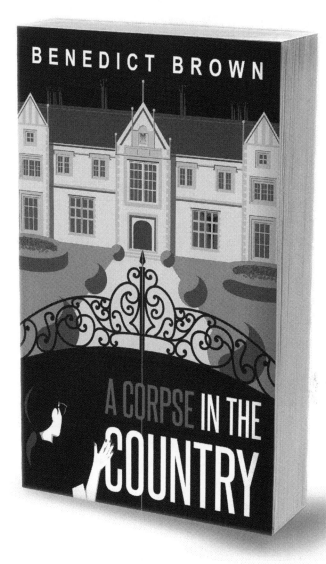

One murdered millionaire, seven suspects
and only forty-eight hours to find out whodunit.

About This Book

My family are total book-junkies and, like Izzy, I grew up on murder mysteries. I'd always planned to write a crime novel so, when faced with a long summer holiday, and feeling determined to produce something that could connect directly with an audience, I dug out a project I'd started five years earlier.

I'd already written a third of **"A Corpse Called Bob"** and had only put it aside because I'd got distracted by life, work and other writing projects. Re-reading the text after so long away from it was a unique experience and I immediately fell in love with Izzy, Ramesh and all their oddball companions. I laughed and gasped and tried to remember who the murderer was supposed to be. When I got to the end, I knew that the time had come to finish the story. A furious summer of writing (and playing with my then one-year-old daughter) ensued and the result is this book.

I hope you've enjoyed the novel as much as I've loved every moment writing it. I adore these characters and have a lengthy plan for the series of books that they will feature in. The second novel **"A Corpse in the Country"** is available now on Amazon and the third is on its way. Make sure you sign up to my **readers' club** where you'll also be able to access free, exclusive novellas depicting Izzy's adventures.

Acknowledgements

Before I go, I should probably say sorry and thank you. Sorry to anyone in **Croydon** if I failed to put across that I actually really like the town I grew up a fifteen-minute 154 bus ride from. Izzy's childhood recollections of what a magical place it seemed are purely autobiographical and I still have lots of affection for the place I would go to for school shoes as a kid and indie records as a teenager.

A second sorry belongs to the whole nation of **Wales**. I spent every childhood holiday visiting my maternal family there and loved it so much that I moved to Aberystwyth when I was eighteen. If I ever make enough money from my writing, I'm going to buy a cottage on the Gower. Despite or maybe because of all that, I couldn't resist Izzy's Tom Jones singalong (my cousins have forgiven me, so I hope you can too).

Which only leaves the thank yous. Thank you to Lucy Middlemass – my favourite person who I never got to meet – for encouraging me over seven years when no one else wanted to read our books. I wrote this book for you to laugh at, I'm glad you got to read at least a bit of it.

Thank you to my wife and daughter for being the greatest humans ever invented and for designing my beautiful covers, to my mum and brothers for reading my books (and picking up packages for me) and to my assorted experts Bridget Hogg **(fiction)**, Paul Bickley **(policing)**, Karen Menuhin **(marketing)** and Mar Pérez **(dead people)** for knowing lots of stuff when I don't.

And finally, whoever you are, thank you for not only reading to the end of my silly novel, but all the way through the author's note. I love you as only a writer can love their anonymous reader. If you can spare the time, **please write a review** on Amazon. It makes such a difference to me as an independent writer to have strong reviews to help my books stand out.

Thank you one last time and, if you're ever near Burgos, I owe you a glass of wine.

About Me

Writing has always been my passion. It was my favourite half-an-hour a week at primary school, and I started on my first, truly abysmal book as a teenager. So it wasn't a difficult decision to study literature at university which led to a masters in Creative Writing.

I'm a Welsh-Irish-Englishman originally from **South London** but now living with my French/Spanish wife and presumably quite confused infant daughter in **Burgos**, a beautiful medieval city in the north of Spain. I write overlooking the Castilian countryside, trying not to be distracted by the vultures, hawks and red kites that fly past my window each day.

I previously spent years focussing on kids' books and wrote everything from fairy tales to environmental dystopian fantasies right through to issue-based teen fiction. My book **"The Princess and The Peach"** was long-listed for the Chicken House prize in The Times and an American producer even talked about adapting it into a film. I'll be slowly publishing those books over the next year on Amazon.

" A Corpse Called Bob" is my first full length novel for adults in what I'm confident will be a long series. If you feel like telling me what you think about Izzy, my writing or the world at large, I'd love to hear from you, so feel free to get in touch via...

www.benedictbrown.net

Made in the USA
Columbia, SC
04 November 2023

25502510R00131